SILVER COLLAR

What Reviewers Say About
Gill McKnight's Work

"A departure from the run-of-the-mill lesbian romance, *Goldenseal* is enjoyable for its uniqueness as well as for its plot. This is a story that will engage and characters you will find yourself growing fond of."—*Lambda Literary*

"Gill McKnight has given her readers a delightful romp in *Green Eyed Monster.* The twists and turns of the plot leave the reader turning the pages to see who is the real victim and who is the villain. Along with the roller coaster ride, comes plenty of hot sex to add to the tension. Spending an afternoon with *Green-eyed Monster* is great fun."—*Just About Write*

"Angst, conflict, sex and humor. [Falling Star] has all of this and more packed into a tightly written and believable romance. McKnight has penned a sweet and tender romance, balancing the intimacy and sexual tension just right. The conflict is well drawn, and she adds a great dose of humor to make this novel a light and easy read."—*Curve*

In *Green Eyed Monster*…"McKnight succeeds in tantalizing with explosive sex and a bit of bondage; tormenting with sexual frustration and intense longing; tickling your fancy and funny bone; and touching a place where good and evil battle it out. …the plot twists, winning dialogue laced with sarcasm, wit, and charm certainly add to the fun. I recommend this satisfying read for entertainment, fantasy, and sex that stimulate the brain like caffeine."—*Lambda Literary*

Visit us at www.boldstrokesbooks.com

By the Author

Falling Star

Green Eyed monster

Erosistible

Cool Side of the Pillow

The Garoul Series:

Goldenseal

Ambereye

Indigo Moon

Silver Collar

SILVER COLLAR

by
Gill McKnight

2012

ISBN 10: 1-60282-764-8
ISBN 13: 978-1-60282-764-6

This Trade Paperback Original Is Published By
Bold Strokes Books, Inc.
P.O. Box 249
Valley Falls, NY 12185

First Edition: December 2012

Credits
Editor: Cindy Cresap
Production Design: Susan Ramundo
Cover Design By Sheri (graphicartist2020@hotmail.com)

Acknowledgments

With love and gratitude to Cate, Cindy K, Jove, and Jo, without whose help and enthusiasm this book would have been done in half the time.

And to my Eds—Cindy, of the infinite deadlines, and Stacia, the immovable object, always wonderful people to work with. Thank you.

Dedication

For Louis, with love, Mum x.

CHAPTER ONE

L uc Garoul squatted under the crab apple tree and watched the lights in the single story farmhouse go out one by one. First the kitchen light, then the living room. She waited until only a yellow oblong of light from a bedroom window poured out onto the yard. With a sigh, she settled in for a little longer. She needed the adults to be sound asleep.

Her stomach gurgled with hunger. She inserted a claw into her wet, bubbling nostril and examined the mucus she withdrew. It was clotted green and streaked with blood. Not good. Her head felt thick and her left ear buzzed with fluid gathering on her eardrum.

She poked at the gutted carcass beside her. She hated domestic cat meat; it was stringy and foul tasting. She had slit this one open out of boredom. Good thing she hadn't gorged on it despite her hunger; its kidneys were rancid. Surprising, as it was a young cat, no more than a kitten really. She flicked the little bell on its collar making it tinkle and hoped it was a much-loved pet.

The bedroom light went out. Luc blinked in the darkness, her perfect night vision adjusting at once to the pitch-dark. Heavy cloud blanked out the stars and the sky hung low and foreboding over the fields. This farm grew wheat, hay, and sunflowers. No animal husbandry at all. That was very disappointing. She was on the run, hunted and famished, and she begrudged the farmer his lack of livestock. It would have been so much easier to pick off a calf or pig than go to all this trouble. Her ears flattened and she growled in discontent. She didn't have time to sit around waiting as her hunger and bitterness grew. She stood and stretched out her cramped muscles. It had been a long wait.

Her keen hearing picked out the dogs prowling back and forth in their run. There were two of them, young and unsure, whimpering in agitation. Earlier, when they were out with the farmer, she had slipped into their run and urinated on their bedding. Now they were cowed by her predator's scent and could do no more than whine in misery all night.

Luc trod through the family vegetable garden. Her huge paws flattened the leafy heads of beet and potato. She knew which window she wanted. She had been watching it all evening. The pink curtains were pulled tight. A picture of a pony was stuck to the glass pane beside a spangled wind chime. She needed that window to open just a crack. Enough to let her claws slide under the sill and force it all the way up. She lifted the collar and tinkled the little bell.

Meow. She mimicked a cat to perfection. *Meow.*

She sank to her haunches under the window and waited. A second later, a bedside lamp suffused the room with a soft pink glow. Luc smacked her lips in satisfaction.

"Tinker? Is that you?" a little girl's sleep-filled voice called out. "Tinker?"

Luc shrunk into the shadows and listened as small, clumsy fingers fumbled with the window latch.

"Tinker? You're a naughty kitty. You know you're not allowed out after dark."

The hinges squeaked as the window opened. Luc reached out. She knew what to do. A single fore claw to pierce the throat and rip apart the vocal cords. The rest of her claws would hook her muted victim under the chin, up into her mouth cavity. Then Luc would drag the child out by her face.

Her father should have kept livestock.

The air thrummed. It rasped around her like a harsh breath. Luc fell to the ground, instinct throwing her onto her belly. Wooden splinters blasted over her. Inches above her head, an arrow shaft sat embedded in the house's cedar siding.

Luc lurched forward in a hunched run. She zigzagged past the vegetable garden into the cover of the orchard. She didn't need to look back to see the arrow barb glinting in the pink bedroom light. She knew it was there, and she knew it was silver. She heard the sting of it whistling toward her. Now all she could do was run. Run from the arrow, run from the hunter on the other end of the crossbow—

Luc jerked awake, her legs scrabbling in the dirt, running at full force even as the dream disintegrated around her. She blinked and finally stilled. Her heart pounded in a sickening, irregular rhythm. She was flat on her back. Overhead, stars shone with sharp-edged indifference. The night was frigid and unforgiving, at its blackest with dawn a long way off.

She was in human form, naked, and shaking with cold and shock. Pine needles prickled her back and matted in her hair. Her chest heaved, and she coughed up thick wads of phlegm. She was ill and frightened, and the dream had terrified her.

Luc's coughing eased and she sucked in chill mountain air. It was too dark to move on, and anyway, there was no point while she was in her human skin. Nauseous and shivering, she curled up into a miserable ball and hoped sleep would soon reclaim her. She didn't care if she never woke up. Let the forest have her bones.

❖

The hinges squeaked as the window opened.

"Tinker? Is that you?" the child said. Luc lunged. She dragged the little girl out onto the grass, and saw it was Mouse—

Luc bolted upright, shaking violently. She had killed her daughter! Wild-eyed, she glanced about her. Sweat trickled down her chest. Another nightmare.

Daylight crept across the pewter sky, and birds began to chorus as the nocturnal world melted away. Luc sat stock-still and listened. She heard her heart thump, and the drum of steady rainfall. The patter of rain on leaves was lulling, but the relentless chill in her bones gave her no peace. Luc stood up stiffly, exhausted and unsure what to do next. She had to keep moving. She had to find food and keep warm. Nightmares plagued her, destroying her sleep. She could find no rest. Her dream felt ominous, and it rattled her. What did it mean? Was Mouse safe? She had done the best she could for her, but it was hard to walk away and leave her at Little Dip. They had not been as close as Luc would have liked, but then, she had engineered it that way. Her sister, Ren, had raised the child. Good ol' capable Ren, as solid as a tree stump. The cub might die of boredom, but at least she'd be well fed.

Luc gazed at the rising sun with its weak, watery halo. The Garouls would come after her soon. She had to head north as fast as possible. Her only ally was the rain; at least it would help dull her scent.

She sank onto her hands and knees and willed the change. She had a better chance of escape if she was wolven. Did she have enough strength to force it? It was a no-win situation. It took all her reserves to mutate to Were form, but the odds of survival against this virus were better as a beast. Luna only knew how long she could maintain the stronger physique. The downside was that her Were body burned up fuel, and she had little enough of that left. She needed a kill, and soon. She needed to feed.

Her dream still disorientated her. Why had she killed Mouse? Did it signify an ending? Luc wished she understood these things and forcibly pushed the dream away. Thinking about Mouse made her heartsick. She didn't need that on top of everything else. Her life was collapsing around her leaving her hollowed out and rudderless. North was the only compass point, the only bolt-hole left. A bone cracked in her hand, and her vertebrae popped one at a time. She fell belly first onto the pine needles, twisting with the pain as raindrops spotted her back. The change was agonizing, slow, and ragged. Not clean, and certainly not pretty. She used to glory in it, powering through her transformation in mere minutes. Now she felt flayed alive. Her bones creaked and cracked, muscles bunched and heaved and ground their way into wolven form. As a werewolf, she felt underpowered and weaker than she did in human shape, but her Were body would be better able to keep the virus in check. The unfortunate side effect of this was that her appetite grew alongside her physique, and she was ravenous. She hoped she had the strength to kill.

Luc rose to her full height of almost eight feet and sniffed the damp air. It was full of possibilities. All she needed was luck... and some easy, careless, half-dead prey. She padded through the undergrowth on her huge clawed feet, crushing everything in her path. Trees swayed and blurred before her. Her ears rang dully, and sweat prickled uncomfortably under her fur. Her tongue lolled from her muzzle, and she used it to wipe her snout clean.

She'd gone barely half a mile and was already exhausted when she smelled it, faint at first through the dampness of the day and the goo in her nostrils. Then the scent came again, fresher, stronger. She staggered on, lengthening her pace, eager now. A small clearing opened up, and there it was, a skinned rabbit, slick and pink in the fine misty rain. It hung from a wire from a cottonwood limb.

Trap. Her mind snapped around the word. She raised her snout to the air. It was useless; she could barely smell the raw flesh, never mind any nearby humans. She circled the clearing with leaden feet. She used to be so fast, so clever. She used to be dangerous. Now she was nothing more than a lump of granite thumping through the forest, waiting for the inevitable. If the virus didn't gut her, the Garouls soon would.

She hunkered down and thought about the rabbit. Her careful examination detected no booby traps or ambush. The immediate area was clear. So the bait itself had to be poisoned, and that confused her. That was not the Garoul way. She shuffled closer, always alert. Nothing happened. Inches from the rabbit, she gave a cautious sniff. Nothing. No poison that she could smell, but could she trust her blunted senses? Her stomach growled; she hadn't eaten in two days. Even small game managed to elude her in this weakened state. She sniffed again. She poked out her tongue and pressed the tip against the rabbit's cold, wet flank. Rainwater moistened the flesh. She licked it clean using the flat of her tongue. Poison? She still couldn't tell. A low growl reverberated in her throat and she lunged. In a flash, her teeth sank into the stringy meat and tore it away from the wire. She swallowed it in one gulp.

Luc sank to the ground, resting on her heels, and waited for the cramps to start. She wondered which organs would fail first, the liver or the kidneys? She supposed it depended on what type of poison she had gorged. But nothing happened. An hour passed. Her fur sequined with raindrops and she flicked them from her ears impatiently. Her belly growled, only slightly appeased with the meal. She needed more food, much more if she was to become strong enough. The gray morning shadows changed shape and lengthened, and still nothing happened. There was no poison.

Luc stood on shaky legs and moved on, surprised to still be alive. Half a mile away, she came across the second rabbit. She went through the same circling routine and found no traps. It confused her. Was she being drawn in? Perhaps the bait was not for her; perhaps the hunter sought other prey, but she didn't understand his method of hunting. She was certain now that this was not Garoul; this was some other hunter. But what was he up to? Luc shrugged and crunched on splintered rabbit bones. What did she know of mankind? She only knew wolven ways. That was all she had ever needed.

With more meat in her belly, she felt better. Attuned to the taste and smell of it, it was easier to pick up a third meal when its gamy scent carried in on the sodden breeze. She turned toward it without thinking. She was following blindly but didn't care. The weak daylight hurt her eyes, her snout poured mucus, and her throat and chest burned. Every muscle in her body hurt. Deep down, she knew she was dying so she might as well quit this world with a full belly. Without care or consideration, she stumbled on toward another clearing and another free meal.

Chapter Two

Oh, Silver. Noblest of metals.
Native of earth yet ruled by Luna.
Bringer of death immortalized in our hearts.
Venus on my left side. Saturn to my right.
Mars before me, Jupiter behind me...

The translation spun away from her, melting back into a language more ancient than the Minoan empire. Emily sat back and sighed. She was too tired. She had labored all weekend to wrestle these lines from the page, and what the hell were they? A song? A poem? Probably another of their goddamn awful recipes.

This was the oldest of all her source books and the most relevant. A treasure unearthed from a run-down auction house in Marseilles. She had thought France was as good a place as any to start, but had never imagined a bounty like this falling into her hands. Luck had smiled on her that day. The battered book was easily affordable for her American dollars, if only because it was so vandalized. The botanical plates had been ripped out at some earlier date leaving a stack of loose leaves and torn binding threads. She would have liked to have seen the plates. She'd heard the illustrations in these books were remarkable, but the text with all its serpentine encoding was all she really needed.

The text borrowed from several ancient languages to hide its true nature. Each runic squiggle was part of a code she hadn't managed to decipher…yet. It didn't help that the content alluded to some ancient, pseudo-scientific art. She had interpreted signifiers for the planets, the elements, as well as other compound metals and was certain the art was alchemy. Silver lay at the core of whatever she was translating. She had seen the sign for it on nearly every page. Silver was a religion to these monsters. They sang to it, worshiped it, and they were afraid of it. And that's what kept her returning again and again to this ripped up, water-stained old book, wasting night after night trying to unlock its secrets. In the end, she knew it would be worth every torturous second. *Know thine enemy.* And by God, she could see right through this one.

Emily sat back and rubbed her dry, stinging eyes. Her back ached; she had been hunched over her desk for hours. Her watch read ten forty-seven. Was it really that late? She stared dolefully at the book lying open before her. As usual, she had lost all track of time once she cracked open its leather cover. It was worth it though. The old book oozed mystery and magic…and clues. They rose into the air like dust motes and danced before her tired eyes. Bit by bit, she was dismantling its secrets.

The leather covers creaked as she closed the *L'Almanach Garoul, 1882*. On the spine, the gilt embossed title was all but worn away. The black cover boards were shabby, but the ornate decoration of moon phases still showed. The eternal moon cycle lay etched along the edges, a crescent moon blooming full, and falling back to a golden sickle. All were beautifully rendered despite the age of the book. It was a masterpiece of craftsmanship. But it was the embellishment in the center of the cover that always drew her curiosity.

She gently touched the indentation and traced the dips and swirls of the tooled paw print. It was massive. The longest claw tips splayed over the edges of the book, and it was a big book. Emily had tried to research the markings. It was of no known animal that she could identify. Either it was an artist's fancy tooled onto the leather for decoration, or it belonged to an animal as yet uncatalogued. She had a good idea which one it was, and it wasn't any artist's fancy.

There was a tap at the door.

"You awake?"

She pulled her hand away as if contaminated. "Yeah, come through," she said, though the door was already opening. She shoved the almanac under some papers.

"Brought you tea, Em." Her uncle Norman came into the room, his concentration fully on the cup and saucer in his trembling hand. "It's late. Hadn't you better be thinking about bed?" He was always clucking over her.

"Thanks." She rose to take the cup from him, guilty that she had left him alone in front of the television. What was the point of visiting him if she skulked in her bedroom all evening studying her musty old books? Except she didn't want him to see what she was reading. He wouldn't understand and would only get upset. "You should have called me to come down. I had no idea it was so late."

"Reckoned you must be busy." He peered past her to the cluttered desk he'd handmade for her too many years ago. It looked diminutive under the stack of books she'd brought with her. She was relieved she'd hidden the almanac.

"You'll wear your eyes out in this light," he said and gave a sniff that could have been disdain or indifference; she was never sure which. Her uncle only held with books if the studying of them promised a decent job, like medicine or law, professions he understood. Her father had been a schoolteacher, and to Norm, that was the pinnacle of success. Everything else, he viewed with suspicion, and Emily supposed she hadn't helped any by returning from college as a scientist, of all things. Worse still, a doctor of something that sounded newfangled and faddy to Norm. In a science he probably suspected diverted good funding money from the real important stuff.

Genomics. She researched genetic mapping. She had explained what she did to him a hundred times, but he was still baffled. However, the fact that she had a doctorate, and his living room wall was filled with her certificates and graduation photographs made him proud. None of his buddies had anyone half as smart as Emily in their families.

Her success was the compromise between her need to get away and his need to worry for her. His savings had gone to making her the professional she was today in a science he was half afraid of. His money, and the small insurance policy left by her father, had given her the education she needed to escape this backwater town.

Emily suppressed a smile; she could read his huffy attitude like the back of a matchbox, all small print and rattling, with an occasional flare-up. Her uncle Norm was a grumpy old malcontent. He hated the modern world and most things in it, except her. He had supported her all her life, and she loved him for it.

"Stay and talk," she said.

"Nah, early start tomorrow. My bones want bed." Already, he was turning away, shaking his head. "Oh, it was the widow woman," he added and looked back at her expectantly.

"What?"

"The widow woman. Lived next door," he explained further. She looked at him blankly. His face closed and his gaze darted away in embarrassment. "In that thing we were watching. The detective thing. It was her killed the boy."

"Oh. Yeah," she answered, feeling ashamed. This was the TV cop program they had been watching hours ago. Before she went upstairs to use the bathroom and never came down again. Before a thought struck her, and she had to come and crack open a book to make sure of some detail or other. Before she had fallen down that rabbit hole an open book always provided, and abandoned him completely. Her heart sank. She had been selfish and she had hurt him. Her visits home were rare, and he looked forward to them so much, and here she was, not giving him even half the time she should.

"I'm sorry, Uncle Norm. I got sidetracked." She flailed her hand limply toward the stacked desk.

"I know. I know. You got work to do. But remember, this is supposed to be a vacation. You need to get out, get fresh air." As ever, he loved an opportunity to scold and fuss. But only a little. He always let her have her own way. Again, she damped down a smile. He was lucky she'd been such a levelheaded, timorous teenager; Lord knew how he would have coped had she been headstrong and wild.

"I'm going hiking again tomorrow," she said to appease him.

"You been trapping?" he asked eagerly. Emily suspected he hunted vicariously through her these days. He had declared several years ago he was too old to go dragging around the woods after vermin, but his interest in it never failed.

"Yeah." She took a sip of her tea. It was too sweet. He never got it right. "I might have some rabbit for the freezer."

"Don't go near that valley." He glowered at her ominously.

"I won't," she said in all honesty. *I don't think I have to.*

He grunted, pleased. "Night, Em. Sweet dreams."

"You, too, Uncle Norm," she said and watched him leave.

She sat back down at her desk, balancing her cup on the last inch of space, and checked over her scrawled notes. More hours passed. Rain rattled hard on the window and broke her concentration. Emily yawned and stretched, studying her skinny midriff reflected in the windowpane. She needed to stop and get some sleep. She was neglecting herself. She should eat better and get some of that fresh air she'd promised her uncle she would. Well, she definitely would be doing that later...today? Was it really that late? In a few hours, she'd be out there, making the rounds and checking on her lures, carrying on with her experiment. She'd told Uncle Norm she was going hiking. Hiking was a nice word for what she had in mind.

From her bedroom window, rivulets of rain distorted the buildings of Lost Creek, weaving their misshapen outlines into one another. She could make out the local gas station, closed because everyone used the mall these days. Next door was Gilroy's Hardware, still limping along because needles and buckets and twine were not worth the ride over to Covington, the nearest big town. Beside Gilroy's stood the pharmacy, and next to that more empty storefronts. This was the lot of backwater towns in hard times. Main Street was practically a mausoleum.

Beyond the rooftops, from her second floor window over Johnston's General Store, she could make out the ghostly sway of poplar trees. Their slender crowns quivered under the onslaught of rain. Hundreds of trees, thousands, tens of thousands, running away from the edge of town and down into the valley as far as the eye could see. All the way down to Little Dip, to the people who claimed ownership of all the land hereabouts. *People? More like animals.* The glass reflected her bitter grimace.

Emily slid open the desk drawer and lifted out a cloth bundle. She set it on the desk and unwrapped the black silk. It pooled around a bright circular ornament. Emily lifted the large silver collar; it glimmered sharply in the lamplight. She regarded it from all angles with reverence, but not for its beauty or expense. It had cost her nearly two months' salary to have it made. Thank goodness it had to be silver and not gold or she'd never have afforded it.

It was a plain thing, no decoration whatsoever, yet its curve and bevel held a simplistic elegance she supposed was beautiful. The silver shone, sometimes sharp as a knife, sometimes soft like a good luck charm. She hoped it was both those things; she needed both. She was unsure of the dimensions so had erred toward oversize. The lock was delicately intricate, and the key was on a long chain around her neck. It nestled close to her heart. If she'd interpreted the almanac correctly, this was a very powerful weapon. A werewolf wearing a silver collar was as powerless and placid as a newborn pup. She set the collar back onto its bed of silk and gazed out at the trees and the black hills beyond.

"I'll get you, you bastard. And if I don't kill you first, I'm going to shackle you and sell you for millions," she swore to her nighttime reflection. It looked back at her, dark and distorted by the rain.

Chapter Three

No. I refuse point-blank. You can't go on this hunt. You're too upset to be objective, and I don't need another loose cannon out there." Marie Garoul was emphatic. "Besides, I have an important job for you and Hope here in Little Dip." She tried to take the edge off her order, but Jolie was having none of it. She continued to bristle.

They were in Marie's living room. Members of the Garoul clan had gathered around the huge dining table to study maps and coordinate strategies for the hunt. The air crackled with energy, and Jolie's toes itched to go over and join them, except Marie barred her way. Jolie scowled at the floor, her face heated with subdued anger. If any Garoul should hunt down that bastard Luc, it was her. It was *her* mate who had been kidnapped, *her* mate who had been endangered. The fine hair on the nape of her neck bristled at the thought of Hope at the mercy of Luc's ferals. Never mind that Hope had run rings around them and easily escaped. She could have been hurt! Jolie had a right to first bite.

A low growl rumbled in her throat, and Marie glared at her. Jolie let the growl trickle away into a moan of discontent and kept her eyes averted. Marie was Alpha, and not to be challenged, but inside, Jolie seethed. It was hard for a werewolf to be denied vengeance. She understood Marie's point of view, but it still felt unfair. She would only bite Luc a little bit when she got her claws on her. Just a little, on the ear, and maybe the nose…and then she would rip her throat right out for so much as looking at her Hope.

"Jolie," Marie said, her tone softer. "You're too wound up. You'd kill her, and that's not what I want. Luc is a Garoul. She's family. We have to find out why she is behaving like a rabid animal. We need to know more about this virus."

Behind them, the hunting party shuffled and shifted. They were prepped and ready to go on Marie's word. This conversation was delaying the inevitable, but still Jolie persisted in a last-ditch attempt to join their ranks.

"Why is Ren going when I can't?" Jolie latched on to what she hoped was a pertinent point that might sway things in her favor. Over Marie's shoulder she could see Ren talking to the others like she was important or something, when she was no more than a blow-in who had brought nothing but trouble. Jolie was angry with her, too.

"Enough." Marie's voice was sharp and determined. "Ren is coming because we are hunting her twin sister, and she has some experience with this disease. Now stop complaining and go see to your mate. I gave you both a job to do. Go do it." She turned back to the hunt pack.

Jolie stomped out onto the porch, seething at her dismissal. She had a right to go! She hesitated, unwilling to leave but uncertain what to do next. She had run out of options. Off to her left, something rustled, and from the corner of her eye, she caught a slither of brown pelt slipping through the snowberry bushes. Anyone but a Were would have missed it, but Jolie's keen senses, heightened by her foul mood, picked up on the shiver of leaves. Someone had been spying at Marie's window. Intrigued, Jolie followed the interloper.

In several strides, she had caught up. Mouse was shrugging on her fleece top when Jolie found her behind a tree. It amazed her how easily the young Were could mutate. When she'd been Mouse's age, it was a struggle for Jolie to change cleanly, if at all. It had come much easier after puberty when her bones were stronger.

"I saw you," she growled at the young pup. Mouse had the good grace to blush.

"I was only looking for Ren," she said.

"You were snooping," Jolie said and folded her arms. "Do I have to go tell Marie?" Marie was always a good threat with the younger ones.

Mouse's face became a sullen mask. "No," she said in a whiny voice. "I wasn't doing no harm." She stooped to tie her shoelaces, and Jolie was unsure where to go with this conversation. She had no idea what to do with cubs.

"Come on." She nodded toward the compound and moved away expecting Mouse to follow.

"Are we going to see Marie?" Mouse fell in step beside her, shoulders drooped and feet dragging.

"Nope," Jolie said. "Hope has made cookies." As usual, when there was a situation Jolie was unsure of, or where she felt out of her depth, she deferred to Hope. Hope would wangle the truth out of the youngster. After all, she always managed to prize Jolie's secrets out of her.

❖

"More lemonade?"

Mouse pushed her glass across the table and brushed cookie crumbs from her cheek with a grubby hand. "Please," she said belatedly.

Hope smiled and filled the glass. "I suppose you miss Joey," she said, slapping Jolie's hand away from the cookie plate. "You've had three already," she told her.

Mouse nodded. "I do. I know he had to go back to the farm, but he was sad. He liked it here."

"He'll be back in a few weeks with the others."

"You'll get to meet Jenna and Noah." Mouse brightened at once. "They're my friends. Joey's my *best* friend, but I like Jenna and Noah, too. They're cool." Mouse reached for a fourth cookie and Jolie looked on dismayed as she got away with it.

"What about Luc? Do you miss her, too?" Hope's question was deceptively casual. Mouse dropped her gaze and stopped chewing for a moment. Confusion and hurt washed over her face.

"Yeah. But everyone's mad at her, and I think they want to hurt her," she mumbled into her chest.

"No, they don't, sweetie." Hope moved around the table and gathered Mouse into a hug. "Don't you worry about that. The

Garouls want to bring Luc home and make her better. After all, she's a Garoul, too, and Marie makes the best medicine in the world. She has to find Luc to give her some. That's why they're going out looking for her."

Mouse perked up at this news. "They have medicine for Luc?"

"You bet they do," Hope said in her most upbeat voice, "and they need to find her to make her take it. Isn't that right, Jol—" She broke off and glared. Jolie tried to stuff the stolen cookie into her mouth in one go, but it broke in pieces down her shirtfront. Tadpole zoned in on the crumbs under her chair, managing to enhance her culpability.

"Mouse, I think Ren will be looking for you. Go say good-bye, and then come back here for dinner. Okay?" Hope pinned Jolie with a stern stare while speaking to Mouse. Jolie cringed.

"Okay." Mouse hopped down from her chair and headed out, Tadpole hot on her heels.

"There's something wrong," Hope said the minute the door closed behind Mouse. "She's holding something back."

"Huh? She seemed fine to me," Jolie answered, dusting down her shirtfront. Hope snorted in exasperation and moved the cookies out of reach completely.

"We'd best keep an eye on her. I'm glad she's staying here while Ren is out hunting," she said.

"I'm the one who should be out hunting—" Jolie began, but Hope interrupted her.

"You're to do what your Alpha tells you. Marie asked us to mind Mouse, and I need you here helping me, not running around the forest after that fool Luc."

"What do I know about cubs?" Jolie refused to let go of her huff.

"Then it's time to learn, and you better be quick. Mouse moves in tonight and we already know she's stressed," Hope said. "Now help me prepare dinner."

"I'm the one who's stressed," Jolie grumbled, but slid off her seat to go peel potatoes.

Chapter Four

L uc found the next rabbit in the abandoned logging camp a few miles north of Little Dip. Her escape route north had disintegrated into a zigzag from one feeding station to the next. She needed the free fuel more than she needed to run for it.

Once more, she approached cautiously. This was different from the other drops, and that unsettled her. There had been human habitation here, but not recently. A delusional entrepreneur had once tried to re-create a Wild West experience for tourists by restoring the original loggers' camp. Luc vaguely remembered the cumbersome court battle he had with the Garouls over plan designs and zoning restrictions. They had not wanted a tourist destination so close to their home valley, and, of course, they had won. All that was left was an abandoned collection of ramshackle cabins, the sturdiest of which was the dynamite store. Even it was teetering on the verge of ruination after all the years of abandonment, nothing more than a damp, mossy home for insects. The builders had been lazy in sourcing their materials and had cut timber from the nearby hillside. They had denuded the sloping terrain behind the camp, and now rivers of rainwater gushed along gullies cut deep in the exposed earth, washing away roots and earth in a muddy scree-filled flow. Water spluttered down onto the camp floor creating a quagmire of muddied pools and puddles.

Luc sniffed disdainfully at the stupidity of man as she stomped through the mire. Her nostrils quivered, zoning in on the scent she was meant to follow. She was enjoying this game. It brought her easy food, and best of all, distraction from her current woes. She turned toward the last standing cabin.

The signs of recent activity were everywhere. The place stank of humanity and mold. Boot prints covered the mud-splattered floor, but just one set. This was not very clever. Luc's ears twitched in annoyance at her hunter. She tried to figure out what was going on here. Everything had been so pristine before; there had been no trace of the hunter in the earlier food drops. Why be so careless now? A half-eaten sandwich sat curling on the windowsill. Luc sniffed it. Ham, and not that fresh, maybe a day old? Perhaps this had been the first drop and she had managed to come upon it last? Who was to say she had found them in the correct order. Maybe the hunter had become more skillful as the game went on? She sniffed the ham sandwich again and ate it. Food was fuel. Then she turned her attention to her main meal. This rabbit was not out in the open like the others. It was hanging from a rafter in the storage room, which was nothing more than a box with iron bar walls, not unlike a frontier jailhouse.

Number four was the trap. It was the fattest, bloodiest, and freshest bait so far. Luc hunkered down and regarded the rabbit and its discreet tripwire until the sun had arched and noontime passed. The rain drummed incessantly on the thin tin roof. So she was meant to lumber up to the free meal, snatch it from the wire, and in doing so slam the barred door shut behind her, sealing herself in. As if she were that stupid! Everything about this trap was a huge disappointment.

Luc tested the bars. They were strong, but not strong enough. She could bend them like licorice if she had to. No big deal. She went to snatch the rabbit then paused. She squatted back down and thought it over. How could she exploit this? Was it in her favor to trigger the trap, and then spend more energy than the bait provided breaking free again? No. Luc was wily. There had to be a better way to work it. Maybe it was time to trip the hunter instead of the trap?

❖

The rabbit was gone.

Emily looked up at the snapped wire. She'd deliberately left it too high for foxes. And it was placed well out of reach of the most agile of wolves and bears. Yet the heavy gauge wire hung limp, snapped like string. At her feet, the ground was a churned up mess. Something had stood here, exactly where she was standing, and contemplated the bait. Something big. Massive, in fact. She placed her booted foot beside a huge paw print. Her footprint looked like a child's in comparison. It had a discomforting likeness to the paw imprint on the cover of the Garoul almanac. Hadn't she traced its whorls and crevices with her fingertip last night?

Emily shifted in unease. She was on the right track. This was her first physical evidence. She took her camera from her backpack and snapped several photographs from different angles. Next, she examined the surrounding area and found more paw prints, which she also catalogued. She was surprised at how easy it was. She had expected it to be so much harder. Why was everyone else not up here in the Wallowas hunting for mythical monsters? But then again, this was the third rabbit drop, and the only one with any evidence. Had the beast become lazier with its effortless feeding? She checked the undergrowth for more prints, or better yet, fur. A piece of fur would be a lovely trophy to slot under a microscope. There was nothing. *Come on. Don't you even poop?* She scratched some fur from a tree trunk very much doubting it belonged to her quarry. Its coloring was far too vivid, most likely a fox. There were droppings nearby, also probably fox. Emily took samples anyway, storing them in her glass vials. Her initial excitement was fading; there wasn't that much evidence after all.

Emily had been hunting since she was six years old and could sit still while her father and uncle sighted their Winchesters. She knew exactly what she was doing out here in the woods. She knew this particular stretch like the back of her hand, and every animal in it, even this one, or so she was willing to bet. Taking it alive would do nicely, but if that didn't work out then she'd settle for mounting its ugly head on her wall and selling freak show tickets. She shivered, pushing down her anger, and glanced around. She felt spooked, as if she were being watched. The birds were silent. Not even the trees stirred. It was as if the entire forest held its breath.

Emily gave herself a mental shake. She needed to concentrate and stop acting like an amateur. Common sense told her the beast would be miles away sniffing out its next free meal. Meals, she corrected. It had scarfed down three so far. It had to be complacent by now, and that was exactly what she'd hoped for.

It was after two o'clock and a long time since she'd set out. She opened her backpack and rummaged through the contents. First a quick snack, then she'd head for drop number four. It was two miles southwest from here, and it was the important one. Number four was the trap. She'd rigged it up at the old logging camp, and she wanted to be energized and ready for what she hoped to find there. If it all went wrong, she was prepared to start over, but she hoped that would not happen. It was hard work trying to outhunt a hunter, but she was certain she could hold her own.

❖

From her perch, Luc watched the woman circle the clearing. So this was her hunter. Not that impressive after all. She looked down at a lanky, scrawny, redheaded thing. She could take her out in two seconds. Not much eating on her though. Not that Luc needed to kill. She had gorged on three elaborately presented rabbits, had even gone on ahead and seen the fourth one dangling delectably on its wire. She was being groomed into eating without thinking. This hunter was sneaky. Luc liked that.

So here she was, hugging a tree like a Christmas ornament, some twenty feet above her adversary. She had returned and stomped all over the third clearing, knowing it would give her hunter pause for thought. She watched with interest as the woman took pictures from one side then the other, and then scratched tree bark and fox poo into tiny bottles. Humans were curious creatures.

Luc's ears twitched. What were her options? Well, option one, she could drop out of this tree onto the woman and kill her.

Pros: there was slightly more meat on her than a rabbit.

Cons: there would be a missing hunter and a follow-up search party. Luc didn't need more humans blundering through the forest getting in the way of her escape.

Option two: avoid the hunter and her traps and keep on moving.

Pros: no dead human.

Cons: she was ill and becoming weaker. Her breathing was belabored and her head felt woozier than ever. Soon, the Garouls would be closing in on her. She needed time out, at least until she regained her strength.

Option three, and this intrigued her the most: find out what the hunter was up to. Why set a series of traps luring her to an old dynamite store? That suggested she was wanted alive rather than dead. Now why wasn't that comforting?

Pros: she'd maybe get her time out. The Garouls would shy away from a human hunter. They always turned tail when one came near, cowards that they were. Plus, Luc knew she could escape whenever she wanted through the licorice iron bars.

Cons: she had to be sure what the hunter's intentions were. A bullet could harm her; it shouldn't kill, but in her weakened state, she had to be careful.

Below her, the human hunkered down under the spread of a basswood to light a small fire and heat some water. Luc zoned in on the backpack and the ammo belt beside it. The woman went down to the stream to refill her water bottle. Luc watched after her for a moment then slid out of the tree like an oiled snake. Keeping an eye on the hunter's retreating back, she hooked the straps of the backpack with one huge claw and scooped the ammo belt onto her other arm. The hunter was still out of sight. Gleeful, Luc beat a retreat with her booty.

❖

Emily froze. She'd barely taken two steps back toward the fire when she knew something was wrong. Her stomach knotted when she noticed the missing items. *Shit. I didn't hear a thing. Is it still here?*

She kicked out the fire and hooked her water bottle back on her belt. Winchester at the ready, she scanned the surrounding area. There were no clues that she could see. No prints in the soft earth, not so much as a bent twig. Sneaky. And alarming. She knew damn well what creature had snatched her goods. What was disconcerting was that it hadn't left so much as a toe tap. She glanced at the churned mud and the walloping great paw prints she had just photographed and felt mugged. They had been made deliberately to detain her here. This creature could move like silk when it wanted to.

Sweat trickled down her spine and the jagged pain in her gut tightened. *Breathe. Nice and steady. Breathe. Don't let it beat you.* Her hand strayed to her pocket and the pack of Lexotanil. Not yet. If she managed her breathing exercises and just took her time, she'd be okay. She could keep the panic under control. She dropped her hand into a large inner pocket and her fingertips touched the silk cloth with its hard metal contents. At least she still had the collar. Her shoulders relaxed. She was in control. All she needed was a little luck, just a little. She quickly reassessed the situation. Even with her ammo belt gone, she still had a full chamber, though that was all. The Winchester was her father's rifle; she brought it along as a kind of talisman. What was more important was her missing backpack. Its contents were invaluable to her success, and she needed it back.

CHAPTER FIVE

Jolie watched as Hope fluffed up the snow-white pillow. With a final plump, she placed it back on the narrow bed and turned her attention to the duvet.

"Grab an end," she said, and Jolie obliged, helping to squeeze the quilt into the duvet cover. A new one, she noted, pastel blue with puppies gamboling all over it. She also noticed the new pink pajamas and furry slippers sitting on the dresser. Hope seemed very caught up with Mouse moving in.

"Has she no PJs of her own?" Jolie asked, struggling not to sound peevish. "I mean she's only going to be here for a night. Two at the most."

"But they're adorable." Hope held up the pink pajama top, more puppies. Jolie was not impressed. She had spent all afternoon helping Hope clean the small back bedroom in their already tiny cabin. Jolie's own log house was in its final building stage but still not ready to be lived in so she and Hope were staying in one of the holiday cabins. They were cramped enough as it was, and the last thing they needed was another body wedged in, even Mouse's scrawny little one. What was Marie thinking?

"Yeah. Cute," she gave Hope the expected response.

The front door slammed.

"I got my bag," Mouse yelled, her footsteps thumping along the hall. She appeared at the bedroom door with a small backpack slung over her shoulder. Tadpole slunk in around her ankles.

"This is cool," she said and viewed the room with interest.

"Hi, honey. I'm glad you like it. We got you some new stuff." Hope held up the pajamas.

"Puppies!" Mouse was delighted. She ran a grubby hand over the new bedspread. "Puppies everywhere. I love it."

"And look, comics." Hope pointed to a pile on the bedside table. "Now come help me fix dinner. But first you have to wash those hands." She looped an arm around Mouse's skinny shoulders. "Jolie will unpack your things," she said, as she led the girl away.

Tadpole skittered after them leaving Jolie alone with Mouse's backpack. So now she was the maid! She opened the dresser drawer and poured the bag's contents straight in and slammed it shut. Mouse wouldn't have done it any different, she reckoned. Then she threw the empty bag on top of the wardrobe. Job done, she slouched up the passageway after the others.

❖

"Okay, so there's one pork chop left." Hope came in from the kitchen, skillet in hand. Jolie gripped her plate, ready to raise it in offering.

"Here you go." Without even a glance in her direction, Hope tipped the chop onto Mouse's plate. "A growing girl needs a little extra," she said.

Jolie was outraged. She got all the extras in this house. She was the growing girl!

"But I'm not hungry," Mouse whined. Jolie's grip on her plate tightened. There was still hope.

"You mean you have no room for pie?" Hope asked. Jolie's heart sank. She knew this trick. And of course, the whelp fell for it.

"Pie?" Mouse said far too eagerly.

Amateur, Jolie groused to herself. *Just slip me the damned chop when Hope's not looking.* She tried to blink the message across the table, but Mouse was incredibly dense.

"Apple cinnamon." Hope continued to bribe. "With ice cream." Jolie groaned. *Kid's a goner.*

"So you're too full for pie?" Hope played her trump.

"No. I love pie," Mouse said.

"Then finish your dinner and I'll get you a slice." Hope swept back into the kitchen. Mouse poked at the chop with disinterest. She took a quick peek toward the kitchen to make sure Hope wasn't looking. Jolie's grip tightened until she thought her plate would snap in two. This was it! *Now or never.* The kid was never gonna eat that chop. She was already stuffed to the gills. *Over here, kiddo.*

Mouse's fingers closed around the chop bone and Jolie lifted her plate. In a lightning move, Mouse slipped the chop under the table into Tadpole's waiting mouth. He was out of the room in a flash, his tail waving in delight. Jolie's plate, and jaw, fell to the table. *The dog! She gave my chop to that shifty, useless, short-assed mongrel!*

"Good girl." Hope was back with a dish piled high with dessert. She set it before Mouse and gathered up the dinner things. Jolie glared balefully at Mouse's heaped dish.

"Where's mine?" she asked.

"You'll get yours after you wash up." And Hope handed her the stack of dirty dishes.

Later, they sat before the fire, Jolie as relaxed and dreamy as the smoke she watched drifting up the chimney. Outside, the rain drummed against the windows and a rising wind whipped the trees into a fretful dance. It was cozy inside, and Jolie watched Hope's knitting needles flash in the lamplight. She had taken up knitting and had begun a pair of mittens for Mouse. Jolie wasn't sure what to make of it, but she had been promised a scarf in colors of her own choosing so she felt less jealous. Hope was changing. Maybe the valley was having an effect on her? They had been staying at Little Dip a lot longer as they built their own cabin, managing to work remotely with the Ambereye office. Soon, their cabin would be ready to move into, and Jolie wondered if Hope would want a more permanent move to the valley.

Across from her, in the big armchair Jolie usually favored, Mouse was flung out with one of her comics. She was squinting at the print, her lips moving as she read. Tadpole lay across her stomach, rising and falling with each breath. He was the picture of heavy lidded contentment, occasionally licking his muzzle in memory of his pork chop.

As far as Jolie was concerned, his betrayal was complete and final. His frequent fond glances toward her were ignored. He was a turncoat. Jolie was Alpha here. She ruled this den, and if he was any sort of guard dog at all, he should be lying at her feet, not snoozing on Mouse's soft belly.

Den. Jolie mused over the word as she glanced at her companions, each engaged in their relaxation after a busy day. She supposed they did make a comfy little domestic pack. And Hope was seriously nesty these days. Jolie eyed those flashing needles again. When they moved into their own home, would Hope channel all this unusual activity into the soft furnishings? As long as Jolie had a space for her fishing gear, she'd be happy enough. Satisfied, she stretched out her long legs and warmed her toes at the hearth.

Luc sat back on her heels and regarded the bounty spread before her. She'd found a nice dry spot under a spreading cedar to rip apart the bag. Already, she'd eaten the Trekker Bars, wrappers and all, as her claws couldn't tear the foil off, and now she was buzzing with a caffeine and sugar hit, two substances her werewolf physiology rarely had to deal with. Beside her, the ground was littered with Glad Wrap from the hunter's lunch. She'd gorged down the ham sandwiches first, having a taste for them after the one she'd found in the cabin. Her ears twitched, and she constantly smacked her lips and licked at her snout. She felt hyper with excitement.

She'd buried the ammo belt ages ago, as it felt like a good thing to do, except she couldn't remember where she'd put it. She didn't care. The backpack was now her favorite thing. It was a huge fun-filled Christmas stocking. She loved examining all the new stuff she pulled out. There were lots of empty little glass vials. These were somehow important judging by the way the hunter fussed over them and put weird stuff in them like fox poop and fur and dirt. It was fun to pop them between her claws and watch the broken glass sparkle in the dirt.

A tube of lip balm spilled at her feet. She knew it wasn't edible, but she bit some off anyway. *Nah*, she spat it out. Her attention turned to the insect repellant. The can dented in her clumsy claws. She managed to whack the nozzle. Spray shot into her left ear and made her jump. She hurled the can at a nearby maple.

The smell of the backpack intrigued her. Everything in it had an underlying scent of creamy, feminine perfume. She found the hunter's cap in a side pocket and chewed on it thoughtfully. It tasted of coconut shampoo and sweaty scalp. She liked the way her spittle merged with the human hair smell. It took the edge off the sickly cosmetics humans used to disguise their scent. Why did humans do that? Wash away what they were, what their bodies said about them? The cap was chewed to mush, and sadly, she spat it out.

Next came an overshirt. It had been worn recently. Luc spent time sniffing the underarms. Underneath the ugly deodorant, she could detect the woman's sweat glands. It would be a nice place to bite when she caught her. The smell was complex. Luc sucked the cloth into her mouth and let the odor dissolve on her tongue. She closed her eyes and concentrated. An image of dark, warm places where sleep was thick and dreamless came to her. But it was unnatural, this dreamless space, dull and heavy, loaded with isolation and emptiness. It felt drugged and artificial. She didn't like the image, but she was intrigued. She went deeper into the taste to see what else it could tell her. The faint taint of foods that were too spicy for her Were palate came next, and then an unexpected blast of sour emotion. This unfolded on her tongue as a terse, controlled anger, followed by an underlying nervous distress. Luc let the fabric drop away and sat in moody silence. The taste unsettled her. She scratched her belly then licked her lips, transferring the taste of the shirt onto her muzzle. She didn't understand the flavor; it was impossible for her to untangle its complexities. It should be easy to break this scent down into components she could understand and ultimately use. These were skills she employed for hunting, except now they weren't working. Luc was unsettled. Perhaps the virus was destroying her diagnostic abilities? Or was this scent somehow unique, holding a message she had yet to understand? She wondered at that. The scent snaked through her sinuses and filled her head with questions. Then she sneezed, and the smell, along with her thoughtful reflection, was lost forever.

Time for payback! Luc lumbered awkwardly onto her feet. She felt dizzy and her joints were stiff. She shook her head violently to ease the buzzing in her ears. She rambled forward in a drunken, unsteady gait; the empty backpack still hooked on a fore claw. She was reluctant to let it go. She dragged it behind her through the brush. It caught and tattered on the thick, prickly undergrowth, leaving a trail a mile wide. She wanted that. It was time for the hunter to see how Luc laid traps.

CHAPTER SIX

Emily slid through the forest, melding with the shadows, flowing through sparse patches of gray, rain-soaked daylight. She felt at ease with her surroundings, but wary of her prey. The biggest game she ever stalked was elk and moose, but that didn't come anywhere close to a Garoul.

She began to make her way to her weapons drop. The Winchester Model 70 was a fine weapon. In its day, it had a lever action to be proud of, and her father had spent many nights fussing over the cleaning of it. But it wasn't Emily's weapon of choice. She was much more of a purist. Deeper into the forest, and on the way to the old dynamite store, she had a backup weapon stash. There was no way she was going on this hunt without a carefully executed plan. She had been doing this for as long as she could remember. The Garouls were not the only ones born to it.

Half a mile on, she found a flattened path in the underbrush. It looked as if an eighteen-wheeler had plowed through it. She was obviously supposed to follow it, so she did. But not directly. Instead, she stayed off track and kept a parallel line. Once she surmised it was more or less leading to the logging camp, she turned back. She didn't need to be there just yet. Let the beast bolt down another rabbit. She had other more immediate concerns.

Emily retraced her steps and followed the trail back to its source. She needed to find the backpack, and hoped it had been abandoned somewhere along the track.

She was out of luck. She found the cedar where the creature had sat and gone through the entire contents of her bag. Emily prodded her forester cap with the toe of her boot; it was chewed to a pulp.

"Weird shit," she mumbled uneasily.

Her favorite shirt lay shredded, the arm ripped clean off. It was a chilling reminder of the danger she had placed herself in. The backpack contents littered the area. A compass lay crushed in the well of a massive paw print. Her wallet was ripped apart. She retrieved that but ignored the dollar bills lying crumpled and squashed in the dirt. The forest floor was littered with her broken possessions. Her glass vials were pulverized in an act of pure vandalism. She found a dented can of insect repellant several yards away, but no backpack. The beast must have dragged it off. Why? This was an unexpected and perplexing development.

Then she saw what she was looking for, the Glad Wrap torn from her sandwiches. Relief poured through her. She hadn't realized how anxious she'd been up until this moment. She was thankful that the creature had developed a taste for cured ham.

"Gotcha." Triumph swelled through her. It would be so much easier now.

With a little more confidence, Emily set off for her weapons dump. Her main stash was wrapped in a camouflage net and hung high in a tree. She had another, secondary backup, but that was in her RV, parked along the logging road on the other side of the camp. She climbed up to the knot, slippery with rain, and lowered the bundle to the ground. Emily filled her pockets with spare ammo for the Winchester, but slung the rifle across her back. It was not her primary weapon any longer. She withdrew her own weapon from the folds of khaki netting. An Excalibur Equinox crossbow. It may not be pretty, but it packed a bone crushing punch that would fell the most monstrous prey. Her quiver of silver tipped arrows glinted at her, promising cruel victory.

The moment she held the crossbow in her hands, a warm, reassuring glow spread through her. Her faith in her plan was renewed, and her base need for revenge hummed through her. She was doing the right thing. This quest had taken up most of her adult life, and it was time to finish it.

The dynamite store was two miles east of her location. Two hazardous miles. Emily had no doubt of what lay in wait for her, but forewarned was forearmed. And she was certain the beast had already fallen into her snare.

❖

Luc was not feeling so good. The floor swam before her. The room spun crazily. She sank to her knees and dry retched. The haunch of rabbit lay before her uneaten. She had managed to tear it from its wire, and sure enough, the barred door slammed shut behind her, locking her in the caged storage room as predicted. It really was a very unsophisticated trap. In some ways, Luc was disappointed that this was the best the hunter could come up with. All she had to do now was wait for the woman to appear, rip apart the cage, and eat her. Then she would rest up and head on out. Luc sighed. She'd wanted a better test, to make more of a game of it. Except her stomach wasn't having fun anymore. She felt ill. With a groan, she rolled onto her back. Had she miscalculated the speed of the virus running through her? She had watched it destroy so many of her young pack. One by one, they had fallen to illness and even into madness, depending on what part of them rotted away first.

Not Mouse though. She had managed to get Mouse away. It hadn't been easy. In fact, it had been a sort of disaster, and now her sister hated her, and the rest of the Garouls would probably tear her apart on sight. But it was worth it for Mouse to grow up in Little Dip. Much as Luc loathed the inhabitants, she had to admit it was the safest place for a young Were to live and be schooled in the wolven ways. Mouse was a Garoul. It was about time they did something right by her.

Luc pushed away further thoughts of Mouse and Little Dip. She was leaving them all behind. Soon, she'd be back in Canada, back to her old ways and roaming her old haunts. The thought didn't cheer her. Her heart felt hollow. Beside her lay the backpack. She pulled it toward her and buried her head in its tattered fabric, breathing in the myriad body scents from the hunter. It was strangely comforting. She closed her eyes and let despair swallow her. She wanted to die.

Time passed. She felt the measure of it by the slant of daylight moving across the worn floorboards and creeping over her fur. She wasn't dying. *Bummer.* Luc yodeled a mournful bellow of self-pity and clutched at her cramped stomach. There was a click, off to her right. A cold, metallic click, not at all associated with her distressed wailing. An alien noise, removed from all the creaks and groans of an old wood cabin and the steady beat of rain outside. Luc opened a bleary eye to see the tip of a silver arrow pointed straight at her snout. *Now that's a real bummer.*

The coldness around her neck started as an eerie chill that became deeper and deeper. She felt the ache of it in her chest cavity constricting her already belabored lungs and making her heart pound harder. She was choking. Her head thumped, and an unparalleled weakness flooded her. Panic set in. For all her melancholic hankering for death, now that it was upon her, she fought back hard, scrabbling her claws against the wooden floorboards, gasping for air in massive, shuddering gulps. Her huge body convulsed and twisted. She heard the clang of the cage door slamming shut, and footsteps hurriedly retreating. The bind broke and she sucked in cool air. Big lungfuls of it, her death wish dissolving with each gulp. *Thank Luna, I'm alive!* The world steadied. She continued to suck in air. The pain in her chest eased and her panic subsided.

Luc grabbed at her neck and patted it with curved claws. Her throat had not been slit. She was so sure that it had. Instead, her claws clinked against metal. They slithered across a hard, smooth surface that encircled her entire neck.

"S-silver," came a voice from above. "A s-silver collar. Just like in the almanac. I got you, you b-bastard."

Luc rolled onto her belly. The room swam into focus. Inches from her nose were rows of iron bars, and beyond them, the scuffed toes of a pair of hunting boots. *And back to bummer.*

Chapter Seven

Emily stood back and fumbled for her inhaler. Her chest felt constricted and her breath whistled tightly in her lungs. After two sharp inhalations, her chest relaxed and her shoulders began to ease out of their tight hunch. She tried to calm herself. She had done it. She had gone into that cage and snared the beast! Her hand strayed to the Lexotanil in her pocket. She didn't need that yet, at least she didn't think so, though her heart was racing and she felt dizzy with both elation and blood-curdling fear.

Finger glued to the crossbow trigger, she examined the creature on the floor, glad of the cell bars between them. It was huge, lying flat on its back moaning pitifully. It was unbelievable that the ketamine hadn't knocked it right out. She had filled the sandwiches with enough to flatten a rhino. Her gaze ran over the huge clawed feet and hands and along powerful limbs. It had a tight, muscled torso, and its chest was padded with a deep, dense musculature that was still curiously female. Somehow, it never occurred to her it might be female. It was covered in a thick black fur that was matted with mud, leaf mold, twigs, and God knew what else. The squashed muzzle was turned away from her, but when she had darted in and snapped the collar around its neck she had glimpsed cruel rows of razor-sharp incisors and the thin, leathery lips trembling against them. She was dismayed to find the collar a tight fit, almost too tight. She forced the ends together until the lock clicked and the silver cut a gleaming welt through the thick neck fur. She'd nearly lost her nerve when she realized the creature was still semiconscious, and had to stop herself from fleeing and abandoning the whole plan. What the hell was she doing? It was a crazy idea, capturing a werewolf. She was mad. Mad to believe in them. Mad to spend her entire life trying to prove they were real, and mad to begin this impossible, life-threatening hunt. The collar better damn well work or she could be dead before nightfall once the beast came around.

She tucked the inhaler back in her jacket. Her breathing was manageable now, and her world re-formed itself into the pigeonholed orderliness she tried to live by. She should congratulate herself! It had not been such an impossible objective after all. On the other side of those bars was a beast of legend. A werewolf, no less. And she alone had trapped it. It had succumbed to a strong opioid like any other big game animal. Okay, so apparently, it needed a ton of the stuff, but there was only so much dope she could stuff in a few sandwiches. A game warden would normally administer ketamine subcutaneously with a dart. Her gaze flickered to the quiver of arrows leaning against the doorjamb. She had several of those, too, if needed.

With a woeful bellow, the beast rolled onto its belly. Emily shuffled back a step, startled by the noise. The beast opened bloodshot eyes, its wet snout level with her feet. A huge clawed hand scratched at the collar around its neck, unsure of what it found.

"It's s-silver," Emily said, her voice hard. "A s-silver collar. Just like in the almanac. I got you, you b-bastard." She hated the stammer, but it always came back when she was under pressure. The hated speech impediment had begun soon after her father died.

The beast ran its watery gaze up and down the length of her. It looked unimpressed. It tugged at the collar. The silver rang against its hard-tipped claws like crystal bells. A strangely melodious sound in the small cabin with its muddy floor and grime-encrusted walls, and far too melodious a sound to issue from a creature of incarnate evil. It groaned again and opened its shaggy maw. She was so close she could see the strings of saliva quivering on its teeth and the elongated flare of its nostrils. There was a queer tilt to its lumpish, misshapen left ear, the imperfection lending character, making it somehow less of a monster? Then its thin lips stretched tight into a wide leer. Time stood still, and for one insane second, she thought it was about to speak. *Do werewolves speak?*

Then it sneezed, loudly and violently; and a huge glob of thick green mucus flew through the air in a perfect arc to land on her pant leg. The beast gave a satisfied sigh and rolled over onto its back, its long pink tongue lolled out and wiped its maw clean before its eyes drifted shut.

Emily stood frozen, looking at the creature, acutely aware of the green muck sliding down her pant leg onto her bootlace. Had she just been dissed? She was revolted and not a little put out at this show of disdain. This was not what she had expected.

What exactly had she expected? A docile werewolf? She found it hard to accept a little thing like a silver collar could calm a beast like the one lying flat out before her.

A riot, that's what she expected; now that she had actually *seen* a werewolf. This creature would awaken maddened from its drugged slumber and quite literally charge at her. Her crossbow was in her hand, armed and ready with a second shot of tranquilizer. She didn't care if too much ketamine would kill it. Dead or alive, it was all the same to her, although alive it was much more profitable.

Her motive was revenge, but there was no reason it couldn't prove lucrative. She looked at the glob of snot on her leg. As far as she knew, this was not a side effect of the tranquilizer. The creature must be ill. It did look pretty ropey. If she had a vial, she would collect this goo and have a closer look at it. Except her lab was at Chicago State University, and the beast had smashed every vial she had carefully packed away. Even now, it had stuffed its matted head inside her backpack and was snoring into the ripped Gore-Tex. Still, a sick creature would be easier to control than a violent healthy one.

Phase one of her plan was complete, a fact that surprised her greatly. Phase two was another matter. Her subject was alive. She now knew ketamine worked and could administer more as needed. Over the next few days, she would take her samples and return to the laboratory she had hired. It would be interesting when the questions began to fly. Where had these extraordinary specimens come from?

Exactly what new species had Dr. Emily Johnston discovered? And best of all, the limitless trajectory her career would take from this day on. This was monumental, the discovery of a lifetime. The discovery of the century!

❖

Luc's tongue was glued to the roof of her mouth. Her eyes gummed closed with a sticky crust, which was probably for the best, as what little daylight that did infiltrate her eyelids cut like a lance. Her head ached, and her breath and mood were equally foul. She growled and the reverberation in her throat came out as a tinny croak and not a satisfying, gut-crunching rumble. *Human again.*

With a sigh, she forced open her eyes and dragged her head out of the backpack. The metal ring around her neck was cold against her skin. She grabbed it. It was loose enough to push up to her chin, but there it stopped, catching on her jaw and ears. She jammed it, and twisted it, shook it, lathered it with spit, but it refused to budge. After about ten minutes, she gave up ramming it against her grazed and reddened skin.

"A silver collar," she spoke out loud in disgust. "What a nut job."

She flopped back on the backpack and absently chewed on one of the long leather buckles as she thought through this latest development. As if a ring of silver could stop her from ripping this cabin and anyone in it apart. She snorted at the preposterous idea. It was the virus that was weakening her. She could feel its burn in her blood. She flicked at the ring indifferently. It hung loose around her neck and lay cold against her collarbone like some useless tribal decoration. In human form, it was nothing more than ugly jewelry. As a werewolf, it was all superstitious nonsense, wasn't it? Still, if this sort of hocus-pocus gave the hunter false courage, so much the better. When she was ready, Luc would strike, and no amount of piddling silver charms would save that bitch's skinny ass.

Luc glared at the iron bars enclosing her and sat up, leaning against the timber wall to sulk over her recent run of shitty luck. In

Were form, she could rip these bars apart and leave unhindered, but in human form she was just a snotball who could barely stand up. What the hell had happened? One minute, she was loping through the forest filled with self-satisfied cunning. Next, she blearily remembered feeling like she'd been hit by a train.

Drugs. The hunter bitch whore had drugged her. Luc scowled at the skinned rabbit on the floor next to her, a cold, gray, unappetizing lump. There had to be something in the rabbits, after all.

The door clicked and Luc watched with interest as the hunter entered. The woman jerked to a shocked standstill, surprised at seeing her sitting naked behind the bars.

A redhead. Luc regarded the woman. *Such an ugly hair color. You'd think nature would have bred it out by now.* Then she threw the rabbit as hard as she could, straight at the hunter's head.

CHAPTER EIGHT

Y ou cow." Emily was still seeing stars. She clutched her forehead expecting a lump the size of an egg.

"What's for dinner? I'm starving." Her captive launched into complaint. Emily blinked and regarded the naked woman warily; she knew she was being kept off tilt. It hadn't really occurred to her that the beast would, or even could, revert back to human form at will. How was that possible? She was wearing the collar? Emily was sure the woman should have been trapped inside her monster's body?

Nor had she expected that the human would be so rude...or naked, for that matter. She'd been shortsighted and stupid. This was a person she was dealing with. A devious, manipulative human being with sneaky, lupine senses. She blinked again trying to clear her head and grudgingly admired the creature's strategizing. She'd have to be on alert for mind games now. This was a malicious predator with many resources. Emily snorted. Then again, throwing a rabbit at her head was hardly genius. She just needed to reassert her control.

"That was your dinner." She toed the rabbit into a far corner, pleased her anger had quelled her stammer. It often worked like that.

"Poisoned rabbit doesn't work for me in this skin." The woman plucked at her bare belly.

"It's not poisoned. The sandwiches had ketamine in them, but you were so busy focusing on the rabbits, you thought nothing of eating *my* food." No sooner had Emily made the boast than she knew she had made a mistake. She should have kept that information to herself, but the arrogance of this…this woman, got her dander up so quickly she was acting brash. She pressed her lips shut.

"You what!" The woman looked stunned. "How did you know I would steal your bag and eat your lunch, huh?" she demanded.

"I didn't. Those sandwiches were for the next drop if this one failed, but you saved us both a lot of time. Thanks for that." That seemed a harmless enough brag. Let the creature know she had contributed to her own demise.

"I need clothes. It's fucking freezing." Unimpressed, the woman changed the subject.

"My spare clothes were in there." Emily pointed at the tattered backpack. "You shredded them, so hard luck." Though she knew she couldn't leave her shivering in the chill air. Damn, the trick was working. Already, she was seeing a woman and not a monster. A skinny, undernourished woman. Her skin had an unhealthy waxy pallor and her dark hair lay in greasy clumps around her thin shoulders.

"Gimme your coat." The shifty black eyes probed Emily for any sign of weakness. Lord knew they were plentiful enough, and she didn't need this hellspawn latching on to any of them. Emily averted her eyes then realized she'd made another mistake. A weakness had just been exposed. She was finding the woman's nudity unsettling. There was a slight shift as the woman subtly rearranged her posture, leaning toward Emily belligerently. In a microsecond, she had picked up on Emily's discomfort. That was spooky. Spooky and clever. Very, very clever. *Oh, she's good all right.*

"Not in a million years." Emily made herself scowl disdainfully at the skinny, dirt-encrusted frame. It worked. She noticed a dull bloom spread across the jaundiced cheeks and the woman drew back. She may not be ashamed of her nudity, but she *was* ashamed of her condition. Emily knew for certain she had a sick creature on her hands, a sick, proud creature. Correction, she told herself, a sick proud *human*. Sickly and belligerent, what a winning combination that was.

"What the fuck's this?" Anxious fingers plucked at the collar, the fingernails bitten to the quick. Emily noted the change of direction. She was being wrong-footed. Forced her to see a human being, and forced to confront what she had done to her. Well, this woman was a monster, a werewolf and a killer, and she'd be damned if she would be manipulated into caring for a—

A loud and uncontrolled sneeze blasted through Emily's ruminations. She watched the woman shiver and wipe the back of her hand across her nose. Her brow was damp with sweat.

Emily sighed and turned for the door. She needed to go get her second stash, the one on wheels about a mile up the road, and drag out some spare clothes. She didn't have it in her to torture. She could disassociate from a monster and extract all the tissue samples she needed to implement the second part of her plan, but she couldn't ignore the needy, morose woman glaring at her from behind these bars. That would be inhumane, and Emily wasn't that. With a puff of annoyance, more at herself than anything else, she slammed out the door to make the short trek to the RV.

"Hey. Where are you going?" The call followed her out the door; she tried her best to ignore its undertone of anxiety. She probably wasn't supposed to hear it anyway.

Jolie heard Mouse go. The smallest sound had woken her, and her human ears pricked to attention. *What was that?* Tadpole lay on his blanket in the corner, his stubby legs stretched out, deep in sleep. The noise came again, a soft click that suddenly fell into place in Jolie's mind. It was the door latch. She had been promising Hope for weeks to oil it. The metallic squeak was enough to get her out of bed and pad barefoot out into the hall so as not to wake Hope or their so-called guard dog.

She was in time to see the door close. Jolie peered out the window into the darkness. Had someone been in their cabin? A soft growl began to rumble in her throat only to be cut off as her keen eyesight picked out a moving shadow. It was not an intruder; it was a guest. A guest leaving.

Jolie opened the door just as softly and stepped out into the night. She followed Mouse into the trees and watched the youngster strip off her pajamas and crouch down. In no time at all, she mutated into her scruffy wolven form and scurried off deeper into the forest. Intrigued, Jolie dropped her drawers and flung off her top and did the same. She had to be quick or Mouse would outrun her in a blink once she hit an open stretch. She didn't know Mouse very well, but like all the cubs in Little Dip, she was banned from running at night unless she was with an adult. Jolie didn't feel that Mouse would be deliberately rebellious. She had a healthy enough respect for her elders, Ren and Isabelle especially, and for Marie Garoul in particular. Marie could put the living fear into any of the pups when she had to.

So what had brought Mouse outdoors so stealthily? Jolie tailed her through Little Dip forest to the edge of the home valley. Mouse hesitated, sniffed the air, and after a slight stall, pushed on out of the Garoul homeland and into, for a cub, forbidden territory. There was no hesitation on Jolie's part. Duty compelled her to follow, but now she felt a rising excitement. A monumental rule had been breached, and she sensed adventure. This was her excuse to disobey Marie and leave the valley. It was her responsibility to catch Mouse and find out what the hell she was up to, and, of course, to bring her back.

Luc rose to her feet and padded over to the bars, her keen hearing picking up the crunch of retreating steps. She gave a snort of derision that turned into a hacking cough halfway through, and spat a gob of mucus at the door.

"Oh, where are you going, big bad hunter?" she called in a high mocking voice, once she knew the hunter was out of earshot. "Don't leave me here all alone."

The hunter was tall, but not as tall as Luc. She was thin, too. Her clothes would fit nicely once Luc peeled them off her lifeless body. Luc slumped back onto the floor and plucked at the chewed buckle on the backpack. It was frustrating to be this weak. She wished she were home.

Her shoulders drooped.

Home. Where the hell was that? For Ren and Mouse, Little Dip was home now. Granted, she'd wanted Mouse there, far away from the virus that was rampaging through Singing Valley, but it meant Luc had little reason to go back north. And Ren would thump her if she ever got her hands on her. Where was sisterly love when you needed it? Luc felt abandoned without that particular safety net. Being a twin was a powerful bond. It felt strange, almost frightening, to be cast adrift without it.

A small whine quivered somewhere in her chest and she quelled it. She was feeling mighty sorry for herself. She lifted the backpack and buried her nose in the coarse fabric and found strange comfort. From a long way out, she picked up the drone of an engine and grew anxious. It came closer and then stopped. Who had just driven in? Did the hunter have companions? She locked in on the silence and soon heard solitary footsteps approaching. She recognized the hunter's footfall. That was a pleasant surprise; she'd expected to be left cold and hungry for at least several hours. That's what she'd do to a victim. And now she knew there was a vehicle out there, too. Her data was building up. A car would come in handy when she decided to leave.

She had some idea what the hunter's plans were. The broken vials from the backpack and the small roll of surgical tools laid out on the windowsill told her this was serious. The hunting trophies this one wanted were a little more complex than Luc's head on a platter. She had to escape before the woman could take specimen samples, or anyone else arrived to help her. If she could stay drug free, Luc figured she had a good chance. All she needed was to stay warm and well fed. If she could build her strength up, she should soon be able to mutate and be out of here in a blink.

The footsteps came closer. She feigned an almighty sneeze to remind the hunter how sickly and unthreatening she was. The door opened and the woman walked in. She carried a small backpack and a thermos. Luc grinned. This was going to be a lot easier than she had thought.

CHAPTER NINE

L uc watched the woman enter. She set the backpack by the door and unbuckled it, pulling out a bundle of clothing. Next, she lifted a long pole from the corner; the sort of thing used to open high windows, and approached Luc's cell. This was interesting.

"Stand back," she said, and dropped the clothes to the floor and began pushing them through the bars with the pole. She was keeping well out of Luc's reach. Luc took a short step back, more a token gesture than compliance. Despite her weakened state, she was still stronger, faster, and in her opinion, smarter, than the average human. Luc lunged. She grabbed the pole, and before the woman realized what was happening, dragged her rapidly forward. There was a lightning fast, unruly scuffle, but Luc managed to snag the woman's wrist and slam her body hard into the iron bars.

"Let go of m-me!" the woman yelled, her face a mask of terror inches away from Luc's. Luc tightened her grip painfully. Excitement soared in her at the struggle. This was fun.

"You're dead." Luc began to play with her prey. "I'm going to rip your—eep!" Luc yelped. With her free hand, the woman began to hit Luc repeatedly over the head with the thermos. "Hey. Stop that!"

A lucky swipe caught her on the bridge of her nose. Blood gushed and her eyes watered. The woman's panicked struggles intensified at the sight of blood. She was babbling nonsense, which Luc finally made out to be a stream of stammering. The woman was so frightened she was barely able to speak; she jabbered, and twisted, trying to jerk free. The terrified wrestling, along with the flow of blood from her nose, soon tired Luc out. Her excitement deflated, along with her energy. Maybe she wasn't as ready for the game as she'd thought. She hauled on the hunter's arm as hard as she could, pulling with all her weight, and slammed the woman against the cell bars. She slumped to the floor and Luc slid down with her, refusing to let go. The woman was out cold. Luc sat there, still holding her wrist, the pulse swimming under her fingertips. She counted the beats for a second feeling the heat of the woman's flesh in her palm. What to do next?

I should rifle her pockets. Wouldn't it be nice for a key to the cell door, never mind this stupid collar, to fall out into Luc's hand? Instead of a key, she pulled out a driver's license, an inhaler, and a strip of pills from the only pocket she could easily reach. Not what she wanted but useful enough.

"Well, hello there, Emily Jane Norma Johnston." Luc smiled at the small color photograph. "That's a bit of a mouthful, isn't it, Emily?" She considered the pale hand clamped in her own. "And I'm sure you will be," she said, sneering at her own joke.

She threw the license into a far corner. The inhaler she slowly examined, twisting it around and around in her free hand, looking at it from all angles before tossing it after the driver's license. The pills were another matter. She needed to think about them. She had no idea what they were but guessed they were connected to the strange odor she'd picked up on the backpack. These weren't ketamine, the drug used to knock her out. Never once letting go of the hand, she set the foil pack next to her. These pills had something to do with that dark, dreamless place she could detect on Emily's skin. Luc guessed they were antidepressants or maybe sleeping pills of some sort. What did that tell her about her enemy? Luc wished she had the emotional sensitivity to know. That would be a useful skill to have right now.

Luc hauled the bundle of clothing closer but didn't feel inclined to put anything on. It smelled of brash detergent and disinterested her. She'd rather be naked and interesting. She examined the hand she was holding. The skin was pale and the knuckles dusted with freckles.

I bet you're dappled all over. She raised the hand to her nose. Even with the blood clotting in her nostrils, she could make out the woman's scent under the sour drug odor. It was…it was… She didn't know what it was, but she sort of liked it. With another surreptitious sniff, Luc pulled a finger into her mouth and sucked on it. Taste flooded her. She rolled her tongue around the finger, drawing in a tinny flavor laced with salt, and a mechanical oiliness that probably came from the handle of the crossbow. Anxiety underlaced everything.

Her gaze slid to the crossbow. It lay well out of reach by the door. It would be nice to have that inside the bars with her, too. She did not fear the silver tipped arrows. That was all superstitious nonsense. But she'd love to see this hunter's face—this Emily's face—when she came to and found herself on the wrong end of her own weapon.

She withdrew Emily's finger from her mouth and examined the palm. It was grimy and red. Acting on instinct, she licked along the lines, cleaning the fine ridged dirt, imagining she was washing away fate and the future, and replacing it with her own divinations, though what they were she had no idea. She squinted at Emily's broken, bitten down nails. If she had the strength to turn Were, she would use her long fore claw to clean the stubby, dirt-laden things. Just look at those cuticles. This human was very neglected and unkempt; she needed a good grooming.

Emily groaned. Luc tightened her grip on her wrist and waited. Nothing happened. Luc sat still, holding Emily's hand, unsure of her next move. She felt as if she was on a cusp but was uncertain which line of action would be for the best. She should kill the hunter; after all, she had wanted to kill Luc, well, sort of. Luc glanced over at the surgical tools lined up on the window ledge. Whatever the plan was, it probably involved some sort of vivisection. But it was in Luc's interest to keep her captor alive. She needed to make sure she could get out of this cell and remove this stupid collar. Then she would decide what to do with the human.

She concentrated on the rain thrumming on the tin roof and on Emily's shallow breathing. The rain came down harder and harder until the whole structure vibrated. Water seeped through the eaves and ran down the walls to pool on the floor. The drumming, the dripping, the steady measure of Emily's breathing became almost meditative. And then she heard it, or thought she did, rolling in under the rattle of rain and the creaking of cabin walls…a lone howl. She sat up straighter and strained her ears, missing her wolven senses more than ever. Was it a howl? She cursed the incessant drum on the cabin roof. After several minutes, she decided she had heard nothing. It was just her mind playing tricks. But the imagined howling unnerved her. She was losing focus. What was she doing sitting in this paltry cellblock waiting to be hunted down and killed? She was ill and needed to recover as quickly as possible. The Garouls were after her, and the torrential rain would not slow them down for long. And what was she doing about it? Nothing, that's what.

She looked at the pale fingers enclosed in her palm. She was sitting here holding hands with a human. She was losing it; that's what she was doing. *Enough!* She had to get out of Wallowa and somehow limp north.

Emily moaned again and shifted but didn't awaken. She seemed content to drift along on the verge of consciousness like flotsam on a tropical shoreline. Well, that was a luxury neither of them could afford. Luc lifted Emily's hand and nipped hard on the soft flesh at the base of her thumb. Emily yelped and struggled to a sitting position.

Oh? That got your attention. Excitement coursed through Luc, and her tongue tingled at the metallic taste of Emily's blood. Emily pulled her hand away and gazed stunned at the bloody indents on her palm.

"You bit me!" she screeched.

"I was all out of smelling salts."

"Y-you bit me. D-does this mean—"

Luc snorted. "You! A werewolf? A w-w-werewolf? I don't think so, somehow." She played on the stammer. "It's only a little nip. If I'd really bit you you'd be looking at a bloody stump." She was losing interest in the histrionics already.

Emily shuffled backward on her bottom, staring at her hand. Luc regretted letting her go, but really, apart from killing her, it was pointless to hold on. There were no keys in her pockets, and the clothes and thermos were already on Luc's side of the bars. In a few hours, she would have recuperated enough to transform and get the hell out. All she needed was a few more hours of rest, Garoul free.

"You're a b-b—" Emily began.

"Babe? Beauty?"

"Bastard," she finished.

"Ah, quit moaning. It woke you up didn't it? What's that for?" Luc nodded at the surgical instruments by the window. "You were planning to cut me open, weren't you?"

Emily had the grace to look embarrassed.

"Who's the bastard now?" Luc said. She lay back down on the dirt floor, uncaring for the cold permeating through it. She was bone tired. She lay there listening to Emily fuss over her piddly little wound.

"Where did you hear about us?" she asked.

"There have always been rumors," Emily answered tiredly. "The black yeti of the Wallowas is famous."

"Liar." Luc's gaze fell on the quiver of silver tipped arrows. "Who goes after yetis with silver arrows?"

Emily ignored her.

"Have you always been fascinated with werewolves?" Luc continued. "Or is it a recent obsession? There's a name for werewolf groupies, you know. It's dinner."

"My name for captured werewolves is stupid." Emily rose to the bait as Luc had hoped.

"So where did you hear about us?" Luc asked again, ignoring the jibe.

"I knew what you were." Emily's voice was sullen. "I have an almanac. I've been studying it for years."

"You read an entire Garoul almanac?" Luc was surprised. "Good for you. I've never got past the first page without nodding off."

"It's a beautiful book," Emily sounded genuinely shocked. "And mine doesn't even have the pictures."

"Wow, no pictures. You really are a scholar. So what was your plan? Cut me into chunks and auction me on eBay? Or maybe sell me to a zoo in one big living lump?"

"The zoo was a last resort."

"Comforting, though I'd prefer the circus." Luc sat up. "I can juggle you know." She watched Emily dab some ointment on her palm. "It doesn't work like that," she told her. "You won't become a werewolf with a little nibble like that." Then a thought occurred to her. Perhaps she wasn't so far off the mark with the groupie thing? "Now, if you wanted to become one, I could help. Just let me out of here and—"

"Forget it. I'm more worried about tetanus than lycanthropy." Emily continued dabbing at her hand. "Have you any idea how many bacteria are in the human mouth, never mind yours?"

"Hey, I'm a natural balm. They say if you rub werewolf spit on the right place it can cure frigidity." She shot a knowing look and saw Emily's face burn. *Ah ha, Miss Prissy took a direct hit.*

"What you've got is lycanthropy, not Spanish fly," Emily snapped. "And your dirty saliva is all over my skin."

"Funny how your stammer stops when you're being a bitch."

"Oh, what a big sense of humor you have, Grandma. Goes well with that big red nose," Emily said.

Luc's hand involuntary reached for her sore nose. The bleeding had stopped, but the throbbing hadn't.

"You broke it." She lied to see if any remorse was forthcoming. You never knew with humans.

Emily snorted back laughter. "You look more Rudolph than werewolf."

Estranged as she was from her pack, it still went against every fiber in Luc's wolven being that a human should know the truth about the Garouls, and especially about her. Survival of the species meant secrecy. She had to fix this mess somehow, which was difficult, seeing as she could not eat the infiltrator.

"Hear that?" She whipped toward the window, diverting the conversation and pumping concern into her voice. She needed to get the upper hand again. This Emily was an all-knowing, spiteful thing.

"W-what?" As she suspected, the stammer came back. Emily was a born worrywart.

"Do you hear the howling?" Luc whispered. "They're closing in."

"The Garouls?" Emily asked, though she looked like she already knew the answer.

"No, that would be Alvin and the Chipmunks." Luc cast her a dirty look. "I bet they want their book back. Is it overdue? Have you been naughty and not checked your library ticket?" She tried to look self-satisfied.

"I c-can't hear anything."

"That's because you have puny human ears." Luc enjoyed the dread that flashed across Emily's solemn gray eyes. "They're going to eat you, and Luna help them because you're one poisonous little toad."

There was a moment of silence as Emily concentrated on hearing, anxiety etched across her face. She nursed her hand close to her chest, rather overdramatically, in Luc's opinion. *Luna forbid I bite her properly; we'd be on Broadway.*

"I can't hear anything," Emily repeated, trying to sound dismissive.

"Try harder."

Luc's tongue clicked against the roof of her mouth. She wished she had her wolf teeth. She'd have loved to run her tongue along the smooth enamel surface and imagine sinking them into Emily's throat and then shaking and shaking and shaking her.

There was a shudder.

The floor they were sitting on lurched. The cabin moaned like an old whaler, and from outside came the snap and splinter of tree roots upending.

"I heard that," Emily whispered, her face went even paler.

"Not that!" Luc barked, though she was all ears, concentrating on this newer, much more dangerous sound.

The roof shook and threw down a shower of debris. Wall planks bent and cracked. Shards of dirt and uprooted plants spilled through the gaps.

"Mudslide," Luc yelled, her gaze locked on the cell's back wall. It heaved and splintered. It tilted to a distorted angle and cracks rang out like gunfire. "Oh crap."

The wall exploded inward, a torrent of mud and stone scree barreled through the planking and poured across the floor in an ear-splitting roar. The roof collapsed to the rear of the cabin, its corrugated tin shrieking as it tore apart. The world around them became a confusing slurry; a sharp-edged torrent of earth and stone and bruising darkness.

Chapter Ten

Jolie followed Mouse as far as the highway that wound all the way down to Route 3. It was the best route through the mountainous region and heavily used by commercial traffic. Eighteen-wheelers and Mack trucks streaked past throwing up dirt and belching pollution. The grass and long-necked weeds swayed crazily in their back draft. She saw Mouse ducked down in the scratchy underbrush. She seemed hesitant, wary, and Jolie realized the youngster didn't have much experience with busy roads or how to navigate them in wolven form. Jolie lengthened her pace, hoping Mouse's momentary indecision would gain her the couple of seconds she needed to stop the cub from running out in front of a truck. Mouse waited, her head whipping from side to side as she watched the oncoming blaze of vehicle headlights, trying to judge a safe gap. Her hindquarters were bunched, ready for a mad dash across the wet pavement. Jolie could see her trying to time her run, unhearing and unseeing of anything else, her concentration fully on the thundering trucks. Jolie snuck up behind her undetected and grabbed Mouse by the heel as she lunged for the road.

Oh no, you don't! Damned if I'm bringing you back to Marie scraped into a paper bag. Her growl was edged with anger. Mouse looked around in dismay as Jolie dragged her backward through the underbrush and deeper into the trees. Her ears flattened and she spat wildly but knew better than to struggle with Jolie holding on to her leg. Once she was released, she scrambled to her feet and stood hunched and hissing.

Hiss at me one more time, missy, and I'll nip your nose off. Jolie was livid and her growling grew deeper. *What the hell are you doing out here? Are you meeting up with someone?*

Mouse averted her eyes, finding the forest floor fascinating. *No one. I was just out running.*

Running, my ass. Tell me the truth, Jolie rumbled, *there's no way you would even think to cross that road except you needed to be on the other side. What's over there? Who's over there?* The cub was out of control, Jolie decided. She had grown up as good as feral with no notion of pack manners. What did Ren think she was doing raising cubs like this? But for Jolie's intervention, the little squirt would be squashed as a fly on a fender. All Jolie wanted was to get her back home before Hope found them missing. Marie and Ren could sort the runt out later. *You came all this way for a run? No way am I swallowing that. Guess Marie can whup the truth out of you.*

I'm following the hunt, Mouse conceded. Jolie smiled inwardly. Marie's name always worked like a charm.

Why? Marie will have your whiskers. Jolie frowned at this news.

I don't want them to hurt Luc.

Luc deserves all she gets, and she's damned lucky I'm not out there with—

The bushes rattled behind them and they both stiffened. *I knew it! You were meeting somebody, you lying little—*

Jolie took a defiant step toward the undergrowth determined to face down whoever was in hiding. With one last snap and shake of foliage, Tadpole bustled out of the bushes. His ginger snout snuffled inches from the ground and he bumped into Jolie's shin before he noticed her. Ecstatic at his find, his tail began to wag and he jumped up on Mouse's leg for a pat of approval.

Jolie's shoulders slumped. Could this night get any worse?

What the hell! Who's guarding Hope? she roared. Tadpole dropped to his belly. *This is ridiculous,* Jolie continued bellowing at him. *You crazy ferret! Do you two realize what will happen if Hope wakes up and finds us all gone? I will die, that's what will happen! She will kill me. Now, back home, the lot of you—what?*

Her last word came out in a squeak of disbelief. She was standing there roaring at Tadpole, and Tadpole alone. Mouse was gone. She had slipped away while Jolie harangued the dog.

With a last hard glare at the dog, Jolie turned and stomped off to begin her search all over again. She snapped branches, and stormed through the greenery until leaves and blossoms littered the ground in her wake. Uncaring, she trampled over new shoots and bent fledgling trees, squashing everything that came into her path. Behind her with his tail waving proudly, Tadpole followed her swath of destruction.

❖

Emily instinctively curled into a tight ball as a wave of mud and stones washed her into the corner. The noise was terrifying, and all she could do was squeeze her body as small as possible and hope the freezing deluge would stop before burying her completely. Stones and forest debris pounded on her back. Boggy water filled her ears, nose, and mouth until she spluttered for air, sure she would drown in the mire. And then the onslaught stopped. The thick, turbid gurgling gave way to the creak and crack of wooden walls.

Emily collapsed onto her aching back, resting on her elbows. Freezing mud covered the entire floor more than a foot deep. She was swamped in it, covered in it, every inch of her. Reclining like this, it came up to her chest. If she stood, it would be knee-deep. Toward the rear, where the roof had fallen in, mud banked up to nearly five feet, and huge boulders and twisted tree roots stuck out of the back wall at all angles.

She sat up, stunned but relieved she could move freely. It was pure dumb luck one of those huge boulders had not pulverized her to bits. Thankfully, she had been far enough back to miss the full onslaught.

But the werewolf hadn't.

Emily splashed onto all fours and crawled as fast as she could toward the cell with its bent bars and bank of solid mud. Sharp stones cut at her palms and knees. It felt like crawling across a riverbed, but her pounded body was too weak to stand in the slippery mess. Wind and rain slashed at her face, whistling in through the flapping tin roof. The sharp smell of pine cut clean and fresh through the sour pungency of the mud. Emily grasped the bars and regarded the mess inside the cell. How could the woman have survived? Emily's heart thumped in her chest and she felt a familiar tightness gather in her body, swarming like bees in her belly. What had she done? She had incarcerated a woman in this death pit, and now she was buried whole. Crushed to death, or drowned.

Emily began scooping away handfuls of dirt from where she had last seen the woman. She had to be here, pressed right up against the bars; there was nowhere else for her to go. She clawed at the earth, but every cavity she scooped out filled up at once with muck and water. Something squirmed and touched her fingers. A hand broke the slippery surface and grabbed at her wrist. Emily reared back with a cry and dragged the woman upright into a sitting position. They sat and blinked at each other in surprise. Then the woman's face cracked into a wide grin, gleaming snow white against her mud-plastered face.

"Hey there, Swampy," she said good-naturedly, as if adventures like this befell her every day. Emily splashed onto her backside, relieved to see the woman alive. They had both had a narrow escape. Above them, the roof creaked, as if to warn that they were not safe yet.

"W-we need to get out of here." Emily eyed the bent roof beams.

The woman shrugged. "I'm going nowhere unless you've got the door key."

But already Emily was pushing her hands into the waterlogged pockets of her pants. She pulled out mud-soaked tissues, coins, and a pocket-sized flashlight. Everything spilled onto the dirt as she searched frantically.

"Here!" She jingled a set of keys.

"Yippee," came the flat reply. "Now get me out."

Emily hesitated. What if her captive ran away? The roof creaked again, louder and longer, and the mud under their feet shifted and flowed as if she were standing in a rolling river. *To hell with it.*

When unsure what to do, Emily followed her gut, which was invariably always digesting moral fiber. She pushed the larger key into the cell door and turned it with a satisfying click. The door refused to open. She shouldered it with all her strength, but it moved barely an inch.

"Let me try." The woman grabbed the bars on the other side, and between them, they managed to wedge the door open several inches. The cell walls shuddered and mud swirled around their legs trying to suck them down deeper.

"I can get through this." The woman began to slip through the gap; she was remarkably thin. "You go. Get on out," she ordered Emily. After a second's hesitation, Emily moved for the cabin door.

"Not that way," the woman called after her. "It's holding up that entire wall. Go through the window." Sure enough, the sagging wall seemed to be resting on the doorframe and nothing else. Alarmed, Emily went over to the window and pulled it open. It was high up, and tall as she was, she had to scuff for a foothold to reach the ledge. She was hanging there scratching the wall with her toes when a firm hand on her bottom pushed her upward and through the opening with dizzying speed. Before she knew what was happening, she landed in a heap outside, a slimy mud bank breaking her fall. With an agile leap, the woman landed beside her. Emily lay sprawled at her feet, shivering with cold and shock. *This is the moment she kills me, proving for all eternity what an idiot I was to trust her.*

"Come on, Tar Baby. We gotta get away from here." A hand scooped under her armpit and she was hauled to her unsteady feet. She gaped in surprise at her former captive who seemed more intent on dragging her away to safety than caving her head in.

"Ouch!" She clutched the back of her thigh and limped alongside her rescuer who wasn't slowing any. They were several yards away when, with an earsplitting crash, the cabin collapsed completely.

"Told you it was going to go," the woman said, and kept on dragging her.

"Stop. Wait, just wait." Emily dug her heels in and refused to move another inch. "Where are we going?"

The woman looked at her, perplexed, then shrugged, dropping her hand away from Emily's arm. "Dunno. Just away." The rain ran in rivulets through her stringy, mud-drenched hair and down her forehead into dark eyes that blinked out rainwater and dirt.

"Well, I'm going to my RV for a hot shower," Emily stated a little huffily, and with that, turned in the opposite direction and limped away.

"Wait. You've got an RV? Where? I didn't see any RV." The strange woman was hot on her heels.

"You would if you'd gone farther north."

"What? How far?"

"About a half mile. I drove it in closer after you were locked up. It's there." Emily pointed to a small, beat up, orange RV on the far edge of the clearing.

The woman gave a low whistle and increased her stride. "Sweet."

"Hey," Emily called, anxiously. "I got the keys." Already, the woman was looking in the windows, smearing the paintwork with her mucky hands.

"This thing has a shower?" she called back. "It's miniscule."

"It's big enough for me." Emily puffed up to the side door and slid it open.

"It wasn't even locked," the woman objected.

"I n-never said it was locked. I said I had the keys." Emily sat on the side step and began to kick off her shoes, grimacing in pain.

"You pulled a muscle?" the woman asked.

"Yes. I was pushed headfirst out a window, remember?" Emily answered tiredly and shucked off her jeans, uncaring about the other woman. She was freezing to death in these mud-soaked clothes. She needed to get clean and drink something hot before she froze into an ice cube. "Once I get the engine started, I can warm the water. It heats up pretty quick."

"Tepid will do." The woman made to push past her into the RV.

"Hey." Emily grabbed at her arm. "Get those dirty clothes off."

The woman looked at her. "I'm naked."

Emily stared at the mud-coated body. Of course, the woman was naked. They were both so slathered in dirt it was impossible to tell the difference in the rain-filled, misty night. The woman pushed past her leaving a trail of muddy footprints.

"Don't touch anything," Emily yelled after her, and shed the last of her clothes. The sound of water alarmed her. Already, the woman had located the small shower and was running it. "Hey. I haven't got the engine started yet." She opened the driver's door and turned on the ignition.

"It's wet. That's all that matters," the call came back. "Do you have any shampoo—oh, here it is."

Emily stepped into the RV, anxious and unhappy that the woman had commandeered her little traveling home. She kept it pristine, but already it had muddy feet and handprints everywhere. The shower door was open and water splashed all over the linoleum floor.

"You're making a mess," she scolded her. Her anxiety tightened in her chest. This was a preposterous situation. A werewolf was in her shower. And using her best shampoo. Except it wasn't a werewolf. It was a muddy, messy, very naked woman who had absolutely no manners. Everything was out of control, and Emily was struggling to corral it back in. Between that and keeping her breathing steady, she was light-headed with exhaustion. She stepped in a puddle of cold water. "Do you have to thrash about like a p-porpoise?"

"Get in here. The water's warming up."

"Just hurry up and I'll go next." Her teeth were chattering. Coming in out of the rain had helped, but her chill went bone deep. She was so cold she felt unwell. A hand reached out and hauled her into the small shower cubicle where a dollop of her expensive shampoo was dropped onto her head. "You can't—ack," she spluttered on the soapy water.

"Where's the key for this?" The woman pointed at the collar around her neck. Emily reached for the chain around her own neck. It was missing along with the key to the silver collar.

"I-I don't know," she said.

"Get it off." The woman was tugging at the collar. "It's annoying."

"The key's g-gone."

"Typical." Then large hands began to roughly lather Emily's hair. "Nothing goes right for me," she groused. The cubicle was far too small and they stood all angles and elbows, and far too close for Emily's liking.

"Ouch." She winced and pulled away.

"You've got a lump on your noggin." Strong fingers probed her scalp. "It matches your black eye. You look like a winking raccoon."

"Well, you look like a p-proboscis monkey," Emily huffed.

"Ah. You caught me with a lucky swipe on the hooter." The hard fingers continued to probe Emily's bruised face and neck, checking out her bone structure for any more sore spots.

"Leave me alone. It hurts." She tried to step away but was blocked by a wet, slippery body, and teasing, challenging eyes.

"But you're not clean yet," the woman said. The suds from the shampoo were massaged over Emily's body. She was scrubbed behind her ears with rough fingertips digging out any muck lurking in the grooves of her ears.

"You need to look after your ears," the woman scolded her playfully. "How else are you going hear the Garouls sneaking up on you?"

So it isn't playfulness, Emily thought. It's torture. She tried to swat the hands away only to have hers grabbed by bigger hands and her palms and fingers brusquely massaged and soaped clean.

"Paws, too," said her tormentor. "Very important for running away."

"Stop it." Emily spat water from her mouth. "I can wash myself."

"Can you now?" The woman grinned down at her. "That might take a while. You got more muck on you than an earthworm."

Her protests were ignored, and Emily found herself too tired for even a token struggle. Her neck and armpits were soaped by calloused palms that stroked down her back to the flair of her hips in broad, stinging sweeps. *God, I'd pay a hundred dollars for an exfoliation like this in a salon.* Emily's unwelcome thought broke off into a squeak as she was spun around and her bottom was brusquely massaged.

"Hindquarters should be nice and silky for a good nipping," the woman said. There was suppressed humor in her voice. "Because trust me, you aren't going to outrun a werewolf."

Emily felt her face redden and turned away, but was pulled back against the woman's body and a huge soapy hand reached around to scrub the apex of her legs until the tender flesh on her thighs glowed pink. Emily tried to slap her hands away.

"I can definitely do this bit!" she said, anger and panic seeping into her voice. There came a deep rumbling laugh from behind her that as good as vibrated along her spine.

"Feels like good nipping there, too," the woman said, ignoring her complaints before somehow managing to kneel in the small space and wash the length of Emily's legs, lifting each foot and soaping between the toes, and tsking all the time at the state of Emily's "paws."

The entire body scrub took all of four minutes and left Emily feeling as if a soap-fueled tsunami had crashed over her, but her skin sang and she was warm as toast, and best of all, thoroughly clean.

She squeezed around in the stall to stand almost eye-to-eye with a gaze as mischievous and sin-soaked as the devil himself. Her heart leapt into her throat. It was too unnerving.

"Me now," the woman said.

Emily tried to slide out without their bodies touching. "Um, I-I'm going to make some tea."

"Me." The shampoo bottle was thrust at her. Emily forgot about decorum and ran for it, her breasts sliding across the woman's torso, belly touching belly, and not caring at all in her scramble to get out. And she was free! Plopped out from the steamy cubicle and into the cool of the tiny RV. She grabbed a towel and wrapped it around herself, trying to ignore the leery chuckle from behind. Tetchily, she reached over and swung the shower door shut, cutting off the laughter with a slam, though the thin plywood provided no real privacy.

Emily toweled dry and pulled on clean clothes. She assembled a spare set of clothing for her guest, a ragtag assortment of whatever she had left, which was very little. She'd be damned if that bitch was going to sit around buck-ass naked and laugh at her discomfort.

Emily was not a prude, but she felt completely out of her depth in every sense. She had so underestimated the nature of this adventure.

This would be the time a smart person would make a run for it, she told herself. But to where? Without her weapons, she didn't have a chance against this predator, especially in the heart of the forest. She'd be chased down in seconds, and she didn't want to find out any more about a "good nipping."

Emily mulled over her options as she lit the gas stove. She had no crossbow, no rifle, and her brain felt as organized as a tossed salad. The woman who was making a mess of her shower could turn back to werewolf at any time and kill her. It was obvious that for the moment, Emily was nothing more than a toy to her, to play with and mentally torture.

She had to get away. Emily eyed the small Tupperware canister lurking at the back of the kitchen shelf. She had one resource left. Thankfully, she would never run out of tea.

Chapter Eleven

Luc rinsed her hair in the cooling water. This was an un-expected turn of events and very much in her favor. Best of all, the crossbow and rifle were now buried under a ton of mud. Her hunter was weaponless. Finally, they were on a level playing field. Luc knew she should make a bolt for it now that she was free, except she too had been under that same ton of mud. She was feeling very beat up and bruised. Not that little Miss Squeaky Clean out there needed to know.

Luc had to look invincible if she was to cow this human into working for her. This was a nice little setup, a sweet little RV that could take her all the way to the Canadian border. All she needed was for Emily to drive her. There'd be plenty of time for her to recuperate on a journey like that. And best of all, the Garouls avoided humans like the plague. They would not be expecting Luc to have a human in tow, never mind one chauffeuring her to freedom. There was a good chance, in fact a great chance, they would miss her altogether as she cruised out of the valley in this orange hippie mobile. *After all, they're looking for a rogue werewolf, not Mama Cass.* Luc was pleased with this new escape plan. It was bold and daring and something new to brag about. She exited the shower to see Emily preparing herbal tea.

"I left out some c-clothes." Emily blushed and nodded at a pile of clothing and a towel on the bench seat. Luc liked that she had an effect on Emily. It was something they could explore on their road trip north.

"Luc," she said, and began pulling on the old jogging sweats, ignoring the towel. "My name is Luc. You can use it."

"Oh." Emily looked flustered, but didn't use the name. "I made some tea." She shifted uncomfortably. Luc supposed it was not every day you had a werewolf for tea, though Emily seemed more than happy to prepare poisoned sandwiches for them.

She slid into the bench seat across the table from Emily and sipped from her cup. It was pitch-black outside, and Emily had lit a small lantern. The rain drummed on the roof, and the windows were all steamed up with raindrops tracking crazy patterns down the glass. She noticed the side door was slightly ajar.

"You're not closing that?" She nodded at it.

"I need to vent the gas from the stove," Emily answered in a terse voice.

Despite the faint draft, the RV had a cozy, intimate feel, and Luc could imagine it was fun to travel around in it, making camp wherever your nose led you. She contemplated the woman sitting opposite her. Her damp hair was dragged back and tied loosely at her nape. It only served to emphasize the angle of her jaw and the long curve of her neck. Her black eye blended with the shadows cast across her face. Luc zoned in on the small ear she had thoroughly scrubbed clean. It brought a sly smile to her lips. Emily shifted in her seat, and Luc noted her high color and discomfort. She still remembered the curves of Emily's wet body under her hands. The woman glowed in the dim lamplight, and Luc felt her blood quicken. She clicked her tongue against her teeth. She had a hunger and it was not for rabbit.

"What is there to eat?" she demanded.

Emily reached in a nearby drawer and pulled out a few bags of chips. "It's all I got. S-someone stuffed themselves with all the Trekker Bars," she said, trying to sound cool.

Luc pulled a bag apart and began to stuff chips in her mouth. She was starving, and at least these were pre-wrapped and couldn't have been tampered with.

"I think you've got w-w—" Emily watched her eat with dismay.

"Wisdom? White teeth?" Luc grunted around a full mouth. "What?"

"Worms," Emily finished.

Luc glared at her. "I do not! I'll have you know my sister's a vet."

"You have a sister?"

"A twin. But she's the ugly one, and we have to lock her away from polite society." Luc crumpled the empty bag and tossed it.

"A twin sister? I'm trying to imagine two of you in the world. It's n-not a pretty picture."

"Werewolves have twin cubs all the time." Luc was licking her fingers clean. "So." She was tired of the conversation. Time to change it. "You travel far in this bean can?"

She watched Emily focus on her tongue curling around her fingers. It was a fine, long, healthy pink specimen, and she was proud of it. However, Emily looked embarrassed. Good. Luc was happy to crank up the sexual tension. Emily looked away and tried to shrug nonchalantly, but it was more like a spasm.

"I-I drove here from Chicago," she said, trying to regain composure.

"Chicago?" Luc was surprised. "You came a long way to collect wolf poop in little glass bottles."

"I'm visiting. I was b-born around here."

"Where here?"

"L-Lost Creek," Emily said.

Well, that explained her hunting habits. Only a local gal could be so slippery in these woods. "I've never seen you before," Luc said.

"I've n-never seen you either."

Luc shrugged. Something was bothering her. Something in Emily's manner, in her speech perhaps? "Well, I went away for a while. I'm visiting, too," she said.

"Visiting the rest of your pack." Emily sounded bitter, and Luc's curiosity rose. Then it clicked. The stammer. It appeared when Emily was nervous, but went when she had her temper up. So what had been making her nervous earlier? Luc was sure it wasn't her simmering sex appeal. Her senses went on alert.

"Pack?" she said.

"I mean the Garouls." Emily snorted in derision. "Don't deny it. I know what the Garouls are. You're all out of the same fractured mold."

I like her much better when she's bitter. "So," Luc said, "what of it?"

"Everyone in town thinks the Garouls are witches," Emily said. "But I knew different. I spent years watching you all."

Oh, this isn't good. Back to plan A, eat the bitch. "And?"

"The Garouls are werewolves and I captured one. All those old folk tales about Sasquatch and black yetis, it's been creatures like you all along, and now I have evidence."

"You do not. All you have is a stupid old almanac." Luc enjoyed teasing her. Emily was such an easy target. She took another slurp of her tea. She was having fun. "And apparently, it doesn't even have pictures. The Garouls will love that. One of their holy moly almanacs vandalized. You are so dead."

"Yes, I have an almanac, and I have you," Emily said, her voice cool and clipped. She was fighting to keep control of the conversation. Luc had to change that.

"No," Luc said with a smile. "I think you'll find I have *you.*"

This was greeted with silence, so Luc expanded on the situation as she saw it. "In fact, I think you and I are going on a road trip. You're going to drive me to Canada. We'll make a holiday out of it and camp along the way like regular folks—"

The RV lurched.

Luc looked around her worriedly. The walls began to blur and spin. Across the table, Emily watched her carefully.

"You drugged the tea!" Luc said. No wonder the devious cow had been stammering. She was waiting to see if Luc noticed. Luc was aghast she had fallen for such a simple ploy…again. Emily said nothing but continued to stare at her with those enigmatic gray eyes.

"You sneaky little bitch," Luc roared. She made a grab at Emily, who bolted from the table and flew out the partly opened side door, slamming it shut behind her.

Luc chased after her, snatching at the door through blurred eyesight only to find the handle had been removed. She fell to the floor. The RV was choking and claustrophobic. The dinky furnishings and garish colors swam in and out of focus. The plastic, unnatural odors contracted her stomach. Sweat saturated her skin, but she knew this drug dose was not as strong as before, or maybe she hadn't ingested as much. In human form, it was overwhelming, but if she could change then maybe it might be manageable in her wolfskin. She grunted as nausea washed over her. She had to force the change, and soon. The clothes she wore were too hot, too tight. She kicked them off. Her body twitched and her guts tightened. Luc closed her eyes and breathed hard into the pain.

A few minutes later, she sat upright. Her huge hulk took up most of the floor space. On standing, she smacked her head against the roof lining. She stood awkwardly and hunched, panting in the constricted space. Enraged that she had been tricked again, and so easily, she kicked against the side door until it hung askew on its metal runners. The cold night air blew through the opening and calmed her. It filled her head with the soothing smell of the nocturnal forest. She raised her muzzle and sucked in the odor of wet soil and rain-laden foliage…and the faintest scent of coconut shampoo. Excitement bubbled up in her. Emily was within reach. With a roar, she leapt into the night and began the hunt.

❖

Emily broke into a wobbly run. Her injured leg was killing her, but she had to keep moving. Her only chance was to keep going until the ketamine took hold. Though Lord knew how long that would take, as she had very little left to dose the tea. She dodged low branches and vicious root hooks trying to put as much distance between herself and the RV as possible. She swerved around low scrub brush, cursing her blackened eye and its partial vision. The twists and turns of her ill-conceived revenge had become catastrophic. Loose shale rattled under her feet, and the harsh rasp of her breathing filled her ears. She was making no headway at all. She needed a change in strategy; she needed to find somewhere to hide.

She hobbled onward and hit a slope, her momentum propelling her forward. Arms outstretched, she felt the soft clay give way beneath her feet. She pitched forward losing control of her balance and speed. The tree loomed out of nowhere and she slammed straight into it, her shoulder taking the brunt. Emily catapulted onto her back and rolled down the steep bank scrabbling for purchase, too weak to slow her fall.

Around her, the forest roared and shook. Leaves and twigs scattered under her. Roots clawed at her and she clawed back, desperate for a handhold. Then the bank dropped away and she plunged into the roaring waters of the Silverthread. The hurtling cold took her breath away. She surfaced and gulped down air. Thrashing and struggling, she flung herself at the shoreline, but the fierce current, swollen by days of rain, washed her farther out. The stars above swirled and lunged crazily, zigzagging across the sky. And then she understood. She was watching them from underwater. She was held by an underwater current. She was drowning. Her body, numbed and useless with cold, floated just under the surface like river weed. She was slipping into nothingness.

I'm dying? I came home and I'm dying—

The water around her exploded. She was hauled by the neck of her shirt out of the river and into the bitter, windswept night. The pain in her body came back tenfold. The river water roared and she was lifted upward, light as a child, and her head came to rest on a broad hairy shoulder. Her face was crushed against dense, wet fur that stank of dirt, water, and bark scrapings and…and…coconuts?

The world spun as she was carried to the river's edge and dumped on the bank. Emily retched repeatedly. At last, she lay still and drew a breath, giddy with the air now swelling her lungs. She was wet and freezing and hurt all over, aware only of a microcosm of wet, pungent earth, the scratch of dirt on her back, and two massive clawed feet inches from her head. The werewolf had found her. It had dragged her from the river and threw her here. It stood immense and panting, towering over her prone body, droplets of water falling from its fur over her.

Then its breath was on her face. *First, a mudslide, then drowning, and now my throat's ripped out.* She closed her eyes. Not that it mattered anymore. Her revenge plan had failed, and she couldn't care less. She was so tired of it all anyway.

Except her throat was not ripped out. Instead, a massive pink tongue trailed along her left cheek, then the right one and across her brow until her face glowed warm and wet. She was again bundled up into a muscular leathery chest. Coarse fur tickled her nose and stuck to the damp on her face making it itch. She was slipping into a thick fog, into a darkness she accepted she might never stir from, accepting this was death...and then...and then...

And then she was opening her eyes, and she was alive?

It was dark and she was warm, too warm. Overheated, in fact. Her mouth was dry and her shoulder hurt. She vaguely remembered running into a tree? Her gaze swam into focus and she found herself staring at the bottom vent of her small built-in fridge. She was lying on the floor of her RV swaddled in a pile of blankets and rugs, and what looked like her gingham tablecloth? Everything was piled up around and over her, like a nest.

She shifted, aware of a weight along her side covering her like a heavy woolen blanket. That was why she was stifling hot. Emily pulled away. A bottle of water sat on the floor beside her, along with a split tea bag, a twig, two packets of pills, and some acorns. Emily frowned at the strange collection of items. Were they some sort of comfort offerings? At the moment, only one mattered. With great effort, she reached for the water and gulped it greedily. She checked out the pills—her standard painkillers and her Lexotanil capsules. She popped two painkillers and collapsed back into the snug hollow.

The weight behind her shifted. A wet snout burrowed into her neck just below her ear. Emily froze. This was not a blanket. She was nestled in with the werewolf! So much for the collar keeping them in a single state and malleable. The beast seemed able to transform back and forth at will.

There was a snuffle, then a sleepy snort that puffed the tendrils of her hair. A heavy, furry arm reached over and covered her, dragging her back into the warmth of a shaggy chest that felt wider than a barn door. She was spooned by an immense body of hard muscle and silky furred smoothness.

She twisted around until her nose was pressed against a furry throat. She levered backward until the arms holding her relaxed and allowed her a little more room. Emily leaned back and examined the leathery maw before her. The muzzle was squat with thin black lips that rested over the sharpest, cruelest teeth imaginable. The canines were so long they curved over the lower lip. The snout was warm and wet, and the elongated nostrils quivered as they drew in her scent even in sleep. A huge pink tongue lolled from its mouth and traced the teeth, licking the thin lips. It was such a hungry, predatory action Emily worried she smelled like dinner. The leather of the muzzle gave way to a smattering of black fur that grew denser toward the brow and small pointed ears. The head, shoulders, and back were covered with a thick ebony coat, except for the chest and belly area where Emily's hands rested on sparse hair that barely covered a heavily muscled torso. Heat pounded off the werewolf's body and she could feel the tremor of its heart against her palms.

It opened its eerie yellow eyes and regarded her with mute caution. She lifted a hand and delicately explored the coarse muzzle. Her fingertips itched under the scratchy texture of its fur, and she found herself exploring swirls and tufts and the crease lines beneath. Its eyes narrowed and the gleam in them softened. Fascinated with the long curve of a canine, she traced it to its razor-sharp point and rested her fingertip there in awe. Its teeth were vicious, monstrous things, and it thrilled her to touch one.

Its gaze darted across her face, equally fascinated at this intimacy. Her touch wandered through thick fur to the next wonder to catch her attention. The left ear was misshapen by a bite taken out of it. She caressed the crimped shape and played with the tuft of crown hairs until the ear twitched and flicked her fingers away. The creature's eye color had mellowed to warm amber, and it pushed its face even closer until the heavy meatiness of its breath blew directly into her face. Emily tried to withdraw, but the arms around her tightened until she thought the air would be squeezed from her lungs. Then the beast's tongue swept across her cheek and forehead, washing her with lathering strokes, and she went limp. There was no fight left in her. She had seen lions do this on TV. She was being marinated.

The arms encasing her became gentle and she relaxed into a sort of…cuddle? The creature gave a final snort and then its eyes drifted shut and, unbelievably, it fell back to sleep almost at once.

Emily watched it sleep for a few moments more until the heat from its body became overwhelming, and the tension within her own exhausting. As she lay there, the ache in her muscles began to melt as the painkillers kicked in and she could feel her body grow slack. She was in a makeshift bed, snuggling with a werewolf. It was all too much for her brain to compute, and her chest began to pinch. She turned away and reached for the Lexotanil, then hesitated. She was sore, and tired, and warm. When had she last felt warm? She felt as if she had been dragged through torrential rain for months on end, not a few days.

Emily closed her eyes and breathed out her exercises. She concentrated on inhalation and exhalations, slow, steady, smooth. She counted, and held, and released, and counted again. Over and over, until she found it impossible to open her eyes as sleep claimed her. The immense size of the creature cradling her was oddly comforting.

Luc, she reminded herself, *the creature was called Luc.* And it was sleeping so soundly because she had drugged it. *I should get out of here. Run away. Now.* But her mind was a jumble of hazy, unconnected thoughts. *I should be scared. I lost Dad's good Winchester. What day is it? Is it Sunday?* Her world was full of troubles and questions, but for this single moment in time, all was suspended. She stopped fighting her anxieties. She was far too tired to reexamine these old and constant companions. And she found that instead of rattling around in her head all night, her anxieties fell away, letting her tip over into dreamless slumber.

CHAPTER TWELVE

Jolie was fed up. These young ones kept a sprightly step, and she was growing tired and more and more cranky trying to catch up with Mouse. Dawn marbled a pewter gray sky. In a few hours, Hope would be waking to find herself in an empty bed. A bed Jolie longed to be curled up in right now. She imagined Hope shuffling sleepy-eyed around the cabin looking for her companions only to realize she was alone. Would she worry? Would she be angry? Jolie's ears twitched and then drooped. Hope would be livid. And who would get it in the whiskers for everyone's disappearance? Jolie would, that's who! Hope would assume they were all out in the woods frolicking and having werewolf fun without her. A wet branch slapped at Jolie's face, and mud caked her fur right up to her knees. She was soaked through and miserable. *Some frolic this is.*

Ears slicked tight to her head, Jolie trudged on. Behind her, Tadpole grubbed along the forest floor, sniffing at this, piddling on that, totally unconcerned that his den mother had been abandoned. *Some affiliate werewolf he is. Useless mutt.*

Jolie's huff was cut short by the rumbling of her stomach. Breakfast time. She raised her muzzle to the cold morning air and sucked in all the exciting smells of daybreak. The nocturnal animals were retiring, sleepy and sated after a night's hunting. The day dwellers were awakening, blinking at the cold morning. Every animal was at its most vulnerable at the crossroad of night and day. Dawn and dusk surrendered the sweetest hunting. Possum musk caught at her nose. It was in the trees overhead. Jolie drew its scent in hungrily and smacked her lips. Breakfast was served.

She found Mouse half a mile away. She had stopped to examine a clearing and was so confounded by the complexity of odors that she didn't hear Jolie approach.

Lesson number one, Jolie snarled, and flung a hank of possum meat at her feet. Mouse jumped back, startled. *Always guard your back. Lesson number two.* She hunkered down to examine the mishmash of muddy footprints Mouse had been so engrossed in. *Eat well and often. Keep your energy level up. Remember, you burn hundreds more calories in Were form.*

Mouse fell on the food. She was ravenous and had not had much luck in feeding herself. Jolie watched her gorge.

Lesson three. Jolie's ears twitched in amusement as Mouse suddenly stiffened, then gagged. *Don't eat the musk glands. They stink.*

That was mean. Mouse huffed, her muzzle twisted and sulky.

That was a learning curve. Now you know, never eat an animal's ass. Jolie turned her attention back to the footprints. *Tell me what you think is happening?*

Mouse had only ever played in the Singing Valley back home. This was a whole new formidable world for her, but she had to learn how to keep safe. Jolie watched as she circled the clearing following her nose. The scent she was tracking was faint and played tricks even on Jolie's sensitive snout. It drifted in on the rain, flat and lackluster, only to fade away on the next twist of breeze. She watched Mouse stumble forward a few steps, zigzagging this way and that, chasing the elusive odor until she caught it again. To Jolie it was a soft and sticky scent, layered with pine and wet loam.

From where she sat, she could easily pick out Luc's scent. It was strong and purposeful. There was almost a cocky gleefulness to it, which surprised Jolie. She had expected a furtive anxiety. Luc knew she was being hunted. Whatever she picked up, Mouse found, too, and it jangled her nerves. Jolie could see it in the hunch of her back and the nervous flick of her tongue across her muzzle. Something significant had happened here, but Mouse couldn't read the underlying story.

Jolie joined her. Werewolf footprints churned up the mud, and a curious wire hung from a tree limb. Nearby, a small fire had been stomped out. Rain pelted down on the drab little tableau, and Mouse hunkered down beside Jolie, unsure what to do.

Humans. Do you think she scared them away? Mouse looked worried. As a pack, the Garouls taught their young Weres to avoid humans at all cost. This was a lifelong lesson. But then, as far as Jolie was concerned, Luc had never learned the lessons, and she certainly had little regard for the rules. She was a rogue werewolf who would put her whole pack, her whole species, in peril through her irresponsibility.

Well, Mouse would definitely learn the rules if Jolie had anything to do with it. She turned her attention back to the cub. For her age, Mouse may be able to change super fast, but she had no idea how to timestamp a scent or read its narrative. Jolie roped in her impatience and began to teach.

One human. Luc may have scared her, but she didn't run away. See how she followed Luc out of here? She left Mouse to examine the markings and went to examine the wire hanging from the tree. She hadn't seen anything like it before but had a good idea what it was.

How do you know it was a she? Mouse asked, twisting and turning around the prints, trying to make some sense of them.

Jolie gave an exasperated snort. *Look at the size of the boot prints. You need to learn to use your brains as well as your snout.* She gave Mouse a rap between the ears with her fore claw to emphasize her point.

There's a wire in the tree, high up. See? She pointed it out, as Mouse had not looked up even once in her investigations, only concentrating on the forest floor. *It's a trap. Luc got away. But barely.* Jolie was worried. This hunter was clever and determined. And as far as Jolie could tell, she was still snapping at Luc's heels.

It was close to daybreak and time to turn back home. Jolie had done all she could do. She would return Mouse to Little Dip safe and sound and report Luc's latest shenanigans to Marie as soon as possible. Finally, she had the situation under control. Jolie breathed a sigh of relief as much as tiredness. All she wanted to do was go home to Hope and curl up in bed for a big sleep. It took stamina to remain in Were form all night without a decent kill for energy. The possum she caught for breakfast barely filled a fore claw, never mind her stomach. *And* she'd had to share it.

Luna knew how Mouse still held her wolfskin. She was one tough little cub, Jolie grudgingly conceded. With a paw planted firmly on Mouse's shoulder, she turned them toward Little Dip.

Come on, whelp. We need to tell Marie about this. She'll know what to do. She was relieved when Mouse fell into step beside her without complaint. She had expected whining and tantrums, but Mouse was as exhausted as Jolie was. It had been a long night for both of them.

Where's Taddy? Mouse asked, her question bringing them up short. A quick glance around the clearing showed no sign of the dog. In fact, Jolie wasn't sure of the last time she'd seen him. She prodded at a nearby bush.

Tadpole? She growled, hoping he would snuffle out from the undergrowth.

Taddy. Mouse yipped. *Here, boy.*

He didn't appear. Nothing moved in the forest except the breeze.

Stupid mutt. Jolie's heart sank. Hope would kill her. There was no going home now. Not until all their party was accounted for. No Garoul was ever left behind.

CHAPTER THIRTEEN

W hat's for breakfast?" a voice murmured close to Emily's ear. "Better be something good or it will be you."

Emily opened her eyes and stared straight into Luc's wickedly teasing gaze. The dawn light shone across the velvety curve of her shoulder. She was in human form and they were both naked. Emily felt only relief. She doubted she could cope lying nose to nose with a werewolf in the brash light of day.

"W-why don't you just kill me and go?" she asked. She was exhausted, mentally and physically, and sick to death of the whole accursed plan. She had been crazy to think it would work.

Luc lifted a lazy finger and tapped the collar around her neck. "Until you find the key, I think we'll be spending a lot of time together."

That was an unpleasant thought. Emily decided not to dwell on it and changed tack. "What's this?" She indicated the blankets balled up around her.

"It's a bed." Luc looked around her, very satisfied with the setup.

"It's a nest, you mean." Emily wriggled uncomfortably, then pulled a budding twig from underneath her. "It's even got leaves. What are you, a big chicken? Since when do werewolves sleep in a nest? Shouldn't you burrow or something?" She had no idea about werewolf sleeping arrangements. She heaved to her feet and pulled on her clothes using the idle chatter to hide her embarrassment.

"I'm a werewolf, not a meerkat. We make nests when we're on the move." Luc began to dress as well, dragging her sweats out from the mess surrounding her.

"Oh," Emily said. "I tend to make up the couch bed when I'm on the move." She looked pointedly at the rear bench seat.

Luc wiggled her fingers.

"Claws. Last night I had claws. They tend to rip the stuffing out of things." She gave Emily a narrow-eyed look that reminded her how lucky she was her stuffing was still intact. "Now." Luc tapped her collar. "Get me the key and maybe, just maybe, you won't be breakfast."

"This is your breakfast." Emily opened the small cupboard over the sink and tossed a chocolate bar at Luc. "It's all I have left."

Luc regarded the bar with suspicion. "No dope?"

"No dope." Emily unwrapped her own bar and bit into it. Partly because she was starving, partly to prove she could be trusted, on this occasion at least. Luc copied her.

"Key?" she asked with her mouth full, still determined to get an answer.

Emily sighed. "I told you before. The key was on a chain around my neck, but it's gone. I think I lost it in the mudslide."

"Okay." Luc finished her breakfast in one more bite and tossed the crumpled wrapper toward the sink. "So we dig."

"Dig?" Emily picked up the wrapper and put it in the trash, frowning with annoyance. "There's a ton of earth out there. No way will we find a necklace."

"We know roughly where you were standing and where you ended up. It has to be in that corner." Luc was on her feet. "Come on," she ordered and stepped outside. With a heavy heart, Emily followed her.

The mud felt cold and gritty between her fingers. Several yards to her left, Luc was hacking at the dirt with a broken plank. Emily dug with slow deliberation, though her mind was working furiously. If they found the key and she was forced to unlock the collar, she would be dead in seconds and Luc would be halfway to Canada in her RV. Emily had no doubt about it. Not that she was exactly sure how the collar was keeping her alive. Her earlier assumption that it "froze" a werewolf in beast mode had proven untrue. If anything, it seemed to be improving the creature's health. Emily considered the state of the woman digging beside her. She had been such a grubby, wretched specimen only a day ago. Now she was just grubby. Did the collar somehow regenerate a werewolf's health? Wouldn't that just be typical of her crappy luck to give the damned woman a cure-all instead of a curse?

"Ah ha!" Luc cried out. Emily looked up sharply, heart in mouth, to find Luc holding aloft a sodden arrow quiver. There was only one arrow left in it and Luc was examining it closely.

"Vicious little thing," she said, looking at Emily. Emily felt her face heat. Then Luc said, "Hey, this tip is hollow. Is that where you put the drugs?" She sounded genuinely interested.

Emily turned away and didn't answer. She went back to digging in the mud and watched out of the corner of her eye as Luc placed the quiver on top of the pile of crap she had pulled out of the mud.

"More treasure," Luc said, sounding pleased with herself, and she patted her latest find. So far, she had collected a boot, a crushed bottle of water, the forceps from Emily's surgical pack, and now the quiver with its arrow. She was the strangest creature, Emily decided, and thought of their nest and the little pile of objects Luc had piled beside it to comfort Emily and aid her recovery. And despite her bed companion being a werewolf, Emily couldn't remember the last time she'd had such a sound sleep. *It just goes to show how cracked I am.*

"You're not putting all that crap in my RV." She pulled her thoughts in a more practical direction. Best play along with this ridiculous Canada road trip until another avenue for escape opened up, and it would. One look at the mud-splattered packrat opposite her confirmed that Luc was not used to playing captor and prisoner. She probably ate her prey rather than try to preserve it. "Why are you going to Canada anyway? Isn't Little Dip your home turf?"

"I'm sort of persona non grata at the moment. Well, at most moments." Luc grinned at her. She was having a good day grubbing about in the mud. "Moments that roll into years that roll into a lifetime."

"Why's that?"

This got no answer. Luc had located an item of particular interest under the dirt and was trying to work it free. She ignored the question.

"What did you do?" Emily asked again.

"Nothing." Luc's voice was harsh. "Aunt Sylvie had to get rid of me in case the police came along with questions. She said I was too wild to talk to any police. There'd only be social services and stuff. She sent me and my family away." Then she fell into a brooding silence still working away in the mud. Emily was unsure of this sudden mood switch, and worked on in silence herself. What had Luc done that made as secretive a family as the Garouls have to hide her away? And why was Luc so upset at their protection? Because it was more of an expulsion than anything? It sounded like it had happened some time ago.

"What age were you when you went away?" she tried for one more question. It felt important to know.

"Nine," came the clipped response. "Hey!" Luc sprang upright, triumphantly waving a scrap of fabric. "My backpack." Her mood had flipped to happy again in a second.

"*My* backpack. Well, some of it," Emily said, making out a flap of Gore-Tex with a buckle attached.

Nine. They sent you away when you were nine years old? It was easy to imagine that child. In a way, she stood there before her, even now. Hurt and bitter, and still as wild. Luc set the tattered mess with the rest of her booty. *What possible use can a scrap of backpack be?* Luc's attachment to the backpack was perplexing. Emily had noticed the surreptitious sniff she had taken before laying the rag with the rest of her "finds." *Well, she is a werewolf. Why should I expect anything like normal?*

Emily nearly missed the glimmer of gold as it slid through her fingers and slithered back into the mud. She plunged her hands in after it; careful not to let Luc see she had found something. After a frantic grapple, she unearthed the broken chain. The key was still attached. Quickly, she dropped it into the top of her boot and felt it slide down to her ankle. Relief poured through her. She had the key. She was still in control.

"You finding anything over there?" Luc called.

"Nope. Guess you got the good spot."

"You betcha. Look what I got." She pulled the Winchester from the mud. "It's a beauty, isn't it?" Filthy as it was, a keen eye could make out the sleek lines of a classic piece of weaponry.

"Give it to me," Emily demanded, voice tight.

Luc snorted. "Sure. I'll give you a loaded gun. After all, you're so trustworthy."

"Give me it," Emily said again. She reached out her hand. With a grim laugh, Luc flicked the safety and pumped out the shells until the rifle was emptied.

"Here." She threw it at Emily who caught it in a white-knuckled grip. Luc looked on curiously. "What's the big deal with the rifle?" she asked.

Emily turned her back with no answer.

"Hey," Luc called. "What's your problem? You got the gun."

She was right behind Emily, breathing down her neck. She had moved soundlessly and at lightning speed. "Have you found more ammo?" she asked, her tone sharp.

"No." Emily tried to move away, but her upper arm was seized. "Let me go. If I had bullets for this, you'd be the first to know." Even as she said it, she knew there was a round left in the chamber. Luc had not checked the chamber, and Emily knew the Winchester inside out. It should not be crudely pumped out. It was one of the first lessons her father had taught her. One shell was always left in, the one that killed the stupid or the unwary. Was this her chance to escape once and for all?

"So why are you crying over an empty rifle?" Luc asked, unaware of the danger she was in.

Emily remained silent, conscious all the time of the key and its fine chain biting into the sole of her foot.

"Why?" Luc pressed. "Tell me."

"It was my father's," she heard herself saying.

"Oh." Luc's gaze fell to the weapon resting in Emily's hands. "Does he hunt, too?"

"He's dead."

"Oh."

"The Garouls killed him."

"Oh." Luc looked both surprised and uncomfortable at this news. "You sure? Doesn't sound like them. They usually turn tail and run."

"I'm sure." Emily let her bitterness run out. What was the point of hiding it, especially from a Garoul? Even as she spat the words, she knew she looked guilty. She had one bullet left, and there was a Garoul standing before her. Wasn't this what she was all about? Revenge? Her grip on the rifle tightened.

"The whole of Lost Creek is sure." She glared into Luc's face, not bothering to hide her anger.

It was a bad tactic, Luc was equally belligerent. Emily realized it was Luc's way, to brazen it out toe-to-toe. Not the smartest of moves given that Emily had the loaded gun.

"Yeah, like the three wise men and all their brothers live in Lost Creek. There's never been an ounce of sense come out of that place. What evidence have you got? Anything could have happened. Hunting is a dangerous sport." Her dark eyes blazed, but she could not hold Emily's stare. Instead, her gaze flitted away.

"I know what's tru—" Emily words were cut short by a low, ominous growl.

Luc stiffened, blood draining from her face. They turned in unison toward this new menace. Before them stood another werewolf. It was huge. Its silver-streaked fur glinted in the morning sun so that its entire body shone hard as steel. Its eyes glowed like amber and were full of sharp intelligence, and now they narrowed into slits of raw anger. Its entire body shook with the ferocity of its growl. An answering rumble of warning came from somewhere in Luc's chest. In her human form, it was not as deep or fearful, but its intention was clear enough. Luc stood between Emily and the newcomer, refusing to back down. The air was laden with tension. Emily's knees weakened. She was unsure what exactly was going on, but knew a fight was brewing. That much was evident in the posturing and growling.

"Is it a Garoul?" she whispered.

"No. It's a big, fuck off raccoon. Now move toward the RV, nice and slow," Luc snapped in a low voice, without breaking eye contact with the other werewolf. "When I say run, do it. And don't look back."

"I have no intention of looking back. What about you?" Emily asked, her voice shaking. "Are you going to fight it?"

Luc gave a curt laugh. "Do I smell stupid?" she muttered. "I'll puff out my chest and strut around for a few minutes, then make a bolt for the woods. It will follow me and you get the hell out of here. Okay?"

"Okay." Already, Emily was sidling toward the RV, her eyes glued on the new werewolf. It seemed content to let her go, concentrating on Luc only. She reached for the driver's door with her free hand, the other slick with sweat on the barrel of the Winchester. This newcomer was a Garoul, and it was after Luc, and Luc alone. Was that why she was being allowed to leave in one piece?

A shadow slid through the tree line to her right. There were more of them! Was it coming after her? Maybe she wouldn't be escaping after all. She pulled herself into the cab. What had Luc done to have her pack come after her like this?

"Luc," she called, her voice shaking. "There are more of them."

"Of course there are more of them. That's why it's called a pack. Get out of here. You're wasting time."

Even as Luc spoke, Emily could see a third Were emerging from the shadows. It slid toward Luc on her blindside. Luc had not seen it. She was focused on the huge female before her.

"Luc—"

"Shut up and go!"

The Winchester burned in her hand. She raised the rifle. There was one shot in the chamber. She was sure of it. Luc had not emptied the weapon as well as she thought she had. Emily aimed at the figure creeping up behind Luc, yet her finger wavered on the trigger. She had a vicious beast in her sights, but she knew from recent experience it was a human, too. She couldn't do it. She couldn't kill it.

She raised the rifle skyward and fired. The world around her exploded. The forest became a whirlwind of action. A riot of birds burst from the treetops and filled the sky with raucous cries. The forest seethed, its shadows boiling over into the clearing in the form of several werewolves. They barreled past the RV ignoring her. Luc bolted for the tree line. The silver werewolf sprang after her with incredible speed. Emily threw herself into the cab and fumbled with the ignition. The RV lurched forward a few feet then stalled. She jerked on the key to restart it and ground through the gears until the old engine screamed and she shot forward, gathering momentum.

To her left, she could just make out the top of Luc's dark head disappearing down the scree slope left by the mudslide. She was sliding over shale, keenly balanced and throwing herself toward the banks of the Silverthread. Menacing shadows pursued her, pouring down the slope, flitting from tree to tree. They slipped through the depths of the forest like wraiths. Then the RV rounded a curve on the logging road and she lost sight of the chase.

Emily concentrated on the rutted tracks and drove on as fast as she dared. She was wracked with fear and worry. Would Luc survive? Could she outrun an entire pack in her human form? Emily suspected she couldn't. But Luc was wily. She would make for the river and let its currents do the running for her. The ferocious waters of the Silverthread would wash her away. And later, somewhere farther downstream, Emily imagined a huge black werewolf surging from the river, shaking its shaggy pelt until the water drops flew like a million tiny diamonds, and the sun cutting clean across that silver collar.

CHAPTER FOURTEEN

Emily was a local girl. She knew the forest well. Like all Lost Creek brats, she had grown up playing under the woodland canopy and splashing about in the creeks and eddies of the Silverthread. Now she drove along the old back roads that hugged the line of the riverbank, searching out the shallow places where a swimmer could easily exit. Well, easily exit if the swimmer were human. Lord only knew where a werewolf could pop up. Anywhere it damned well wanted, she supposed. She was anxious to make sure Luc had gotten away okay. *Because she's worth a fortune...and intrinsic to my research*, she reminded herself. But it rang hollow. Her worry was genuine, and it was not centered on career prospects.

She was running out of options when she turned into the last waterhole before hitting the main road through to Lost Creek. She parked the RV and got out to walk along the riverside. The bank was dappled with golden splashes of sunshine and the silvery waters rumbled below, swollen and violent from last night's rain. She wandered several yards in one direction and then the other before giving up the search. It was a hopeless task. She was fooling herself if she thought she would stumble across Luc.

Emily perched on a toppled tree trunk and shucked off her boot. The gold chain with its key spilled into her palm. It winked up at her in mockery. What the hell had she been trying to do? Her fingers fumbled as she fixed the broken links. Revenge herself against the Garouls for the death of her father, garner acclaim, and project her otherwise mediocre career skyward? *Jesus, I spent last night snuggling with a werewolf. It licked my ear. It saved my life.* Emily sighed and dropped the chain around her neck. The key lay cold again her breast. If Luc had survived, she would be miles away by now. What would she do about her collar? Emily broke off bits of bark and threw them at the water roaring past her feet. One way or another, Luc was gone. Disappeared out of her life forever. The thought left her feeling hollow.

It was time to head home. Uncle Norm would be worrying himself sick. It was okay to be out all night when she was on a hunt, but usually she'd return in the early morning with a kill for the freezer and begging for a hearty breakfast. With one last searching glance up and then down the river, she made her way back to the RV.

She fished her keys out of her pocket when suddenly, he was there at her feet from out of nowhere. The little ginger dog sat blinking up at her. His chocolate brown eyes swam with a sad, sweet hopefulness that melted her heart instantly. His long ears were littered with twigs, leaves stuck to his matted coat, and his muzzle was covered with dried mud. His silky whiskers quivered under a wet, oversized shiny nose.

"Where did you come from?" she asked, looking around for his master. No one appeared. She turned her attention back to the dog. He didn't have a collar and sat with perfect patience staring up at her, a picture of utter dejection. "Are you lost, my love?"

Her friendly tone got an immediate response. The little dog raised his paw and patted her knee. His tail wagged once then flopped, as if the energy involved had been too much. He looked exhausted.

Emily opened her RV door. "I guess I—" In a flash, he had scrambled past her and up into the front seat. Seemed he could find that bit of extra bounce when needed.

"Okay," she said, a little surprised at this sudden enthusiasm. "Looks like you got yourself a lift, mister. But your paws better be cleaner than your snout."

Bemused, she climbed in after him and started the engine. They took off, swaying down the rutted track. Beside her, her companion sat bolt upright in the passenger seat keeping a vigilant lookout through the windows.

❖

"Where, in the name of Pete, did you find that?" Uncle Norm scowled at the dog sitting at Emily's feet.

"Found him in the woods. Do you recognize him? I thought he might belong to someone in town," Emily said.

Uncle Norm shook his head. "Sure don't look like no hunting dog to me. All folks have around here is hunting dogs, and he ain't no hunting dog. Look at those legs. I seen longer on grasshoppers."

"Well, I can hardly take him back." They watched the dog as he wandered around the kitchen, sniffing for crumbs, shedding dead leaves with every movement. "I suppose I can always take him to the pound at Covington," she said. The dog continued to circumnavigate the kitchen, his tail waving high and happily, unaware of the dire conversation going on overhead.

"I'll get him a can of dog chow for the meantime. He won't find much to eat down there. I was cleaning yesterday," Norm said, glaring at his leaf-littered kitchen floor. With a solemn shake of his head, he made for the door that connected his house to his store. He cleaned every day. His house was always spotless.

"Okay." Emily plonked down at the kitchen table. Her legs had begun to tremor, and she was exhausted. *I've just seen a pack of werewolves.*

"Don't worry," Norm called back. "I'll pick something out for you, too. How about some eggs?"

"That would be great, Uncle Norm," she said, aware her voice was weak. "I'll make coffee." *Werewolves. Dozens of them.*

She sat for a few minutes, too tired to make coffee just yet. *And they let me go?* The dog came over to her and sat on her right foot. She reached down and scratched his head with a shaking hand. *I can't believe I'm still alive. Will they come after me? Is Uncle Norm safe?* The dog leaned into her touch and licked her fingers.

"You are a real cutie, aren't you?" she said, thankful for the distraction. She could feel her chest tightening. The old panic was gathering, ignited by her thoughts. An unsavory aroma itched at her nose. "Phew, I think someone needs a bath." She smiled as he slunk off to the farthest corner and shot her a hurt look. Already he was a remedy.

"Did I say a bad word?" She laughed. If he knew what a bath was, he was definitely someone's pet and not a stray. Someone somewhere was missing him. Maybe she should call the local police to see if a small ginger mongrel had been reported missing?

"Here we go." Norm was back, moving slowly around his kitchen. He opened the dog food and spooned it into a dish, then stood and watched as it was gulped down in seconds. "He was hungry."

Next he threw bacon in the skillet and began cracking eggs into a bowl. Emily did her share and started up the coffee maker. She plopped back into her seat and watched her uncle prepare breakfast.

"Good night out there?" he asked.

"So so," she answered.

"Nothing for the freezer?"

She sighed. "Nope. So-so is a gross exaggeration."

He grunted and turned his attention to the stove. The dog was now glued to his leg hoping for scraps. "Did you sleep in your RV?"

"Yeah. Best money I ever spent buying that thing."

"You look like a hippie driving that."

Emily smiled. It was an old, soft argument. She waited for Norm's usual spiel about camping under canvas when he was young. How hunting was somehow a tougher pastime in his day. He always forgot she had been there, too, on special nights, snuggled down in her sleeping bag between him and her father.

"I can go under canvas, if I need to," she said. "I have all the equipment. It's just the RV is safer if I can park it in a good spot." The last good spot had been the logging camp. It had been a lifesaver after the mudslide. A sense of desolation crept over her. It had been a little sanctuary for both her and Luc. Well, until she poisoned her way out of it.

"How'd you get that shiner?" Norm asked.

"Walked into a tree." She gingerly touched the puffiness around her eye. "Can I use the washer?" She changed the subject. "I got a heap of dirty clothes."

"Sure. I'm done with it. Yesterday was laundry day. I did your bed linen."

"Thanks, Uncle Norm. I don't know what I'd do without you." She watched him slip a piece of bacon to the dog. While his back was to her, she quickly swallowed down her Lexotanil. Her hands were shaking badly and her T-shirt was sticking to her back with sweat.

"What's his name?" Norm nodded at the dog.

"I don't know. He doesn't have a collar or name tag."

"Dog needs a name." He set her breakfast plate in front of her.

"He'll be in the pound tomorrow. If someone's looking for him, they'll find him there." She lifted her fork and made short work of her breakfast.

Norm moved around the kitchen sorting out this and that and generally fussing over her. All the time the little dog stuck to his heels, crisscrossing the floor, content to follow him anywhere.

"You better go get some shut-eye," he said at her second yawn. "A nap won't kill you. I'll clean up here." He began clearing the table.

She struggled to her feet. Her whole body felt as if it were encased in lead.

"Thanks, Uncle Norm. I'll just put the Winchester away and sort out the wash first."

The gun cabinet was in Norm's office. Emily set her father's Winchester back in its place. She was too tired to clean it now. That was a job for tomorrow. Norm's old shooters looked pristine beside it. And even though they were spotless, she knew she'd clean them, too. Norm would like that.

She collected her bag from the hallway. Not that there were many clothes in it. Luc was wearing the last of them when she made her run for it. Emily's stomach cramped. Flashes of Luc's ragtag escape down the scree slope cut at her until her breathing began to hurt. It was a physical pain that Emily could only explain as shock.

Back in the kitchen, she found the breakfast things washed and put away. The dog snoozed on an old blanket by the kitchen radiator. The debris had been brushed from his coat and a plastic dish filled with water had been placed beside him. Emily checked the clock. Uncle Norm would be opening up his shop. Not that Johnston's General Store had many customers these days. A few locals still went there, though their shopping lists were getting shorter and shorter. It was cheaper to go down to the mall at nearby Covington. Johnston's could never compete with the big chain store prices. Norm's old hunting buddies dropped by most mornings and took up space for their daily complaining session. A few grouchy old men were always to be found jawing on about this and that at the coffee counter.

Emily unpacked her bag and loaded the washer. The little dog didn't move once. *He must be done in.* It wouldn't take much walking for those little legs to wear out. Next, she went out to the camper to empty the tiny fridge and clean up in general. The blankets were still heaped on the floor, grubbed into the nest Luc had made for them. Her pills lay where she had left them, along with the bottled water, an acorn, and all Luc's other little offerings to make her feel better.

Emily hesitated. Luc had also slept here with her. Shouldn't she pick through the blankets for stray werewolf hairs? The nest would be littered with forensic evidence. Instead, Emily crawled into the heart of it and curled up. The fluttering anxieties that had unsteadied her immediately lessened. The churning in her gut ceased, and the muscles along her back relaxed. It was better than any pills. Emily lay there considering the past few days. She had set out with such determination, most of it bedded in the hard rock of revenge. And nothing had gone to plan. Absolutely nothing.

Emily wormed down deeper and drew a blanket over her head to create a sort of cocoon. The blankets were stiflingly hot and smelled of a musk that reminded her of rich loam and fall leaves… and ink black pelt.

She had set out on her mission with such anger against the creatures she just *knew* had killed her father. Except the beast she had captured turned out to be a woman, a woman called Luc. A smart-mouthed, totally annoying, ass of a woman, who had unfortunately managed to capture Emily right back, but then everything had seesawed haphazardly over the last few days. Like Emily rescuing Luc from the mudslide, only to be rescued in return from the Silverthread. They had even abetted each other's escape from the Garoul ambush. Strange powers were at work. Nothing moved in a straight line anymore. Everything was twisted and convoluted, and Emily had no idea if she was coming or going. She wondered if Luc had escaped. Had she managed to shuck off the collar? More questions she'd never get an answer to. She secretly hoped Luc was on her way north, but part of her wanted her to be still in the valley.

Emily sat up and pushed the blankets from her. It was too hot in the camper. It was cooking her head until she thought stupid things. She climbed out and walked into the woods behind Norm's house. The air was cooler under the trees, and Emily leaned back against an old oak and let the breeze wash over her sticky skin. Above her head, the blue of the sky peeked through the leaves and sunlight dappled the trees in splashes of gold. *Sometimes the forest is so beautiful.* Emily rubbed her back against the tree as if she had an itch. *It changes its face and its mood like any living thing.* She moved to another tree and smoothed her cheek and neck against the bark, smiling at the prickling sensation and breathing in the rich sap scent.

"Em?" Norm called. "Where are you, Em?"

She started. Pulling her face from the tree was like awakening from a dream. She frowned. It was not like her to space out like that. Norm called again and she turned back the way she had come. In a few yards, she was by the picket fence that marked out Norm's yard from the woods beyond.

"I'm here. What's up?" she called back.

"Come lock up this gun cabinet. That's what's up. You know I don't allow it to lie open." His crankiness was apparent; she dug in her pocket and found the cabinet key.

"I'm sorry, Uncle Norm." She appeared beside him. "Guess I was tired and forgot."

He took the key from her. "Leave the washing," he said. "I'll do it for you. Go get some sleep." His bad mood was gone in a blink, melted away at the thought of being able to do something for her. Of being useful.

She kissed his stubbled cheek. "Thank you, Uncle Norm," she said as exhaustion washed through her. He was right. She wasn't even thinking straight. She turned to the house and to bed.

CHAPTER FIFTEEN

L uc let the current wash her downstream until she was sure she was out of sight of her pursuers. One Were had launched itself into the river, splashing and blustering too high in the water to make any true progress through it. The rest loped along the banks, hoping to track her by sight alone. She shed her clothes and let them tumble away with the water, surfacing and then submerging like the red herrings she intended them to be.

As slick as an otter, she reversed direction and cut the current back upstream. Luc was an excellent swimmer no matter what form she took, werewolf or human. She lived by a lake and swam in it every day come hell or sunshine. Now she carved her way through the murky under waters, weaving through the weed, blending with the pebble-strewn shadows of the riverbed, making it almost impossible to spy her from above. The sun was high and blazed across the tumbling waters. On the riverbed below, it danced with splashes of silver and dappled light. Even this worked for her, melding the metal of her collar with the fanciful patterns.

The Garouls would expect her to use the river to get as far away as she could. So she didn't. With great effort, she hung on to a submerged branch and held steady in the buffeting undercurrent. She clung tight as the waters billowed over and around her until she felt her lungs shrivel from lack of oxygen. It was now or never. Either her pursuers had traveled on ahead, or they were waiting above for her to surface. Had she fooled them? Her head cleaved the surface of the water. Blinking rapidly, she glanced all around, swirling a full three hundred and sixty degrees to be sure. She was alone.

Luc swam to the bank and crawled free. In a crouching run, she doubled back the quarter mile to the logging camp, where her scent was laden over everything. She would hide in her own scent. In a half-collapsed cabin, she hunkered down and willed the change. She forced it out of her. She wrenched her body apart until she fell weak but fully transformed to the muddy floor and lay there panting, ears alert for any sound of the hunting party returning. And they would return after they realized she had eluded them. They would come back to the last place they had seen her. They would return, regroup, refresh on her scent, and start all over again, and they would never stop because she had humiliated them. Luc's ears perked in pleasure at this thought. Only to immediately twitch with anxiety.

Where could she go? She was too weak to outrun them. Her exploits in the river, and the harsh rapidity of her change had seriously depleted her. Thankfully, the virus no longer ran rampant through her. That was at least one thing in her favor; she wouldn't sneeze and give herself away. Her only real option was to remain here where the camp reeked of her. Could she camouflage herself with herself? It was ingenious, she decided, a dangerous gamble, but oh so sweet if it worked.

A distant howl startled her. Several more followed. They were regrouping. Were they coming this way? She listened. More cries and howls. Closer this time, very close. They were returning, and fast if the forest acoustics were to be believed. Luc bounded over to the dynamite store, a complete mess after the mudslide. She climbed over the debris to the rear of the cabin and slid in under the twisted tin roof. There she dug frantically until she had made a hole deep enough to slip inside. She scooped the mud back in around her, drawing in big pawfuls to smother her head and muzzle. She sank down as far as her breathing would allow and sat chin deep in mud, perfectly still.

They broke into the clearing in an agitated squabble. Circling and snapping at all and anything that held her scent and might give a clue. Then the silver streaked female bounded in. *Marie Garoul.*

Luc remembered her, though she had been much younger then. And the other one, the huge male. That was Claude. She was almost certain of it. It was strange to see them after all this time, and again under thoroughly miserable circumstances. Her only relief was that Ren was not with them. She knew Ren was in Little Dip and sort of hoped she'd stick around at least until Mouse was settled. She was glad her twin had not been part of the Garoul hunting party; that would have cut deep. Though it would have made no difference to the outcome, she'd still have run rings around these hounds, for that was all they were to her. Part of her was enjoying this chase, as long as she stayed one jump ahead.

Luc sank even lower until her snout barely cleared the mud. From her vantage point, she could see but not be seen. Or so she hoped. Marie snapped her Weres into order, and in seconds, they left the clearing heading north.

Luc sat in her mud bath for an hour or more until she was certain Marie had left no one lurking behind. Then she surged from the mud hole and ambled down to the river for a good rinse. She missed the little RV with its hot water shower.

She found a sheltered spot under the bank where the current was peaceable, and floated on her back, cloud watching and making plans. So the Garouls had decided to head north and block off her route home. What a lousy plan. She'd have expected better of them. So what were her options?

Option one: she could make her way north to the border and try to avoid any Garoul ambushes along the way.

Pros: she was aware they were out there waiting for her.

Cons: it was hard to preempt an ambush no matter how prepared you were for one.

Option two: she could head in any direction other than north and loop around to the border.

Pros: she'd be making a very circuitous way home.

Cons: she'd be making a very circuitous way home.

Her choices were shit. With a snort of dissatisfaction, Luc burst from the river and angrily shook the excess water from her body. It streamed from her thick pelt and puddled around her feet. Leaving a trail of great wet paw prints, she stomped over to the dynamite store and hunkered down to dry off in the sun. Beside her, her pile of treasures lay undisturbed. The Garouls had not been interested in the mud-caked rubbish she had unearthed. Idly, she reached over and shuffled through them. A boot. A button. A silver arrow. She sniffed the silver point. *She was going to skewer me with this, and I let the little bitch get away.* She'd never have let the Garouls take her, though. Emily was hers.

Option three: she could stay where she damn well was! Here in the forest, and let the Garouls fart about in the north waiting for a traveler who would never pass by. At least not while they were there.

Pros: she knew these woods, and for the moment, they were Garoul free. That gave her plenty of time to set up a bolt-hole. *And she'd know the minute the Garouls returned.* Once they trailed back with their tails between their legs, she could make her own way north unhampered. Excellent! She lifted a filthy scrap of backpack with her fore claw and sniffed at it. *Coconut shampoo.* She shifted on her haunches and thought about the cons to her plan.

Cons.

There were no cons.

She sniffed the rag again. A mild euphoria spread through her making her lips smack and her toe claws tap on the dirt. It was a great plan. She would take up temporary residence in the forest and wait out any danger. Luc sighed happily at her own cleverness.

Emily came down from her nap an hour later to find the house empty. The dog's blanket was heaped under the kitchen radiator, but the dog was no longer on it. She made her way through to the shop to see her uncle and grab a cup of coffee from his food counter. The swing door between the house and the store opened and she heard the grumble of old men's voices.

"Says here bichon frise."

"He ain't no bichon frise, you blind old coot. Look at his goddamn tail," Uncle Norm snapped. "Nothing French about that tail."

"Color's all wrong," another voice chimed in. "And he ain't curly. What you have there is a dachshund. A German dog."

"He's an American dog. We found him here in Oregon, didn't we?" Norm was belligerent as ever. "And he's too short for a dachshund."

"Ah, come on, Norm. He's the shortest runt I ever seen."

"I meant lengthwise. He's too short lengthwise. Them dachshunds are wiener dogs." Norm was not going to give an inch.

Emily came further into the shop to find the newly washed dog standing on top of the coffee counter, tail wagging. Sitting around on stools was an assortment of old boys intently assessing him. One had a copy of *Dog's World* magazine lifted from the newspaper stand, and they were flipping through the pages comparing the pictures with the specimen before them.

"He's got the body of that French dog and the head of a dachshund—"

"And the tail of a squirrel." They all laughed, and the squirrely tail wagged wildly.

"He's as ginger as a pine squirrel—"

"And he's for the pound." Emily stepped up to join them. She lifted the dog from the counter. "You're breaking Lord knows how many health and hygiene laws here," she told her uncle, tucking the animal under her arm.

"I was just telling the boys how you found him in the woods and they wanted to see him. None of us knows him. He's not from these parts."

"Perhaps a tourist lost him?" one of Norm's cronies spoke up.

"It's a bit early for tourists. And he's not the type of dog you'd take hiking. You'd have to carry him most of the way," she said.

"Guess he's from Covington, then," another crony said.

"Yeah. I'm taking him down to the pound. I need to go to the bank anyway," she said.

"Not today, you won't. Pound shuts half day on Tuesdays," Norm said and placed a cup of coffee on the counter for her. "Gimme here." He took the dog from her. "I'll take him outside to do his business. You mind none of these boys leaves without paying."

❖

Luc found the tree.

The special tree.

A big leaf maple, to be precise, that stood about fifty feet high. It was the branch spread that caught her eye, and that was nearly thirty feet across at its widest. She didn't care how tall the tree was. It only had to be high enough to afford a view and offer safety from the forest floor. Other than that, she wanted a wide and level spread of branches where she could build a nest and snuggle down for a long wait. She imagined it would be a long one because the Garouls were really stupid and it would take a while before they realized she wasn't heading north any time soon, and that she had outwitted them yet again.

She dug her claws into the soft bark and pulled herself upward. Luc prided herself on her climbing skills. She enjoyed climbing as much as she enjoyed swimming. Once she reached the lower canopy, she snapped off some branches and began to construct a crude platform. This she lined with medium sized branches to make the skeletal platform sturdier. Then she padded that out with smaller branches that bore wide, pliable leaves. Finally, she whipped and wove some longer, stronger branches into sidewalls a foot deep to encircle the entire base, plugging any gaps with wads of ripped up leaves.

Pleased at her efforts, Luc sat in the center of her creation and wriggled her hindquarters into the matting, digging out any sharp, pokey twigs and making a large Luc-sized indentation. Satisfied, she lay back and contemplated the slivers of sky that trailed and twisted through the greenery above her like pale blue ribbons. She was relaxed and almost content. She had made a nest, a temporary home as such, and at last she felt secure and in control. This was the second nest she had made in the last twenty-four hours. The first one had been for Emily, to keep her safe and warm. The thought made her solemn. Where was Emily now? Ah, yes. Lost Creek. She said she came from Lost Creek.

Luc launched herself from her nest full of frantic activity. Okay, so it was cozy enough. Now all it needed were a few home comforts. She leapt the last fifteen feet or so to the ground and bounded off, weaving through the trees, sometimes bouncing off a tree trunk here and there to maintain her hurtling momentum. It took her no time at all to pinball her way back to the logging camp.

Chapter Sixteen

Emily returned from her bank visit a little after dinnertime. "Uncle Norm," she called, closing the front door behind her. "How'd you feel about Mexican tonight? I got stuff for fajitas."

There was no answer. She pushed on through to the kitchen, but it was deserted. Where was he? The shop had closed an hour ago. Her eye fell on the dog's makeshift water bowl, and she frowned. WILBUR was scrawled unevenly along it in black marker pen.

"Wilbur?" she murmured in disbelief.

"Here, boy. Fetch." Norm's voice came from the back porch. Emily found him in his rocker throwing a ball for the dog, who ran and fetched it every time.

"Good boy, Wilbur," Norm crowed as the dog dropped the ball at his feet and waited, tail thumping, for the next throw.

"Wilbur?" she said again. He looked up, pleased as punch to see her.

"This is one smart pup. Look what I taught him in no time at all," Norm announced.

"Maybe he already knows this game." She might as well speak plainly. "I don't think he's a stray. I think he's got someone out there missing him. And *Wilbur*, for God's sake?"

"It's as good a name as any. He looks like a Wilbur." Norm was grumpy now.

"If he belongs to someone else, you can't keep him. If you really want a dog, well, why don't we go down to the pound and you can pick one out?"

"Seems stupid to go all the way down there just to dump one dog in and take another out." He was not going to be mollified, so Emily changed tack.

"Did you hear me ask if you wanted fajitas?" she said. He brightened, and she was thankful for the truce. They could talk about Wilbur another time. *Jeez. Wilbur. He's got me doing it now.*

After dinner, Emily pored through the local newspapers for the region. There was no mention of a swimming fatality on the Silverthread, or an incident in the forest. With a sigh, she set the papers aside. Just another day in the kill or be killed world of the forest werewolves. How disassociated mankind really was from nature. If we realized there was a bigger, better predator out there that didn't need guns and knives and higher technology to kill, we'd napalm the entire forest. Anything to stay on top of the food chain.

Disgruntled with the lack of information, she decided to go for an evening stroll.

"You taking Wilbur with you?" Norm yelled from his La-Z-Boy before the television.

"If you like," she called back. How could he sit there with the TV at full volume and still be able to hear her pull the zipper on her fleece? "You have a leash for him?" she asked. "I wouldn't want him wandering off. He was lucky I found him last time."

Norm appeared at her elbow, sucking his teeth in thought. "Use a bit of rope," he said. "No point buying him a collar and leash if he's bound for the pound."

In the end, Emily didn't need a rope. The little dog seemed almost timorous of the dark, and quite content to amble around the woods behind the house keeping close to her. It was a chilly night. Winds from the north brought in cooler air, and the cloudless skies gave a fresh crispness to the stars above. They hung silent witness in the dark, their constellations holding a million stories and countless secrets. Emily stood and looked up at them until her head spun. She could understand how ancient man worshipped the stars and modern man craved to walk among them. They shivered with the promise of knowledge far beyond any celestial dream of man. Emily ached with her own questions, and thirsted for her own answers.

Was Luc still alive? And why was she so fretful about it when in the first place all Emily had wanted to do was harm her? Perhaps Luc was looking up at this same canopy of stars, though hopefully with Canadian soil under her feet.

Emily surrendered her weight to a young cedar, and with her eyes still heavenward, gave in to a primitive need to rub her cheek against the trunk. The smell of bark was a balm, its roughness pulling the itch out of her skin. Without a second thought, she squatted and urinated at its roots. She moved on to a basswood and raked her palms along its surface, punch drunk on the scents of the night forest. The earthy musk of damp loam hung heavy around her. Bracken fern split the air with its sharp acidity softened only by the sweeter underlay of thimble and salmon berry. Above her, the maple leaves rattled and fir needles hissed in the rising wind.

Wilbur wandered over, plopped down near her feet, and gave her a soulful, prophetic look.

"What do you see, little buddy?" She reached down and rubbed his silky ears. In answer, he leapt to his feet and headed for the distant porch light and home.

"Ah. You see supper," she said, and followed.

❖

Luc was thick with mud again, but she was certain she had dug the entire corner clean. She could now account for all of Emily's surgical instruments, including the fabric pouch. She had also unearthed a bundle of spare clothes, a whole clutch of silver arrows, *and* the thermos. The arrows now lay at her feet gleaming dully in the faint moonlight. She looked at the huge mound of earth and shattered cabin before her. If there was anything else left in there, it was well back and under more mud than she cared to lift.

No key though. She could have missed it, but she doubted it. She had gone through that corner of the cabin like a sieve.

Luc slouched off to the river to wash away another ton of mud and consider her next move. She lay back and let the water stream over her and contemplated the constellations, every one of them a childhood friend. She had been a clever pup. One of the smartest Little Dip ever had, in her opinion. She knew she had been Aunt Sylvie's favorite. And then it all turned to crud and they had sent her away. Sent her whole family away, and they had never forgiven her. She knew they hadn't. Her parents had soon grown ill and died, and Ren...

Well, Ren had tried her best to get away from her, too.

Luc rolled onto her belly and swam a few strokes. This maudlin behavior was not going to solve her current problem; namely, this stupid silver collar. She felt like a fool wearing it. Where was the damned key! Why hadn't she found it? Of course, a light item like a key and chain could be washed away anywhere. But it had last been on Emily, and Emily had been in the corner. It was also possible Emily had found the key already and kept it hidden. That's what Luc would do if the tables were turned, and Luc always deemed what *she* would do to be an excellent measure of others' actions. The irony was she had let Emily go. Then again, there was only one place Emily could run to.

With a grunt of pleasure, Luc dived under the swollen waters. Weed tickled her flanks and steelhead trout zigzagged before her, silver flashes through the dark current trying to avoid the lazy swipe of her claws.

Feeling totally refreshed, Luc climbed back up the riverbank. She had a brace of trout for supper and a sturdy nest to gorge them in. Full of renewed determination, she strode over to the broken down cabin and the stash she had unearthed. She scooped and clawed as many items as she could into her arms, cramming objects into an unruly heap against her wide, furred chest. It might take two runs to get all her booty back to her new hidey-hole, but with the Garouls chasing their tails to the north, she had time to settle in properly. She'd take every item to her nest and arrange her treasure all around her. Then she would eat her fishy supper, and afterward, she could give everything a well-needed lick and sniff. Some things still had traces of Emily on them.

Chapter Seventeen

Luc was settling into her new home nicely. Her new favorite things were scattered all around her and had given her hours of pleasure examining each one for traces of Emily. Now she lay well rested and content sprawled across her nest, the morning sunlight dappling her warm fur. It was a good way to start the day, she decided. Luc could wear her wolfskin a long time, much longer than most wolven who changed back during sleep. But then she had grown up this way in the wilds of nowhere. She knew she was as good as feral. Ren was always rhyming on at her about it. Ren and her stupid traditions and stupid almanacs. Some use it had been when the virus came along and the young ones began to grow ill. Where was the mighty Garoul almanac then? Useless piece of pulp.

She scratched at the collar around her neck. It was a prime example of almanac nonsense. Emily had hoped it would subdue a werewolf. That it would make Luc weak when in fact it did the opposite. It had made her strong, strong enough to shake off the virus and escape the Garouls. *Interesting.*

She tapped out a little tune on the metal band. It was time *she* was in control of the collar. First, she needed the key, and it would do no harm to take back that almanac. Stupid as they may be, Garoul almanacs should not be in human hands. With a new plan in place, Luc stood and stretched her claws up into the heart of the tree. She embedded them in the trunk and tore at it until her shoulder and arm muscles were tight and pumping blood. Leaves whisked across her forearms and tapped and tickled at her muzzle. The smell of sap was strong and invigorating. It was a glorious sunny morning after the downpour of the last few days. The entire forest was drunk on sunshine. And Luc was, too.

She had survived the hunt and was holed up nice and secure, *and* she had a new course of action. A course of action that involved Emily Johnston, and somehow that felt right and relevant. Content she was no longer rudderless, no longer at the mercy of the virus, or fate, or the Garouls, and especially not a scrawny redheaded hunter, Luc climbed down from her aerie and struck out for Lost Creek.

Emily rose early after a night of violent dreams that left her feeling rattled. Her mind was muddled with images she could no longer fully recall, but which left a jagged imprint on her nerves.

Sometimes her medication did that to her, made her hyper alert so her subconscious became a churning morass of anxiety. At other times, the blessed times, it knocked her flat out, pushing her down into a dark, dreamless pit, asphyxiating in its stillness, as cloying as black tar when she reemerged to face the morning. She was far too agitated after these last few days to even hope for a decent night's sleep. Her skin felt tight with worry, and fretfulness furrowed her brow and crawled across her scalp.

Emily tossed aside the twisted bed sheets and headed straight for the shower. A blast of hot water would revive her and get her brain working again. A long day stretched ahead of her. She needed to get back to her books and see what she had overlooked or miscalculated. The silver collar had not worked as expected. In fact, it had been a complete failure. She needed to bury herself in Garoul lore, as if she hadn't spent enough time there already, and try to understand where she had gone wrong.

Emily's bedroom window overlooked the woodland to the rear of the house. This side of the forest was the last to catch the morning light. It lay in shadows until the sun crested the roof of Uncle Norm's house. Now the dawn mists swirled and eddied around the trees as fluid as tidewater. Dew still clung to the stems of low-lying wiregrass waiting for the sun to burn it off. It would take maybe another hour before sunlight would penetrate the gloom. Meanwhile, a soft, soapy brume curled along the forest floor. Slender aspen and shivering ash rose eerily out of it like the ghostly masts of sunken ships. Chokeberry and bitterbrush lurked in incoherent, menacing silhouettes at the base of trees.

From the corner of her eye, Emily noticed an uncommon movement. She hesitated by the window and gazed out at the hauntingly distorted woodland. What had she seen? Her gaze flickered over everything. Apart from the drifting mist, all was still. And then it rose from out of the vaporous mire to stand upright a full eight feet or more. A huge, shaggy werewolf. It had been hunkered down examining the earth and now stood to sniff the air. The creature looked up toward the house scanning the windows, and Emily stepped back out of sight. Its amber eyes glowed bright in the dark density of its fur. Wide-eyed, she took in its stance, the curve of the muzzle, and the short ears. Then it turned and melted into the surrounding forest as if it had never been there at all. As if such things did not, could not, exist. But Emily knew they did. And she knew that this werewolf was not Luc.

Had it come for her? Or was it the almanac it wanted? At least her questions about Luc's safety had been answered. She must have been captured, and the silver collar would have told them that a human had access to the Garoul magic, the Garoul world.

What could she do? She had brought danger to her own front door. Would Uncle Norm be safe? If she took the book away from here, would they know? Would they follow her? Either way, she had to remove the bait from this house, whether the bait be the almanac, or her.

Her shower forgotten, Emily threw on some clothes and grabbed a grip bag and crammed the almanac and several of her notebooks into it. She had to get this material out of the house and as far away from Uncle Norm as possible, and hope for the best.

She pounded down the stairs and made a grab for her light raincoat from the hall coatrack.

"Where you going this early?" Norm emerged from the kitchen. "And you don't need that raincoat. It's gonna be a sizzler."

She slung the coat back on the rack. "I need to get to the post office at Covington," she lied.

"What about breakfast? I was doing us some pancakes." Norm sounded very put out at this change in plans.

"I'll grab something at the mall." She headed for the door, bag in hand.

"What about the dog?" Norm called after her. "Ain't you taking him to the pound today?"

She hesitated for a split second. "I can't today. I'm in too big a hurry." She didn't even look back. His hurt expression would have only compounded her guilt tenfold. But she needed to do this to keep him as safe as possible.

"Okeydokey then." He sounded positively cheerful. "See you later, Em." And with a chirpy whistle, he went back to the kitchen. "Just you and me for pancakes, Wilbur," she heard him tell the dog.

I'll never peel that dog off him. Emily started the RV and did a neat reverse turn out of her parking space. The bag sat on the passenger seat beside her as she made her way through the quiet, early morning streets of Lost Creek, heading for the main road out. The sun was already beginning to heat up the day, but to Emily's eyes, for every patch of sunlight, there was a darker, more ominous shadow.

❖

Luc found Emily easily.

The faintest scent caught her as she skirted the small town. Even if she hadn't been looking for it, it was impossible for her to slink past it. Normally, she would avoid places like Lost Creek in daylight, but she was on a mission, and a sickly sweet chemical smell tugged at her snout and drew her in. Her brain registered the odor as the flowery detergent that clung to the clothes Emily wore. All it took was that precarious link to make her lope toward the town's western outskirts. If she stuck to the tree line and waited her chance, she might just get lucky and see Emily. *And if I see her, I'm grabbing her and making her take off this collar and give me the damned book.*

Lost Creek was a desolate, rundown place, but it was an easy town to negotiate, being so close to the forest perimeter and with not much to keep its residents on the streets for any length of time. Luc vaguely remembered it from her childhood, before her family had been packed off to Canada. She shook that particular memory from her mind. It always made her heart harden, and she did not need that now.

She avoided the main street, keeping to the alleyways and abandoned backyards. There were many of them, overgrown with weeds and screaming of neglect. The few dogs that were out in the early morning heat stopped barking as soon as she drew near, and they cowered in corners until she passed. Cats too, ran for safety and hunkered down to watch. She made her way across town, yard by yard, alley by alley, street by street, dragged along by her nose.

In no time at all, she'd zoned in on laundry flapping on a clothesline behind Johnston's General Store. With a quick glance and an even quicker sniff to make sure no one was around, Luc vaulted the fence.

The air was alive with the smell of Emily. Her dirty boots on the back stoop were delicious. The cushions of a porch chair where she had rested stank of her freshly washed, coconut-scented hair. Even a dishtowel looped over the porch railings smelled of her... and some nondescript casserole. Luc was thrilled. This was Emily's den.

From the front of the house, she could hear a radio at high volume blaring out the morning news and weather reports. A screen door creaked and Luc slid around the porch corner, her back tacked to the siding. She heard an old man's voice muttering and then the clip of claws on the porch boards. Luc's ears flattened. The screen door slammed shut again, and around the corner trotted a small dog. Luc stood still, her claws ready to gut the animal if it so much as squeaked. Instead, much to her surprise, the dog wagged his tail excitedly on seeing her and came over for a friendly sniff. This was strange. He should be alarmed. Luc didn't have time to ponder; she had to get rid of him before his master came out to join him. Beside her foot lay a florid pink, well-chewed tennis ball, she lifted it and flung it as hard as she could across the yard. The little dog took off after it, his short legs a blur. By the time he returned with his prize, she'd be long gone.

The passageway upstairs was in darkness. The window shades had been pulled against the harsh noontime sun. In three silent strides, her long legs swallowed the staircase and she was on the landing. Downstairs, the radio continued to blare, and outside, the little dog barked in disappointment.

Which room was Emily's? Luc gazed along the narrow corridor with its closed doors. The whole house reeked of her, but one area drew her attention in particular. Here the scent of coconut was strong. It was either the bathroom or Emily's own room. Luc pushed at the door.

She slid into a bedroom. It was cozy, with a single bed, warm pine flooring, and walls painted a soft buttery yellow. She was assaulted by the smell of Emily, hard and fresh. It made her so giddy she feared she'd sink to the floor. Luc sucked in all the scents through greedy, quivering nostrils, and soon realized Emily was not wholly embedded in the room and its furnishings. Not like in the little RV, for instance, where her perfume clung to cushion covers, and curtains, and even the plastic tableware. Here it was present, but fainter. This was a temporary lair, but then Emily had said she was visiting.

The window was open to the sun-filled day, and cream curtains billowed dreamily in the breeze. There were books everywhere, some piled in high, unsteady stacks, others lying open, their pages occasionally fluttering in the breeze. Books smelled of books and not much else. Luc clawed through them all and didn't find a Garoul almanac. That was disappointing, but as she was here, she might as well explore. She turned away eagerly, glad to leave the teetering piles of books behind.

The pine dressing table caught her attention first. She lifted a hairbrush and stuck her snout deep in the bristles; the smell of shampoo and human scalp assaulted her, along with that underlying sourness of anxiety she had come to expect. The brush oozed it, and it vexed her that Emily was so haunted. She set down the brush, discontented.

The bed, however, drew her like a devotee to an altar and cheered her up immensely. She fell flat on her back onto its soft blue coverlet and wriggled in delight as her fur grabbed Emily's sleep scent. The little bed squeaked under her writhing weight, but she did not stop until she was satisfied enough of her own musk had been left on the sheets for Emily's own delectation. The bedside table held a paperback, hair clips, a box of tissues, and more of Emily's pills. Luc sniffed them all, intrigued, trying to build up a mental picture of Emily's bedtime rituals. Then something else caught her eye. Shoes.

She picked up a dress shoe, buried her snout inside it, and inhaled deeply. First one shoe and then the other. She licked the leather and rubbed it all over her muzzle. She nipped the heels. Nursing the shoes to her chest, she decided to investigate the dresser drawers. She hooked the handle with her fore claw and clumsily slid the top drawer open.

Inside was a scented treasure trove. Soft sweaters in all colors tumbled toward her and snagged on her claws. She sniffed a few then jammed them back in any old way. The next drawer held underwear that ripped to shreds at her slightest touch no matter how gently she pawed at it. She slammed the drawers shut, hiding the carnage.

She moved away from the dresser. It was too dangerous to play with, but the laundry hamper was another thing altogether. It was pay dirt. She tossed the contents on the floor and rolled on them, growling softly, throwing towels and T-shirts playfully in the air, enjoying her game. In her ecstasy, it took her a moment to realize the house had become very quiet. She stopped throwing around dirty linen and listened. The radio had been turned off, and her sensitive hearing could pick out the creak of the staircase. Someone was coming upstairs. Luc's ears flattened. This was not good.

Lying prone on the floor, she could make out the shadow of approaching feet under the door. And now she could hear an old man muttering to himself. The shadow moved on along the landing. Luc relaxed. It had been a close call, and now it was time to go. She decided it best to slip out the window rather than go through the house. Even as she looked toward her escape route, the window blind lifted and the curtains whooshed in a blast of wind, and a precariously balanced book toppled to the floor. It landed with a hard slap on the bare pinewood. Luc froze.

The shuffling footsteps halted and then came back.

"Em? You in there, Em?" an old man asked.

Luc flung herself under the bed as the door handle began to turn. Slow footsteps entered and moved toward the bed. Luc heard the book being lifted with a fussy tutting and replaced on the desk.

"Look at the state of this place." The tutting continued.

If he finds me, I'll have to eat him. Luc barely breathed as slippered feet shuffled inches past her snout. *I bet he's all gristle.*

The old man turned to go. Luc watched his feet move away.

"I never raised her to be messy," he continued grumbling to himself. "She needs a good talking to, that girl."

The laundry basket was pulled upright and the scattered laundry shoved back in it.

"There's rules in this house," he grumbled on, "and she best remember them." He moved off, dragging the basket with him. "Better wash this load now. It'll dry by lunchtime in that wind." And the bedroom door clicked closed behind him.

Luc slithered out from her hiding place and bolted for the window. She perched on the sill and took a last lingering sniff. *Emily.* But she needed a souvenir! She couldn't just leave without one. She scanned the room and made her selection. She grabbed the dress shoes and, clutching them to her chest, scooted out the window onto the porch roof. An excited bark greeted her from below. She looked down to see the stupid ginger dog barking happily up at her.

Piss off, she hissed, but he barked back, if anything, even happier. Didn't he know she was a predator who ate his species as appetizers?

"Wilbur?" the old man's croaky voice came from downstairs. "What's wrong, Wilbur?"

Any minute now, he would come around the corner and see her stuck on his roof like a freakin' weather vane, and all because that stupid dog wouldn't shut up.

Reluctantly, she lifted one of the shoes, her prized possessions, and hurled it as far as she could in the opposite direction. As she had hoped, the mongrel went after it full tilt. Luc leapt from the porch and ran for the fence in the opposite direction, keeping the billowing clothesline between herself and the house. She cleared the fence in one leap and was bounding into the depths of the forest before the mutt had even snatched up the shoe.

Chapter Eighteen

Emily came to the fork in the road where the signpost for Covington pointed off to the right. She turned left.

Sure, she could sail on down to the Covington Post Office and mail the books to her address in Chicago and get them safely out of the way. But part of her could not give up on her almanac. It was perhaps the only bargaining chip she had, and something told her to hang on to it. She had waited too long, searched too hard, and probably paid far too much for the tatty old thing. No way was she just going to hand it over to the Garouls unless there was some sort of deal involved. She was not going to give it up, at least not yet. Instead, she was going to hide it well. Somewhere that would not endanger her uncle. He was her only family, and she had to look out for him. She would surrender the book only after she was assured of his safety.

If the Garouls were watching her house, it was a reasonable assumption they were watching her, too. She had to act like she was unaware of their presence. First, she would go out and examine her old traps. Luc had all but obliterated them anyway, so she could make a reasonable pretense of cleaning them up. It would give her an opportunity to wander in the woods and stop by one of her old hunt stashes. She would hide the almanac there. Her stash holes were sturdy, weatherproof places, and a book could easily be hidden there for a short period of time. As for her notebooks, those she would burn. She had computer backups anyway.

❖

One shoe was not enough.

Luc begrudged having to share her souvenir with the dog. She hunkered down in a quiet glade and brooded. Her fur was thick with pollen from the flowers she had brushed against or ploughed right through, and bees hummed around her, crawling through her coat. She hardly noticed them. Sunlight illuminated the forest in rich, golden swaths that in turn cast soft-edged shadows. Plant life unfurled and stretched toward the gentle rays, and insects droned drowsily. The noontime was heavy with a lazy, luxuriant heat. Birdsong thrilled high in the leafy canopy, and the breeze idled by, filled with bittersweet scent and the heady promise of summer. Luc didn't give a rat's ass. One shoe was not enough.

That bedroom had been a treasure trove and she wanted more. Why hadn't she grabbed all she could while she'd had the chance? Luc carefully dug a shallow hole between her feet and buried her shoe. She thumped the earth back in place with her claws until she was satisfied it was well hidden. Then she stood, flung her arms wide, and roared, shaking the bees violently from her pelt. Luc bounded back the way she had come with grim determination and angry buzzing all around her.

The white picket fence loomed ghostly in the dim forest interior, and beyond it, the sunny green lawn with its thick, colorful flower borders shimmered like a distant fairyland. Luc stopped several yards back and approached cautiously. She didn't want to run into the little yap-bucket again. If she did, she would stomp on him this time and see how he yapped then. She crept in, watching out for the dog, when a ginger flurry caught her eye. He was in a central flowerbed digging like fury. Muck, flowers, stems, and roots flew through the air. Luc noticed with disgust he was burying the shoe she had tossed him. *Stupid mutt. Burying a perfectly good shoe.* Burying *her* perfectly good shoe.

Now that she had a fix on him, she could orchestrate her entry point. She needed to be obscured from the house and also from the dog, and that meant using the neighboring outbuildings. It was not the most direct route, but it would have to do. Luc hated being out in the open any longer than she had to. Her plan involved a quick dart across the lawn and then a run alongside the clothesline, using the clothes to hide her. Then with a quick hop onto the porch roof, she'd be through Emily's bedroom window in a jiffy.

Her sprint across the garden was powerful and swift. Her leap to the porch roof flawless and clean. Her fumbling with the locked window was time wasting and pathetic, her huge claws were useless with such fiddly things. The window had been locked since her last visit, and she had neither the time nor the privacy to break the glass or rip the wooden frame from the wall. The old man and his crazy mongrel could come along and spot her at any moment.

Luc retreated, slinking down into the shadows of the porch. This was most unsatisfactory. She would have to go in through the back door as before, except this time, she knew there was an occupant, and she had no idea where he was. Her muzzle twisted with discontent. Just then, she heard a familiar click-clacking on the porch boards and her heart sank. The stupid dog was coming back.

Luc opened the screen door a sliver, took a quick peek, and sidled inside. The kitchen was bright and cheerful, if a little dated. Spotless Formica surfaces held gleaming chrome appliances. The wooden cabinets were painted a jaunty primrose yellow with white trim, and gingham curtains fluttering at the window matched the tablecloth on the dining table in the center of the room. There was a cozy smell of buttered toast and good coffee. A dog bed and water bowl sat in the corner, but Luc was confident her furry friend could not get in through the screen. There was no sign of the old man.

A sudden metallic rattling came from the room to her right and startled her, but it was only the utility room with a creaky old washer working through its cycle. The old man had taken the laundry hamper with him, and now Luc watched mesmerized as Emily's clothes swished around the circular glass door, but soon she shook herself out of it. She needed to secure the surroundings before she helped herself to anything. At the back of the utility room stood another sturdier door. This one had locks and bolts. It was currently unlocked, and Luc carefully pushed it ajar. From her viewpoint, she could make out rows of shelves filled with cans and boxes of food items. There was a strong smell of fresh coffee and baked bread. A shop? A diner? Then she picked up the moan of old men's voices, and in particular the old buzzard she had heard this morning. She grunted happily. The old man must work in the shop. The rest of the house was hopefully clear of people. With a little more confidence, she slipped into the hallway and upstairs to Emily's bedroom.

She made straight for the dresser and opened the top drawer, pulling out a pretty pastel sweater. Next she swiped a handful of underwear. More shoes! She definitely needed those. She went to inspect Emily's footwear. There was nothing quite as exciting as the dress heels she had stolen earlier, but a slipper would do. And the hairbrush! The glorious hairbrush. She couldn't help but bury her snout in it again. She was busy sucking in the powerful smell of Emily's scalp when she heard a vehicle pull up. A quick glance out the window confirmed the RV had returned. Luc was as upset as she was excited. She didn't want to go just yet, but she did not want to be seen with her booty either. She was confused at this urge to steal Emily's stuff. Not that Luc didn't steal. A hen, a pig, anything bright she liked the look of. Luc stole from all over the place, and always had. She acted on her urges, but this one was different, and she needed to think it over more, but this was not the time or place. She had to get away before old men, small dogs, or Emily spotted her.

She hesitated long enough to see what path Emily took. It looked like she was heading for the shop. Good. That meant the back was clear.

On her way through the kitchen, she grabbed a few other random items from the countertops. It all added to the excitement. Outside, the dog was nowhere in sight, but she could hear his barking from the front of the house. He had also spotted Emily's arrival. Having Ratty running around her heels should slow her down some giving Luc an extra minute or two to get away.

Luc loped past the laundry and snatched at items from the clothesline. She recognized a shirt Emily had worn yesterday. She grabbed that, too. And weren't those her jeans? She yanked them off the line as well.

Heaped high with plunder, Luc leapt the fence and thundered into the woods panting with excitement. There was no having to share this time. This loot was all her own.

❖

"I'm home," Emily called. The shop bell tinkled, and she entered carrying a squirming Wilbur in her arms. A chorus of hiyas from Norm's buddies greeted her. As usual, they were sitting around sipping on Cokes and coffees.

"Did you catch it in time?" Norm said.

"Catch what?" she asked.

"The mail." He gave her a funny look.

"Oh," she said, relieved. At first, she thought he was referring to werewolves. "Yeah. It's all okay," she answered then swerved for the connecting door to the house.

"Here." Norm reached out his arms for the dog.

"You can't have a dog in a food store," she said.

"It ain't a food store. It's a general store," he said.

"You serve food, so no dogs. In fact, you need to get a No Dogs sign," she said and kept on walking. "I'm grabbing a shower then I'll start on lunch. See you soon."

"We do coffee, cake, and some sandwiches," Norm said. "That's not food," he continued to argue, but she let the door swing shut on his grousing and deposited Wilbur on the kitchen floor. He made straight for the screen door, wagging his tail excitedly.

"In one door and out the other, that's all you're good for," she said and followed him out onto the porch.

"Oh no!" The destroyed flowerbed immediately caught her eye. "Don't tell me you're a digger. Uncle Norm will skin you alive. He loves his garden." Emily suspected the love affair between Norm and Wilbur had run its course.

The flowerbed looked like a small meteorite had hit it. Remnants of marigolds, begonias, and petunias lay strewn around a crater that seemed almost too large for the small dog to have dug. Most of the soil and plant debris littered Norm's immaculate lawn.

"You'll be in the pound quicker than a blink. What the—" The shine of patent leather peeked out from the heap of soil. With a sinking heart, Emily leaned over and pulled out a shoe. "These are my best heels, you little booger!" The Wilbur story was history as far as she was concerned. Wilbur stood nearby wagging his tail harder than ever.

"I should have left you where I found you." Emily stalked back to the house, rigid with disgust and holding her chewed up shoe at arm's length. Wilbur proudly followed her.

Norm met her in the kitchen. "I sent them old boys home and shut early. What ya got there, Em?"

"One of my best shoes, that's what. He buried it in the garden. What was he doing upstairs? These were in my room."

"Oh." Norm looked guilty.

"Did you let him upstairs?" Emily asked.

"I thought he was in the garden. When I went up for the laundry hamper, he must've followed."

"These were my best pair. They're my interview shoes. They cost a fortune." Emily waved the slobbery, muddy shoe at the dog before tossing it in the trash. "You've just blown your get out of jail free card, mister. It's the pound for you."

"Look, go get your shower and I'll make lunch." Norm tried to placate her. "How about soup?" He began to usher her toward the stairs. She allowed herself to be bustled out. Her nerves were already at the breaking point, and she needed the restorative powers of hot water and scented soap, and she was not coming out until she was as shriveled as a prune.

Upstairs, her bedroom looked...odd? Things had been touched, rearranged, poked at even. Her books! She had not left her books like that. She went out to the landing.

"Uncle Norm?" she called down the stairwell. "Did you say you were in my room?"

"Yeah," he called back over the burble of the kettle. "I got your laundry."

"Were you moving my books about?"

"Yeah. Some fell over. I picked 'em up. Do you want mushroom soup or tomato?"

"Mushroom, please. I'll be down in ten." She relaxed a little.

"Em?"

"Yeah?"

"Have you seen my wallet?"

"No. Try looking under the shop counter. You sometimes leave it there."

"Okay."

Her shower was a quick one after all, and things still weren't right. She took clean underwear from the freshly laundered pile uncle Norm had left on her bed, but she couldn't find her hairbrush anywhere, and a slipper was missing.

"I'm gonna kill that mutt." She went down for lunch.

"My hairbrush has vanished," she said, dragging her fingers through her damp hair. "And one of my slippers. Did you find your wallet?"

"Nope. Not in the shop." Norm shook his head. "I found a dead squirrel on the stoop though."

"A squirrel?" Emily looked at Wilbur. "He must have moved like lightning to snag a squirrel."

But Norm was too busy scratching around in the kitchen drawers to care. "I was sure I left my wallet here," he said.

"Do you think Indiana Jones has been doing more digging?" She nodded at Wilbur who was eating his third meal of the day as far as she could tell. Norm shrugged and sat at the table.

"I'll wander around the yard and do a spot check after lunch," she said, tasting her soup. "Thanks for taking care of lunch, Uncle Norm."

They listened to the local radio as they ate.

"I hate getting old and forgetful," Norm said and scraped back his chair, heading over to the sink to wash his bowl. Emily brought hers over, too, and put her arm around his slumped shoulders. They stood for a moment and looked out at Norm's well-tended yard with its stretch of crisp lawn and bright flowerbeds and the vegetable plot with its small greenhouse already bursting with spring produce.

It was immaculate, bar the mess Wilbur had made in the central flowerbed.

"No, you're not, Uncle Norm," she said and gave him a gentle squeeze. "We've both lost things. Dollar to a dime the answer is out there." She nodded at the garden, but her gaze drifted over it to the shadowy tangle of forest that lay beyond.

CHAPTER NINETEEN

What is it? Jolie frowned up at the tree.
  An initiation tree, Mouse said.
An initiation what?
  Mouse scuffed her paws, then sank to a squat on the ground. She looked exhausted. Her ears drooped and her muzzle was slack. *No Taddy here.*
  An initiation what? Jolie repeated, all thoughts of Tadpole pushed to the back of her mind. She looked in amazement at the big maple. She had never heard of such a thing. Above her, the bizarre tree was decorated like Christmas come early. Only creepier. The weirdest things dangled from it. A hiking boot strung up by its laces. Bunches of keys swayed like wind chimes. Colorful scarves waved gaily alongside pantyhose and an assortment of odd socks. Shirts of all colors and in all conditions streamed from the tree limbs. Some were ripped to slithery ribbons; others, intact, billowed like sea sails. Pants strung up by their legs hung heavy and sullen, while sweaters waved their arms crazily in warning. Her hackles rose just looking at the macabre sight.
  Mouse slid further down until she lay flat out on the ground, and Jolie realized she couldn't hold her wolf shape any longer. She had drained every ounce of energy in her small wolven body and now had no option but to turn back to human form. Kudos to the kid for lasting so long, Jolie thought, and hunkered down beside her.
  Okay, go for it, kid. She patted Mouse clumsily with her huge claws. Then she sat and kept guard as Mouse slithered and squirmed

her way back into the body of a grubby, mud-caked little girl. Again, the almost painless ease of her mutation amazed Jolie. She supposed Mouse had been transmuting since she could crawl. A sure sign of a wolven thoroughbred, and Jolie could only watch and admire.

Jolie was exhausted herself. She could go another couple of hours if necessary, but she didn't see the point. She lowered her head and grunted out the discomfort as her bones ground together and her ligaments stretched to the popping point. When she raised her head many minutes later, Mouse had already recovered and was poking around the immediate area.

"Luc was here," she said excitedly.

"Luc *is* here." Jolie stood and stretched her cramped muscles, shaking out her human shape. The scent of Luc was overpowering. This was an inhabited hide, not some long abandoned bolt-hole. Everything about it was too fresh, too urgent. Energy bounced off the very fabric of the place, and it made Jolie's skin prickle. She did not like being in another Were's den uninvited, and especially not Luc Garoul's.

"So what is all this?" She pointed at the tree.

"Told you. Initiation tree. It's what you do if you got a new Were to bring into the pack. I'm hungry." A whine had entered Mouse's voice. "And I'm cold."

Jolie had to admit she was also hungry and cold. It was not the best idea to be wandering around naked. It might have been a sunny day, but here in the depths of the forest, the shadows were long and the air held a late springtime chill. She dragged her thoughts away from the tree and its strange meaning for the moment. It was more important to keep Mouse warm and get her fed. Now that she was in human form, she was a small child and a vulnerable one at that, and Jolie felt an inarguable urge to protect her.

"Okay. Let's get you warm," she said. The most obvious thing was to dress them both from whatever they could salvage from the tree. Some of the garments hanging there were in a pretty sad state. Most were chewed to bits. Whatever was going on with Luc, she was expressing it in the weirdest way. Jolie had no hope of understanding it. She had no idea what an initiation tree was. As far as she was concerned, if you wanted to introduce a new pack member, you brought them home for dinner and to meet the family. You didn't have a garage sale in a tree.

She took a running jump and grabbed at a low-hanging branch, heaving her way up into the tree in an ungainly scrabble.

"Can I come, too?" Mouse called up.

"No, you can't," she barked down. "Stay there." There was a shiver of branches and leaves all around her, and Mouse appeared beside her.

"Whatchya doing?" Mouse asked.

"Getting us some glad rags," she growled. Would this kid ever do what she was told?

"Get me that T-shirt." Mouse pointed. "The one with the horses."

Jolie grabbed the garment and thrust it at Mouse.

"Now get back down," she ordered. She wanted to crawl a bit higher and look at the platform she could just make out several feet above their heads. It was well camouflaged, and Jolie was certain it was important and might contain more clues to what Luc was up to. But, trouble magnet that she was, Mouse was already scrambling toward it. With a tsk of frustration, Jolie grabbed the nearest shirt and a pair of overalls and followed her.

The platform was bigger than she had at first thought. In fact, it was quite cozy. To one side was an assortment of swag that was no doubt destined to litter the tree. Where had Luc acquired all this stuff? Mouse was already poking through the odds and ends strewn all about.

"Cool," she said. "A Were nest." She picked up a well-chewed scrap of what used to be a backpack. With a quick sniff, she tossed it aside and moved on to the next bit of junk.

"A Were nest?" Jolie echoed her. "What the hell is a Were nest?"

"It's what we use back home when we go away for long hunts. It's so we can sleep nice and safe," Mouse said.

"You mean you've been in one of these before?" Jolie was amazed.

"I love sleeping in nests. Though this one's full of garbage." She sounded very disapproving.

The wind gusted and the tree swayed. The nest creaked and moved under Jolie's feet making her stomach lurch.

"Doesn't feel so safe," she said. "It's weird to be up this high." Her stomach was swirling now, and she felt dizzy. She didn't dare look down. She was certain she'd puke even though there was nothing inside her to throw up.

"Nests don't have to be in trees," Mouse said. "They can be on the ground if you want them to. They can be anywhere."

"Someone should tell Luc that." Jolie decided she had developed vertigo. Who knew? She had never been this high up a tree in her life and wasn't going to again if she could help it.

"Put on that T-shirt," Jolie said, dragging on her own plaid shirt and well-worn overalls. The pants were far too short and swam around her hips. Mouse obeyed for once and slid into her top. It was a small adult size but still managed to hang from her slender frame right down to her knees.

"Here." Jolie picked up a belt and cinched it around Mouse's waist. "That's better. Looks sort of like a dress, I suppose." Mouse did not look impressed, and Jolie gave her shoulder a brisk pat to compensate for the fashion faux pas. It was the best they could do, and at least they were clothed.

"Hey." Mouse spied something from over Jolie's shoulder. "A wallet!" She pounced on it "And it's got dollars in it."

"Give it here." Jolie waved Mouse to hand it over. She counted the bills. There was more than enough for what she had in mind.

"I'm hungry." Mouse chimed in again, and Jolie could hear her stomach rumbling from a yard away.

"Okay," Jolie said, snapping the wallet closed. "Time to get some food."

"Burgers?" Mouse said hopefully.

"Maybe burgers. Lost Creek is near here. It's got a sort of coffee house thingy." She took one last look around. "Let's get out of here." She would inform Marie of Luc's loopiness once they got home. *If* they got home. It would be hard to go back without Tadpole.

Jolie sent up a quick prayer to Luna for the return of the pup, not that Luna gave a damn about stupid dogs, and pushed the problem away. She had more than enough to contend with for the moment.

Mouse went on ahead, scrambling down the tree as agile as any monkey. Jolie swung her legs over the edge of the nest and felt an uncomfortable surge of wooziness that made her overly defensive and angry. Trust Luc to get her into a situation she wasn't comfortable with. Luc was a pain in the ass and nothing but trouble.

"Nests are for the birds. But then your mom always was a cuckoo," she muttered.

"My mom?" Mouse's voice traveled up from the ground below. Jolie had forgotten the pin-drop precision of her hearing. "Luc is my mom?"

Oh freakin' hell no! Panic shot through her. She had just made a monumental error. She had breached a confidence she'd been told in the highest secrecy and a terrible sense of shame overwhelmed her. Her foot slipped. Jolie grunted, she grappled for purchase, her eyes bulged…and then she crashed through the branches to land in a heap by Mouse's feet. Leaves and twigs, a baseball cap, brassieres, a tampon, and a lot of dead insects showered down on her. She lay winded, listening to the blood thump through her. And then Mouse's wide-eyed face was hovering over hers, and above the blood thundering in her ears she clearly heard Mouse say, "Luc's my mom!"

❖

The RV smelled like…Luc sniffed. It smelled like…like… secrets, she supposed. Yes, secrets. But were they her own or Emily's? That's what she had to work out, which was probably why the RV had become her new thinking place.

The little orange vehicle had sat beside the house under the shade of a cedar all afternoon. Sunlight winked off its chrome, teasing her, beguiling her. No one had come near it for hours. Emily was inside doing Emily things, and Luc could not resist sidling closer for a quick look through the RV windows.

It was lucky that Emily didn't lock it, though the skitter of Luc's claws on the paintwork around the door handles looked suspiciously like a break-in. As if someone with shaky hands had taken a screwdriver to the locks. Still, she was inside now, and delighted to find the heap of blankets still on the floor where she and Emily had slept...before the Garouls came and ruined it all.

But first, she had to make the place just right for thinking. The RV was old and stunk of cheap plywood and brittle plastic. Even the brown upholstery with its horrible, knobby texture reeked of fabric cleaner. Luc rubbed her damp muzzle on the bench seat to wipe off the yuckiness and replace it with sexy werewolf. Then she lay down in the makeshift nest and sucked up Emily smells and let her mind drift. She had felt a little bit bad about all the stuff she had stolen, so she had returned to bring a few gifts of her own. But it was her secret. No one must ever know she had done it. She had a bad reputation to maintain.

Secrets.

Hers and Emily's.

She considered her own first. Namely, why did this human affect her so much? At least she could dissect her scent now, separate out the woman from the chemicals that polluted her. Luc remembered the first time she had encountered Emily's scent with its stink of antidepressants and sleeping pills. She had stolen her backpack and pulled it inside out to get a nose for her hunter. The true essence of Emily's scent had eluded her then, pungent with her anxieties and medications. No matter how intrigued Luc was, she could not interpret the telltale odors of Emily's body. At first, she had worried that the virus had decimated her sense of smell. The hunter in Luc studied scent the way a human savored wine. Luc *tasted* scent. It flavored her sinuses, exploding on her tongue with a million messages, impressions, directives. Sly suggestions swilling around her teeth until she snapped them away like flies. Sometimes, from the corner of her eye, she would make out a shadow, a fleeting vision that, if she held her breath might manifest itself into her quarry and she would know where and what it was and how to kill it.

She squirmed further into the nest, each rustle of the blankets releasing a waft of Emily's skin scent. Luc wanted to wrap herself in it. Her collar dinged against the linoleum floor, and she rubbed the metallic edge against the soft fur of her neck until the flesh underneath protested. This was her secret. The collar was the cure. The collar had contained the virus, and all her stunted wolven powers had flooded back, and she'd bet anything that had not been Emily's intention.

What was her intention? Luc lay back and stared at the stained roof liner. *To cut out my gizzard, that's what.* Her muzzle creased as she rumbled out a growl, but her heart wasn't really in it. She liked that Emily was after her gizzard. Luc demanded one on one attention. *So let's look at little Emily's secrets.*

Emily wanted a werewolf, a live specimen to cut up. Luc remembered the vicious surgical instruments. But not any old werewolf. Emily had captured a Garoul. She knew about the Garouls. She had studied them and blamed them for her father's death. Luc's ears flattened. She knew about this hunting incident. She had been a witness to it. It had been a catalytic moment in her life, and in the lives of her immediate family. Emily's secrets weren't so secret after all; they were all about revenge. Revenge for a death Luc had already paid for.

Luc flopped over onto her belly, and the small RV rocked on its springs. Her snout was level with the fridge vent, and she idly picked the dust from it with her fore claw. She should have killed Emily. There had been countless opportunities. Okay, so she had needed things from her, like cell keys and collar keys. She had even planned to use her as a human shield to drive her out of Garoul territory and on to the border. *Then* she would have killed her. Or would she? And this maybe was the biggest secret. Luc couldn't kill her.

Instead of destroying the almanac and its human owner, she was sneaking into bedrooms stealing scent. Luc flicked the dust bunnies from her claws and rolled back to stare at an oblique sliver of blue sky through the RV window. Yes. She was drawn to Emily in a way she couldn't understand, and could never harm her. And that was the biggest secret of all.

CHAPTER TWENTY

E m. Have you seen my glasses?"
"No." Emily had to work hard not to snap back her answer.
"Can't find my car keys either. Can't find a danged thing without my glasses," Norm muttered to himself more than Emily, and went back to shoveling around inside the kitchen drawers, his nose inches from the opening, squinting in at the jumbled contents.

Emily was having enough frustrations of her own. Her own reading glasses had gone missing. There was a trail of hairclips all the way down the stairs, and another pair of shoes had disappeared. A quick look around the garden did not produce any clues as to what Wilbur had done with them. They were well and truly hidden.

"What about my wallet, Em? Did you see my wallet anywhere yet?" Norm asked for the umpteenth time.

"No." She did snap this time. "Stupid dog's a magpie. I can't find anything."

"Dang," Norm muttered again, and shuffled off to water his vegetable patch with his danged dog in tow while Emily stomped back upstairs to put away the laundry.

"Em?" Another holler followed her up the stairs. "There's clothes missing off the line. Did you bring any in?"

"I'm putting the laundry away now," she called back, disinterested. Without his glasses, she was surprised he could even find the clothesline. *The whole house is in an uproar since that stupid dog arrived.* She lifted the clean laundry from the foot of her bed and took it to the dresser. *It was madness to bring him here. I should have taken him straight to the pound.* She yanked open the top drawer. *Lord knows how much of our stuff is buried in the garden. If I ever—*

Emily froze. Her sweater drawer was in chaos. She picked up a woolen Aran sweater. It had been a favorite. Now it was in tatters. A huge hole gaped at its side, and broken threads of yarn stuck out in all directions. It looked as if a great white shark had taken a bite out of it.

A quick rummage showed that nearly all her sweaters had been damaged in some way or another, either holed with huge chunks missing or plucked to bits as if a million chickens had attacked them. Emily slammed open the next drawer and found the same carnage in her underwear drawer. Everything had been folded away but now lay in an unruly mess, tattered and torn. This was not the dog's doing. Emily's blood ran cold. Something had been snooping in her room. Throughout the whole house in fact! Was it a Garoul after the almanac?

"Em! Em!" Norm's shout brought her to the top of the stairs anxious that something awful had happened.

"What? What is it?"

"There's a goose on the doorstep," he called up.

"A goose? Is it dead?"

"Of course it's dead."

"Well, did the dog kill it?"

"It's bigger than the dog."

"The damned squirrel was almost as big as the dog and he killed it."

"Well, okay then." With that, Norm turned around and wandered outside again leaving Emily on the verge of tearing her hair out. *We're all going mad.*

She went back to her room to recheck her desk. Uncle Norm said he'd picked up her books when they'd toppled over. Emily riffled through her collection. No books were missing. Nevertheless, she was relieved she had already removed the almanac to safety. But her reading glasses were gone, and now she noticed her pen, the gold one Uncle Norm had bought her for graduation, was not where she'd left it. What the hell was going on? Why were things going missing? And why were other weird things appearing, like dead geese and squirrels?

Emily sat on the edge of her bed and tried to arrange her thoughts. She sniffed. There was a musky, foxy sort of smell. She checked the soles of her boots. Nothing. She sniffed again. It was still there, definitely an earthy, muddy sort of...oh no! Emily buried her nose in the bed sheets and breathed deeply. No! It couldn't be. She pulled back her bedclothes to find a second dead squirrel and several acorns. Werewolf gifts! Luc's werewolf gifts.

"That bastard's been in my room." She couldn't believe it. "In my house. In my uncle's house!" And the sneak thief had pilfered its way from room to room stealing anything that caught its fancy. It was all so obvious. She recalled Luc's bizarre habits of acquisition; her little piles of loot, her need to grab at anything that caught her eye. Rage streaked through Emily like hellfire. *How dare she come into my home and steal from my family!*

She reached under her shirt to touch the silver key where it nestled on her chest. Her hands shook. She'd hidden the almanac and burned her notes. The only link left was the key to the collar. That had to be what Luc was after. Emily had to thwart her and hide it. She had to hide it well, in a place Luc would never want, never mind think, to look.

A snuffle came from the doorway and an inquisitive Wilbur stuck his nose through the gap and pushed the door open all the way. He came into her room slowly, as if aware he should not be upstairs. Emily noticed Uncle Norm had been gifting dog again. He wore a brand new collar. She knelt and held out her arms.

"Come here, boy. Who's a good boy," she crooned. "I need your help with something."

Seconds later, Emily wandered to the window. She was more relaxed now. Her problems walking up and she was dealing with them as best she could. But the biggest problem was still out there. She glanced at the forest. Somewhere out there Luc Garoul was laughing.

Something was wrong with her RV! Emily zoned in on her vehicle. Something was different. She had parked it under the big cedar. The narrow driveway only had room for Norm's truck so she used the clearing beyond the house. And she knew she hadn't left the side door open a crack. And she knew she hadn't pulled down the back window blind either, especially not at that lopsided angle!

Emily tore down the stairs and out to the driveway that ran by the side of the house. She stopped beside her RV and had a quick look around the yard for Norm. He was nowhere to be seen, probably back inside opening up his store for the afternoon. She wanted him well out of the way.

The paintwork on the side door of her RV was scored around the handle. Her blood boiled even harder. Luc was destroying her beloved RV piece by piece.

Carefully, she approached and peered in through the crack of the open side door. There, on the nest of grubby blankets, lay an equally grubby Luc, curled up into a ball. She was naked and snoring. Her mouth was open, and the pink of her tongue trembled against her teeth. She looked pale and unkempt. Emily could only surmise she had been on the run since she had last seen her, and that this tatty RV was perhaps her last hope, her last sanctuary. Emily swung the door open with a resounding crash and leapt on the reclining figure.

"You bastard! You stole my things!"

❖

"I sort of k　　　anyways." Mouse sucked on her lower lip, concentrating on h　　　et as she and Jolie walked through the forest.
"Yeah. I suppo　　wasn't much of a secret." Jolie tried to let herself off the hook.　　till felt awful that she had been the one to reveal the truth to　　She supposed it was to be Ren's job at some point, but in Jolie　　n, Ren was doing a very shoddy job when it came to rearing　　The child was half-wild, and not in a good wolfie way, but in　　he child mugger type of way. At least Mouse wasn't as h　　unk, child mugger type of way.
　　　high tech gadgetry like most

of the kids back in Portland were. *So how do we talk about this? Should I even attempt to?*

They walked along, both kicking up dirt and leaves with their bare feet.

"Why does the pack want to hurt her?" Mouse asked out of the blue.

"Ah. Well." *What would Hope do?* "They don't want to hurt her. She's sick and they need to find her quick. Okay?" Jolie said, remembering Hope had said something similar.

"Has she got the same virus that killed Patrick and the others?"

"Um. Um." This was hard. Jolie decided to stop stalling. If she were in the kid's place, she'd want the truth. And they were from the same pack after all; they were family, and that had to mean something. "Yes, I guess so. But this time Marie's involved, and she's pretty damned sharp when it comes to medicines and stuff. She used to be a doctor before she became Alpha." She snaked her arm around Mouse's shoulders. "If they find her in time, at least your mom will have a fighting chance. That's more than the others did."

"But she's running away from them. She's scared they'll blame her."

"Blame her for what?" Jolie frowned. She had only breezed in near the end of this saga when Hope and Isabelle were already safely returned to the Garoul compound, and Mouse and Joey were everyone's heroes. It had been too late to blow off steam. No one cared that Jolie had her mate stolen. Hope had handled it all with great aplomb, but that did not stop Jolie from having nightmares for weeks afterward.

"Blame her for what Patrick did. He's the one who grabbed me and Hope," Mouse said.

"Oh?" Jolie said. This was news. It put a whole different slant to the "touch my mate and you die" thing she had going on with Luc. Jolie could feel a sulk starting and battled it down. She wanted Luc to be the baddie. She wanted to be angry with her and Ren, but she also wanted to hear more of Mouse's story.

"He started ordering everyone around when Ren left, but we just laughed and then he grabbed me and took me away to a cabin and locked me up with chains and he had his own pack, but they were stupid." Mouse barely drew breath. "They all got bad guts, but Patrick had it in the head. I knew because his eyes were all red with goo coming out."

"Lovely." Jolie grimaced.

"Plus he was talking crap, but Patrick always talked crap."

"Hey! Language."

"Joey says crap."

"Joey needs a good nip on the ear talking like that around you." *Sheesh, what was Ren thinking of? These kids needed taking in hand.*

Mouse laughed at that. "I nip Joey's ears all the time. He's silly."

"So," Jolie tried to keep Mouse on track. "You think Patrick did all those things because he was sick?"

"He was mean even before he got sick. He was bossy."

"Did he want to be Alpha?"

"Patrick an Alpha?" Mouse snorted. "He's too crap. His pack was crap, too."

"I told you. No more bad language."

"Okay." Mouse didn't look the slightest bit bothered.

Jolie gave up on the cussing lecture and tried a different tactic. "You know Patrick's dead, right?" she said as gently as she could.

"Yeah. Luc killed him." Mouse perked up. "I heard Ren tell Marie what she did, and I bet it was 'cause he hurt me. He stole me from Singing Valley and she never knew. I bet she killed him 'cause he was bad to me and way too sick anyway."

So much for pricking her conscience. Mouse had the hard snout of the Garouls through and through.

"Why didn't Luc just tell you she was your mom?" Jolie asked, though she suspected the question would have been better asked of Ren. Why had she and Luc both kept it from her?

Mouse shrugged. "Dunno. I saw her all the time. She never lived with us, but she came nearly every day to teach me how to hunt and do stuff. We had fun. She's the best hunter ever, and builds the best nests. I built a nest in our barn out of hay. Joey said hay is for horses, not Weres, and I said we had no horses so I could sleep in it if I damn well wanted to."

"And don't say damn either." Jolie had no wish to talk about nests; she hated them unequivocally. Besides, they were fast coming up to the outskirts of Lost Creek and her stomach was grumbling louder than a grizzly. She took hold of Mouse's hand and guided her to the edge of the tree line so they could skirt along it and into town. Jolie knew roughly where she wanted to go, toward the west side where hopefully Johnston's General Store was still in business and still served food.

They padded along a side alley then out onto a dusty sidewalk. The streets were empty. The houses ran in rows, and all had blank windows; most with the shades pulled against the afternoon light. The only vehicle Jolie could see was a small orange RV parked far up ahead, near the woods. It rocked violently from side to side, which she found strange but was in no mood to investigate. It was the only sign of human activity in the otherwise tranquil afternoon. There was no one else in sight, and Jolie was thankful for it.

The store door opened with a cheerful tinkle. Jolie's eye level was higher than the store shelving, and a quick glance around ensured they were the only patrons in the place. Behind the coffee counter, an old man sat fiddling with the radio, trying to tune in a sports station. His nose was almost touching the dial. He looked up as they entered only for his face to fall into a scowl when they were not who he had been expecting.

Jolie led the way over to the counter where she and Mouse slid awkwardly onto the high stools.

"What'll it be?" the old man asked, squinting at them suspiciously.

"Two Cokes, and what sandwiches do you have?" Jolie said. A refrigerated stand was wordlessly pointed out to her. She retrieved a selection of sandwiches and set them before Mouse, who pulled the wrapper off the nearest one and took an enormous bite.

"You passing through?" the old guy asked, still glaring at them through what Jolie could only imagine to be a mist of myopia. He seemed fascinated with what they were wearing, and squinted hard at her overalls. Jolie couldn't really blame him. They did look rather hillbilly.

"Yeah." She took a large mouthful of sandwich and decided to play dumb.

"Where's your vehicle?"

"We're walking."

He seemed to consider this. "Hiking? Where's your gear?"

That was more awkward, but Jolie was on her second bite now and concentrating on the joy of actually eating. "With friends."

"Who's your friends? Anyone local?"

"Yeah, local."

He paused, waiting for more information. When it didn't arrive he said, "Well? Who? Are they from Lost Creek?"

"Near here." Jolie wished he would go away and let her eat in peace.

"Where then?"

"Little Dip," Mouse piped up.

Jolie frowned. *There goes my digestion.* The kid knew nothing about the bad feeling between Lost Creek and Little Dip, and Jolie was annoyed she hadn't thought to school her on the way over.

"You mean that witch place?" The old guy's face darkened.

"What witches?" Mouse asked with great interest. Jolie began to shove the unopened sandwiches into her pockets and reach for the wallet. It was time to go, and not a moment too soon.

"Them Garouls are all witches." He wagged a finger at Mouse who scowled back at him. "There's no good goes on out there."

"That's crap," Mouse said.

"Why you little brat—" he began, but the click-clack of paws distracted them all from the ugly scene for a split second.

"Taddy!" Mouse cried, and jumped off her stool to hug the little dog who appeared around the corner. He was in a little green tartan coat with a matching collar, and gave a delighted bark to see her. His tail went into overdrive.

"Wilbur. Come here, boy—Hey! That's my wallet. Hey!"

Crap! Jolie threw the loose bills, wallet, and all at him and grabbed Mouse by the arm. "Run!" she yelled.

"Hey! Stop! Those are my clothes!"

"Keep running." She was dragging Mouse behind her, and behind Mouse came the excited click-clack of Tadpole as he ran to keep up with them.

"Hey! That's my dog!"

They burst out into the bright afternoon. Jolie kept her death grip on Mouse's arm and hurtled down the street to the side alley they had come in by. From there they headed for the cover of the trees. Jolie pulled them deeper into the forest for another fifteen minutes before she stopped to draw breath. *Luna! What a bucket of crud.* But they were safe now.

"Taddy. What have they done to you?" Mouse was on her knees beside Tadpole hugging him half to death. "I thought we'd lost you forever."

Jolie took a deep breath; her nerves were shot to pieces. She looked at the dog in his jaunty tartan coat and couldn't believe her luck. They had found him, and in the oddest of places. Luna only knew how he had ended up at Johnston's General Store, but Jolie didn't care. She had rescued him and now they could all go home.

CHAPTER TWENTY-ONE

"Y ou hairy little shit!" Emily lunged.

Luc barely had time to open her eyes before Emily was upon her. She struggled to get away, not that there was anywhere to go. The RV was cramped enough with only her inside it, never mind a psychopath. To make matters worse, she had transmuted back to human form while asleep and was now very vulnerable to attack. She tried to scrabble toward the back of the RV, but Emily grabbed her by the stupid silver collar and nearly garroted her.

"Stop that!" she gasped. "You're choking me."

"Good. You damn well deserve it." Emily started to shake the collar until Luc thought her head would drop off. "I should have choked you ages ago when I had the chance," she ranted. "I should have poisoned you like a rat. I should have left you under the mud like the evil slug you are."

Luc twisted around and grabbed. She had to fight back or be beheaded. She wrapped her arms around Emily and pinned her to the floor. "Stop throttling me."

Emily stopped throttling and bit her instead. Luc had to admire her resourcefulness.

"Stop that, too." Luc flinched as her shoulder felt the imprint of Emily's teeth. She seemed so unreasonably angry, and something else. A something Luc couldn't help but respond to. Her skin flushed and her heart rate increased. She liked the bite despite her protestations. It tingled through her; her senses were swamped with the smell of Emily and the heat of her wrath. Luc was used to people being angry with her. She never allowed it to annoy her. She couldn't afford to. But this was different. Emily was a squirming bundle of irritable, passionate, righteous anger, and it was hot!

"What's got your craw?" Luc growled, and found she was holding on tighter rather than trying to shrug Emily off.

"Let me go." Emily tried to wriggle free.

"No. You let me go," Luc countered. She liked the situation now that she had Emily under control. She rolled her onto her back and lay on her with her full weight. "You put this stupid collar on me, and you can take it off. I'm going nowhere until you do."

"If you were looking for the key then why did you steal all that other stuff from my house?"

"You'll get it back." Luc knew her answer wasn't satisfactory. To be honest, she wasn't certain why she had this urge to steal from Emily's den. She just knew she did. It excited her. She liked decorating her nest with bits and bobs that belonged to Emily, that smelled of her or reminded Luc of her in some way. Luc knew it was weird and obsessive, but she couldn't help herself. It felt good and she didn't want to think too hard about it. Emily intrigued her. Luc knew she was acting on instinct, but so what? She had always done whatever she wanted to do. She was feral. She answered to no one! If she wanted to steal stuff from Emily's room, then she damned well would.

The bite mark stung. Emily lay looking up at the welt on Luc's skin, somewhat affronted that she had caused it. Luc wriggled her shoulder to stretch out the pain and clicked her teeth. She wanted Emily to bite her some more. She wanted to teach her all about biting. About the patterns teeth could make on a lover's pliant flesh. The crescent moons and rows of tiny bruises, the stars and sickles all raised and lumpy, or maybe soft and swollen, wet with spittle or seeping beads of blood. The pupils of Emily's eyes were eclipsing her flat gray irises, darkening her gaze and pulling Luc into their depths. Her skin was clammy with small beads of sweat glistening on her upper lip. She was upset, but curiously not frightened. Luc could smell that off her. There was confusion, but no fear. A slight tremor ran along the length of her body where it pressed against the weight of Luc's. Emily moistened her lips and Luc felt her own heart lurch in response. It fluttered irregular and weak like a wounded bird. Her chest tightened and then released, and she sucked air forcefully into her deflated lungs. She lowered her head and placed her mouth on Emily's mouth. She would be careful with this seduction because she wanted it so much. She would be gentle.

"Fuck!" she yelped and pulled back. Emily had bitten her again. She touched her bruised bottom lip. Emily bucked her hips, trying to bounce her off while she was distracted by this newest affliction. She managed to pull her arms free and mesh her hands in Luc's long hair, twisting huge hanks of it into her fists.

"Hey. I was being nice," Luc complained, trying to wrestle Emily back under control, her seduction plans temporarily aborted.

"A lettuce could kiss harder than you," Emily said, and tugged harder on Luc's hair.

Luc paused, uncertain she had heard right. Emily tightened her hold and dragged her down into a kiss that would wither lettuce on the stalk, that would crystallize ginger and implode chilies and burn sugar and melt Luc Garoul like summer Popsicles.

"Why are you doing this?" Emily broke their contact and left Luc floundering. Her head swam with the intoxication of their kiss. She was stupid on it, so how then was Emily so cool and in control?

"Is this some sort of trick?" Emily continued to demand in a tight, thick voice.

Trick? Luc could barely focus. "I was under the impression *you* were kissing me," she said. *Trick.* She began to flare up. How dare this woman accuse her of trickery? Emily had been the one who had trapped and tricked her. She was the one who had chained them both with this damned collar. Luc would be in Canada by now but for Emily's interference. Thievery was one thing, but trickery? This woman had more tricks than Halloween.

"You have some nerve." Luc's thoughts popped into some semblance of order. "The last thing I need is to be hanging around here stealing your panties with those Garoul bastards breathing down my neck." She felt Emily's fingers toying with the nape of her neck. "You've been nothing but trouble." Her touch was silky cool and gave Luc a delicious shiver all over her body. "I mean...You're the one who's been manipulating *me*." Her head dropped to kiss along Emily's jawline. "I mean...I mean, look at what you're doing to me now." She trailed her lips to the well in Emily's throat and rested on the thumping pulse. "You're pitiless. Who needs this?" Her fingers twitched, fighting the urge to dig her nails into Emily's flank and mark her. Her kiss on the fluttering pulse deepened, she became hungrier, more demanding. She laved the pulse point with the flat of her tongue. Below her, Emily shifted and moaned. Her fingers meshed in Luc's hair to massage—

"Ouch!"

Emily twisted Luc's hair around her fists in great hanks and pulled. She rolled them over in the tight confines of the RV floor until she was on top. She looked very determined, and once again, Luc found herself struggling to keep up with her through a fog of lust and little else.

"Are you going to change?" Emily asked.

"Into a werewolf or sexy lingerie?" Luc answered. That got her an extra tug on the hair and she yelped. She liked Emily's bitchiness. It was kind of cute.

"Werewolf. Are you going to change into one and go crazy and bite my head off?"

"No. I'm going to stay right where I am and go crazy." Her hands snaked under Emily's top and found the warm flesh of her belly. Luc was already naked, but she burned to feel Emily's skin next to hers. She began plucking and pulling at Emily's clothes. "Are you going to change and get naked?" she asked.

There was a slight hesitation on Emily's part and Luc saw it. She pulled her to her and kissed her with open-mouthed, smoldering passion.

"I want you," she murmured, lest there be any misunderstanding. She tugged harder at Emily's clothes. "I want you right here on this floor." A stitch burst and elastic snapped, and then Emily was helping by shrugging off her top and kicking her legs out of her jeans. Luc clawed the underwear from Emily's hips. She wore no bra. Luc would have bitten it off anyway.

The touch of their skin on each other was electric. They sparked and twitched and moaned, gliding over each other like silk, like static. The RV floor was too small and knees and elbows slammed into cabinets and table legs as they wrestled for space. Luc smoothed her hands down Emily's back to cup her rump and squeezed. Her mouth found a raspberry red nipple and she drew on it with relish feeling it harden under her tongue, straining for her attentions. Emily moaned and Luc bit gently until she heard a hiss of pleasure. Her forefinger traced the groove of Emily's bottom and she brought her other hand around to play with the soft crease between Emily's belly and groin and down to where the warm swell of her pubis pushed into the palm of her hand. Her fingertips found wetness and heat and a low growl rumbled in Luc's chest. Her skin was burning and her head was heavy with heat. The wolfskin was close to the surface. Her feet were cramped and hot, and the tightness in her face warned her how close she was to changing.

"Question." Emily's cool hands cupped her face and brought her up to meet her gaze, now darker than a winter night. "What happened to your ear?" Now that her hair was pulled back, the crooked ear was exposed.

"My sister bit it," Luc said.

Emily digested this without comment, her gaze flicking over Luc's still face.

"Your eyes are flecked with gold," she murmured, and lowered her mouth to kiss the corner of Luc's lips. "I've never noticed that before." Then her mouth found the softness of Luc's throat. She bared her teeth and grazed the flesh; Luc arched her head and pushed up into Emily's claim. She knew what it was even if Emily was clueless as to her act. The fact that either of them was doing it, was laying claim where there was no history to bind them, no love to hold them, did not make Luc hesitate. Luc offered herself with no thought, just the pure, blind instinct that always drove her. She closed her eyes, and somewhere deep inside, she made her dedication…and heard a joyful, whooping woof.

Oh no. Not him again.

Luc opened her eyes and slid out from under Emily to peep out the back window with its lopsided blind in time to see the stupid ginger mutt scramble up the street hard on the heels of a ramshackle child and hobo woman. Was he chasing them off or following them? Then Emily's crazy old uncle spilled out onto the sidewalk.

"Hey. That's my dog." His shout answered her question. The dog was making a run for it, and who could blame it. The old man turned away from the escapees and began to trundle toward the RV. Luc heaved to her feet, whacking her head on the low ceiling and muttering curses.

"What is it?" Emily was upright, dragging on her clothes.

"Your uncle is on his way over."

"Get the hell out of here before he sees you."

"But I'm human." Luc felt hurt, not that she wanted to meet Emily's uncle anyway, grizzled old geezer that he was.

"He doesn't know I'm gay. Get out!" Emily was shoving her out the sliding door. Luckily, it faced the forest and Luc could easily run for cover before the old boy got close enough to see his niece's naked lover making a run for it.

A few yards into the thicket, she paused and looked back to see Emily's anxious face scouring the wood line for her. She was clawing her clothes into place even as her uncle reached the rear of the RV and began slamming on the side for her attention. Emily couldn't see her. She was too far back in the shadows. For a second, Luc relaxed and watched. Her throat was still damp from the touch of Emily's tongue. She placed her fingers on her pulse point where Emily's teeth had been. There would be no mark. Emily didn't know how to bite, but Luc would teach her that. Luc watched the sunlight shine on Emily's auburn hair as she slouched on the step of the side door and waited for her uncle to find her. That was Emily sitting there. Her Emily. Her mate.

Chapter Twenty-two

A nd then they stole Wilbur and my overalls."

"Your overalls?" Emily said. She was perched on the side step of her RV feeling hot and very, very bothered. Norm was giving her a hell of headache with all his nonsense.

"I'm sure they were my overalls. They had a paint splotch on the bib, right here." Uncle Norm tapped his chest.

"Okay." Emily had no idea why she said okay when nothing was okay. The dog was gone. The damned dog had run away. She had assumed he would be here forever. Norm had bonded with him, for God's sake! She heaved herself to her feet and walked away from the RV a little unsteadily.

"You sure you're feeling all right, Em?" Norm asked.

"Sure. Sure," she said. He had nearly given her a heart attack banging on the RV like the hordes of Armageddon seconds after Luc had streaked away from it. "It was hot in there." She waved at the RV and kept on walking to the house. She needed to stand under a cold shower, or a fire hose, or something. She had to think.

"It's too hot for cleaning out cars," he said, and fell into step beside her. "What are we gonna do about Wilbur?"

"Did they grab him or did he just follow them?" Emily had a good idea what had happened. Wilbur had found his rightful family.

"Them Garouls grab anything they want." Norm sounded defeated, as if he too knew the answer. The dog belonged in Little Dip not Lost Creek.

"Can't argue with that." Under her shirt, Emily's skin itched all over. Luc's nips and scratches stung, but in a good, secret lover sort of way. Emily felt overheated and depleted, and also irritable. She wanted Luc, here, now. They needed to talk.

"It's so hot, why don't we light up the barbeque tonight and eat on the porch?" She decided to change tack with Norm. He needed to calm down. She had brought total chaos into his life, if he but knew it. "I'll make that potato salad you like."

His eyes lit up. "The one with the onion bits in?"

With one last look at the tree line, Emily gently ushered him toward the house. There was nothing out there. No shadow that looked deeper and more menacing than the rest. No wraith-like sliver of pale flesh vanishing through the tangle of trees. Luc had gone and left a lit keg of explosive emotion and a million questions behind her.

❖

"Look at all these rib bones." Norm cast a sorrowful eye over his plate. It was piled high with his leftovers. Emily knew what was coming next. "If Wilbur were here, he would have loved these," he said mournfully.

"I think we need to go down to the pound and adopt a dog," she said. It was clear to her that Norm was lonely. Despite all the hangers-on at his coffee counter during the day, it must be depressing once the shop shutters came down and he went home to an empty house. "It's a sin for all those animals to be lined up on death row when all they need is a decent owner to save them. There are some wonderful dogs there. Good guard dogs, too."

Norm looked over. "Guards dogs?"

"Well, you have to admit Wilbur never guarded a damn thing." She felt sorry for blaming the dog for the disappearances, but better that than tell her uncle they'd had an intruder. A hairy one. "Look at the stuff that went missing. Bet it's all buried out there somewhere." She nodded over the fence to the forest. It was only half a lie.

"A guard dog would keep an eye on the clothesline," Norm said. He was warming to the idea.

"You only think that woman was wearing your overalls," Emily said. "You didn't even have your glasses on. I bet the dog pulled the overalls off the line and hid them somewhere." She warmed to her theme, false as it was. "I mean, why would a grown woman steal your messy old paint pants and then wear them into your shop? You must have scared the wits out of her yelling like that."

Norm looked a little shamefaced. "She had my wallet."

"No, you said she threw some dollars on the counter and then you *found* your wallet, exactly where I told you to look earlier." Emily was pleased at her problem solving. Norm was easy to manage with logic, even if the logic flew in the face of reality. But the less inclined he was to march down to Little Dip with his Winchester to reclaim his dog, pants, wallet, and whatever the hell else Luc had pilfered, then the better it was for all of them. As far as Emily was concerned, she was in the middle of a disaster recovery exercise and doing rather well at it.

"Another beer?" Norm asked, indicating his own empty bottle. It was a peace offering that Emily was glad to accept.

"Please," she said and watched him go fetch a few more. She sighed and relaxed back into her rocker, lifting her face to the last rays of the sun. She rocked back and forth enjoying the pearly pink play behind her eyelids and the gentle heat caressing her face. The motion of the chair was soothing, like the sway of a cradle, and she allowed her fatigue to seep through her bones and melt her muscles to honey—

Her chair jarred to a shuddering halt. A shadow blocked out the mellow sunglow as her rocker was roughly tipped backward, so far back her feet dangled doll-like off the floor. Emily's eyes flew open. A huge werewolf loomed over her, its menacing frown leered only inches from her face. This was not Luc. She could see the dark brown flecks in its amber eyes, each individual hair bristling from its leathery maw.

This was the Were she had spotted lurking in the dawn mist. Its nostrils quivered as it delicately inhaled her. Her ear, her hairline, and down her neck to her breastbone. The moisture of its breath brushed along her skin. Then it growled, low and cunning, as if it had learned something, and Emily's guts jellified. It released the back of her chair abruptly, and she was flung forward, the runners crashing down on the wood planking, the soles of her feet slapping on the floor. Emily looked over her shoulder, but the beast was gone. She was alone, shaking with dread. What the hell was happening? Werewolves were everywhere. Lost Creek was crawling with the things.

"Here ya go." Norm waved a sweating bottle of beer under her nose. She hadn't even heard him return. She took the bottle, thankful for the coolness and solidity of it in her hand. It grounded her a little.

"Maybe we can go have a look in the pound tomorrow?" he said, and sat in the rocker beside her and took a sip of beer. She copied him, letting the cold liquid trickle down her tight, dried out throat.

"Yeah, let's do that," she said, her voice rasping as she struggled with her panic. All the time, her gaze flickered from the porch to the yard to the forest and back, never once finding a trace of her visitor.

❖

"It was like a great garage sale in the sky," Jolie said, waving her hands at the surrounding trees for emphasis.

"With lots of neat stuff," Mouse added. "I got this T-shirt and some glasses." She was wearing the glasses, which made her eyes huge and owl-like. Jolie swiped them from her nose.

"I told you not to wear those. You'll damage your eyes."

"A nest?" Marie frowned. Beside her, Connie looked bemused. Jolie had found them in the central compound and made a beeline for them. She had to spill her news before she burst with it. As usual, Mouse was at her heels butting in all over. The cub had no respect.

"It's been years since I saw a nest. We don't bother with them here." Marie smiled at some private memory then shook it away to fix her errant pack members with a stern gaze. "Hope has been looking for you two."

Jolie shifted under her scrutiny, and Mouse edged in behind her, far more sensitive to Marie's mood than she'd ever been to Jolie's.

"We were going there next," Jolie said glumly. She did not expect a warm welcome. Marie looked satisfied with this.

"So Luc has styled an initiation tree and is sleeping in it?" she said.

Mouse nodded mutely, her gaze prodding Jolie into being spokesperson. Jolie was highly suspicious of this. It was not like Mouse to voluntarily step out of the limelight, and Jolie had the distinct feeling she was skating toward thin ice, with a helpful push.

"Well, yes." Jolie cleared her throat. "It was dripping with clothes and jewelry and stuff."

"And these things were hanging from it." It was a statement not a question. Marie indicated their patched up, barefoot ensemble. "So you removed items from the tree." Again, it was not a question, but Jolie felt obliged to answer.

"The cub was tuckered out so we went back to human form. It was freezing. I thought it was the best to get dressed," she said. Every word she said made sense, yet an unshakeable feeling of foreboding descended on her. Marie looked troubled.

"The tree is an ancient courtship ritual. To remove an item from it is to contest the declared union," Marie said, frowning.

Jolie looked at Mouse, aghast. Why had she not warned her? Mouse just shrugged. It was obviously news to her, too.

"I didn't want to, Aunt Marie. She made me dress like this," Mouse declared. Jolie was outraged.

"Well, I never told you to take those glasses. You stole those all on your own!" she said.

"But I need glasses for reading." Mouse put on her best wheedling voice.

"You only read comics." Jolie was furious. Once again, she was in trouble and Mouse was at the epicenter of it. "And even then you move your lips."

"I do not!"

"If it isn't Huckleberry Finn and the littlest hobo!" Hope's voice cut through their bickering.

"Hope." Jolie was delighted to see her mate, and at the same time full of trepidation.

"Hello, Auntie Hope," Mouse trilled happily, totally unconcerned.

Oh, so it's Auntie Hope is it? And I'm just plain old Jolie? I see how it is. Jolie's mood darkened. "I can explain," she said and pointed at Mouse. "She—"

"Oh, you'll explain all right," Hope interrupted her. "Explain, repent, and compensate. And the first thing I want to know is exactly who is this woman you want to fight Luc for. I don't see you as the harem type." She folded her arms and tapped her foot.

Jolie vaguely noted the parody in Hope's show of annoyance, but she was in hyper-defensive mode and determined to redeem herself, so once again pointed at Mouse.

"She didn't tell me how the damned tree worked," she said.

"She dragged me miles in the cold and rain until I was starving." Mouse fought back.

"She ran away," Jolie almost squeaked in indignation.

"She lost Tadpole," Mouse almost shouted.

"Oh, you little—" Jolie flushed scarlet with mortification.

"Tadpole?" Hope's voice filled with alarm. On hearing his name, Tadpole wandered over from a bush he had been exploring and pressed his fore paws on her knees begging for a head scratch. His tartan coat stretched along his body and the little bell on his new tartan collar jingled. "He's in tartan?" Hope blinked in confusion.

"We've had to listen to that bell for the last ten miles," Jolie grumbled.

"What have you done to him?" Hope demanded.

"Jolie lost him," Mouse piped up, "and she made me eat possum butt."

"I did not!" Jolie protested. "The damned dog followed me following her and he got lost, as usual. And the possum was a lesson about anal glands and—"

"We get the idea." Marie had a little smile on her face. A few Garouls had gathered around her and were being entertained by the series of denouements.

"It was ick," Mouse continued to complain. "I was poisoned."

"I bought you sandwiches and a Coke didn't I, you little weasel." Jolie was not letting her get away with it.

"With money you took from the tree!"

"You never told me not to take from the tree!" Jolie shouted.

"Did the tartan jacket come from the tree?" Hope demanded. "Did *you* do this to him, Jolie?"

"No." Jolie felt ashamed. "Norman Johnston from the general store dressed him like that."

"What!" Hope was aghast. "That horrible old man tortured my dog?"

"*And* he called me a brat," Mouse heaped on the drama. "*And* he said we were witches *and* he chased us and we had to run away and Tadpole followed us *and* Jolie told me Luc was my mom."

Chapter Twenty-three

L uc raced to her tree and stopped to draw breath. She slumped to the ground and rested against the gnarled trunk, ignoring the prickling discomfort on her skin. She hated running through the woods in human form. It always made her feel so vulnerable and so...hunted?

It was blissfully cool under the leafy branches of the maple and she sat for a moment watching the knickknacks she had pilfered dance in the breeze. Sunlight glinted off buttons and buckles, insects droned, and the forest floor smelled sharp and resinous where her feet had churned up the dust and debris. Her skin was still flushed from her sprint through the forest, and the silver collar lay cold and lumpish around her neck and shoulders.

The rest allowed her time to think. Had she made a mess of things? Probably. She usually did. But then she remembered Emily was the one who had initiated intimacy, and in her own way was as clumsy as Luc in that area. She let her stronger emotions lead her, heart over head, instinct over logic. It was comforting to Luc that Emily could lose control. And Emily had bit her! Okay, so she had no idea what she was doing, but a bite was big news in Were world. Luc felt rather smug about that. It was nice for someone to try to make a claim, especially when she was feeling so confused and low herself.

Emily would make a great mate, and that was the trouble. Luc chewed her lip. She had not planned on finding a mate, was not even looking for one, and especially not this close to Little Dip. She needed to get away from here as fast as possible, and instead she was building nests and decorating trees. Why was that? Was it because Ren had made an initiation tree for Isabelle? Luc hoped their petty jealousies weren't that trite. She liked to think of herself as above Ren and her petty pack politics, but had to admit sometimes she did feel lonely and left out. As twins, Ren and Luc had their share of rivalries. In Luc's opinion, she was the self-styled adventurer, the independent, lone wolf type, while Ren was the nerdy party pooper, always worrying about this and micromanaging that while Luc just got on with it.

Those first few minutes that Ren had all to herself in this world did not give her the divine right to boss everyone else around. And definitely not Luc. As soon as their parents had died, Luc had set out on her own and was doing quite well in her career as a loner, thank you. Sometimes she did miss the twin connection. Like now for instance. It would be nice to talk to Ren about her problems, especially the emotional ones. Not that Ren was an expert. If anything, she was even less qualified.

Luc pondered the problematic route her sister's love life had taken. *If she had just done what I said and bitten Isabelle, then it would have been much easier.* Luc was all for the bite 'em, love 'em, and leave 'em school of relationships, believing in the old adage that a true mate would follow her Were to the ends of the earth. At least Luc used to believe that. Since meeting Emily, she was having a lot of problems with her old mottoes. She could bite and love Emily easily enough, but leaving her was impossible. The woman was Super Glue.

Maybe I'm still affected by the virus? Why not? Or maybe she was just tired of running. Little Dip was her birth den, no matter how much she detested the fact. It would always have a hold on her. And now it held Mouse, and it was harder than Luc expected to leave her behind. She was having a lot of trouble walking away these days. She missed Mouse so much she swore she could smell her…Luc frowned. She sniffed harder but was unsure. To her human nose, the scents of the forest were strongest. Pine and cedar with their high, sharp tones hit her sinuses first. But something tugged at Luc, something skirted on the edge of her memory, taunting and elusive. She was rested now and crouched down to grunt into wolven form, ignoring the popping and tearing in her body, pushing through the change until she stood upright, tall and bold and sniffing the breeze. And there it was, under those sappy, resinous high notes, and the fuggy herbaceous cut of the surrounding greenery came the subtler spiced scent of her daughter…and of another Were.

In three short bounds, Luc pressed up through the boughs of the big maple to her nest. The growl in her chest was deep and venomous. A Were had been here with Mouse. A Were she did not recognize. Panicked thoughts of when Patrick grabbed Mouse bombarded her. Had some remnant of Patrick's pack come after Mouse? Luc had thought them all dead. She had tracked down as many as she could. They'd all been infected with the virus, dying on their feet and cruelly abandoned by their creator. It had been a pleasure to catch up with Patrick the pretender, and remove him permanently from her life, and Mouse's and Ren's, too. He had caused enough trouble.

A quick glance around the nest told her things were missing. Things suffused with Emily's scent. There was no doubt in her mind, this new Were was posturing for a fight. It had Mouse and was after Emily, too. Her growl bubbled into a throaty hiss and her ears flattened to her skull. She would rip its throat out.

With one almighty leap, she flew from the nest, landing on the ground below with a resounding crash that threw the forest's inhabitants into silence. Unhesitating, she thundered through the shadows in a direct line to Emily's house. She had to reach her before the other Were did.

"You blabbed that Luc was Mouse's mother?" Ren looked furious and Jolie felt her muzzle twitch under the muscles of her jaw. If this newcomer thought she was going to throw her weight around, Jolie would soon snap a bit of order into her. It made no difference to her that they were now in Marie's cabin trying to sort out a way forward. Jolie was sick and tired of Ren and Luc. The twins had been a royal pain in the ass when they were young and were an even bigger pain in the ass now that they'd grown up.

"I did not blab," she said. "It just came out in the heat of the moment, and *you* should have told her ages ago anyway. It's not as if the cub can't cope. She could face down a grizzly if she needed to."

"Even so—"

"Even so nothing," Jolie interrupted. She did not like Ren. Hope had been placed in danger because she had helped Ren's mate, Isabelle. If anything, it was Ren who owed Jolie's den some respect. "I was the one who went after your charge when she high-tailed it out of the valley," she said hotly. "Where were you, huh? Off hunting shadows, that's where." She alluded to the failure of the hunt with relish. They should have taken her with them. And where had Ren been anyway? She had returned to Little Dip long after the pack had come home. Jolie didn't like Ren having secret missions she knew nothing about.

"Mouse was worried for Luc. That's why she ran away," she continued. "She was trying to find her before you did. So maybe she didn't know Luc was her mom, but she sure as hell acted as if she was. The instinct was already there." Jolie was pointing at Ren now that she was on a roll. How dare she treat Mouse that way! "It's ingrained. You can't lie to the cub, or hide the scent of her own goddamned mother from her."

"Jolie." Hope spoke softly and placed a hand on Jolie's arm to calm her. Jolie turned to her.

"And let me tell you something, Hope. Our cubs won't be wandering around the woods all night without a chaperone. They'll be brought up right, and know how to cross roads and do as they're told and goddamn know who their parents are!" Silence greeted this outburst. Marie and Connie looked amused, and Hope blinked up at her in surprise.

"Our hypothetical cubs, I mean," Jolie quickly added, and felt a flush covering her cheeks. She was excruciatingly embarrassed. "Anyway," she continued, much more subdued. "I didn't plan to tell her. I was tired. And up a tree." Her scorched face mercifully began to cool down. "And it was windy."

"Well," murmured Hope, "if you were up a tree. That explains it." She rolled her eyes and Jolie scowled at her.

"Thank you for looking after Mouse," Ren said stiffly. "I'm glad you were there when she needed help." Then her voice relaxed to its normal tone and she said, "It seems you and Hope always manage to save the day where she's concerned. No wonder she loves staying at your place."

Jolie's hackles subsided. She had been a hero, of sorts. She had cared for the cub, and struggled to get her back home. In a curious way, she already considered Mouse an extended member of her den. A bond had been struck somewhere along the journey, and Jolie was pleased. Emotional entanglements were not her strong point, but she had easily managed with Mouse. Something had shifted inside her. Maybe living with Hope was changing her, too?

"So what do we do now?" Hope asked. "Mouse is all tucked up at our place playing cards with Paulie, but she knows Luc is out there. It won't be long before she sneaks off to go looking for her again."

Marie turned to Ren. "What did you find out? Is Luc still in the vicinity?"

"Very much so," Ren answered.

"How would she know?" Jolie asked. "Is this some twin thing?" Because if it was, she and Andre didn't share it, thank Luna.

"I had Ren split from the pack to do some scouting for me," Marie explained.

"Luc's going nowhere fast and that confuses me. Normally, she'd be away in a blink," Ren said.

"Jolie and Mouse found an initiation tree," Marie said. "I think that affects a lot of things." Ren looked stunned.

"It had a nest in it." Jolie enjoyed knowing something super scout Ren did not. "That's why I was up a tree." She needed to underscore that point. It was not every day Jolie Garoul climbed a goddamned tree and Ren had better appreciate that.

"A nest takes time to build, and it explains some of the things I've seen," Ren said. "You remember the woman at the logging camp?"

Marie nodded. "It looked as if Luc was shielding her?"

"How the hell did Luc get away?" Jolie couldn't hold it in any longer. Now if *she* had been there it would have been—

"It was deliberate," Marie said with a challenge in her eyes. Jolie backed down.

"Oh?" she said. "That's…" She had no idea what it was. "But why?"

"Because we knew Luc had a human with her," Marie said. "We found traps all over the place. Someone was trying to catch something big, and that big thing turned out to be Luc."

"We have to be careful if humans get involved. You know that," Connie added.

Jolie snorted. Every Garoul knew that. But who was trapping whom?

"At first, we thought Luc had a hostage. Turns out she was doing her utmost to protect the woman who was hunting her? Which is just weird. So now I need to know who she is and what the hell's going on," Marie said. "I let Luc escape for now, so that Ren could follow the woman. Luc may be as slippery as snake oil, but I'm the rattler the oil came from. Do you think they're in this together?" she asked Ren.

"That's my bet," Ren said. "The woman oozes Luc's scent. I'm sure they've mated."

"What?" Connie looked shocked. "Luc's on the run. How the hell did she have time to hook up?"

"And you're sure this woman knows Luc's a werewolf?" Hope asked.

"Looks like she was trying to trap one," Marie said.

Ren looked troubled. "That's the weird part. The woods to the back of the woman's house are full-on with her scent. It's as if she's been marking the area?"

"In an aggressive way?" Marie asked. "As if she's marking a boundary?" She did not look happy at this news.

Ren shook her head. "No. It's more like in a come hither way."

"Come hither?" Jolie echoed. "Like a sex scent, you mean?"

Again, Ren shook her head. "Maybe. To be honest, I'm not sure if this woman knows what she's doing."

"It's hardly wise to knowingly seduce a werewolf. They're not very good with the old flirtation thing, more like leap, bite, and maybe smooze a little later. And we have no idea who she is?" Hope said.

"No idea," Ren said.

"I wonder if she has something to do with that curious collar around Luc's neck. I've never seen anything like it before. Have any of you?" Connie asked Marie and Ren.

Ren shrugged. "Luna only knows with Luc. Could be a piece of jewelry she snatched that happened to catch her eye. She's a law unto herself."

"This woman she's mooning after, she lives in Lost Creek?" Marie said.

"It's hard to tell who's mooning after who. Between come hithers and initiation trees, it sounds like they're both a bit addled." Ren looked troubled despite her throwaway comment.

"I think it's time I paid a visit to Lost Creek," Marie said. "I haven't been in town for ages, and I have some library books to return."

"Well, don't take Tadpole anywhere near the general store," Jolie muttered. "You might end up in an ownership dispute."

Chapter Twenty-four

Luc hurtled toward Lost Creek slowing as she approached the outskirts, swerving toward the general store and Emily's house. She crept in directly from the backwoods this time, rather than her usual oblique line of approach where the neighboring outbuildings shielded her. Nightfall would obscure her now; no need to slink behind woodpiles and outhouses to plot her final sprint to the house.

Luc entered the thicket of trees just behind the house. She could see Emily's bedroom window from here. There were no lights on, or anywhere else in the house. It must have been much later than Luc supposed. She couldn't detect the little dog either. That meant he had kept on running. Either that or they locked him indoors at night. Luc hoped he was out of the picture. She did not need a dog barking at her, even if it was about as dangerous as a dust bunny.

As was her habit, she hunkered down by a tree and contemplated the yard, waiting to make sure all was quiet before she made her next move. She was still rattled. Her hackles raised at the thought of the Garouls running around out here with Mouse, and now zoning in on Emily. Maybe it was a trap?

Her nose twitched. She turned her head slightly and sniffed. She made for the nearest tree and examined the trunk. She snorted in the brackish bark smell. There was an underlying scent. She growled at the familiarity of it. It was Emily's scent, but altered. Befuddled, Luc traced the smell up and then down the rough surface of the tree.

This was not the Emily she had first come to know, the Emily with the Winchester and crossbow and the dubious ham sandwiches. This was the Emily of the RV. The woman who had leapt on her and covered Luc's throat with her bare teeth and scratched at her back with blunt nails. The same woman who had lain in her arms chilled to the bone, who had stroked the fur on her face and tweaked her ears while they both slipped into drugged slumber. The scent was intoxicating and sexy and it made Luc's blood run riot. She buried her claws in the bark of the tree and clawed deep parallel lines into the living wood, enjoying the flex of her muscles and the rip of wood under her claws. Saliva moistened her muzzle. She was excited at this unexpected waft of Emily's scent. She rubbed her face against the splintered trunk, uniting their odors. Emily's was seductive, beckoning, coaxing even, as if she was expecting her—*It's another trap.* Luc's euphoria spluttered to a halt and she slumped onto her hindquarters. *Bitch never gives up.*

If silver had a taste, it would be Emily. If it had a scent, it would smell like her, too. Emily confused her. Sometimes Luc couldn't quite make out who was hunting whom? She was definitely drawn to the woman, and if she were being honest, which she rarely was, she'd have to admit to being fascinated with someone who could give her a run for her money the way that Emily had. Her claws strayed to the metal collar snug around her neck and pinged softly against the shiny surface. She could kid herself that all she wanted was the key to this contraption, but she knew she wanted more. She wanted Emily. She wanted her by her side running through the woods, stalking prey, sharing a kill, and afterward, rolling in meadows of sweet grass until their coats were thick with seeds and pollen dust. She wanted a mate. She wanted Emily wolven.

Was this more of Ren's actions rubbing off on her? They were twins after all, and twins tended to develop simultaneously. Luc had decided not to answer the blood call and mate for life. Ren had found Isabelle. To be honest, Luc had never expected to find anyone until Emily came along with her snares and weaponry, and sneaky stealth skills and sheer bloody-mindedness…in fact, she was everything Luc ever wanted in a girl.

Another scent came to her on a twisting, turning breeze. And this one was much more exciting. Luc crawled on all fours toward another tree several yards away and found another scent, and this one agitated her even more. It was pure sex. A come-on that had to be for her and her alone. Emily had urinated here, but the ground had been disturbed. Luc was not the only one to have found this secret message. The forest floor was churned with the unmistakable paw prints of another werewolf. It had zoned in on Emily's scent. Luc's ears slicked to her head and she bared her teeth in a savage snarl. She recognized this scent, too. She had known it from the cradle. It was as familiar to her as her own scent. It was her sister's.

It was clear to Luc the Garouls were not waiting up ahead for her to make a run for the Canadian border. They had not been tricked. They knew she was here, and they were using the people who mattered to her the most to flush her out. They were closing in on her using every weapon they could. They had her daughter, though that she had allowed because Mouse needed the security of Little Dip. But they could not have Emily. Emily was hers alone. Luc threw back her head and howled her outrage into the night.

Emily shot out of bed. The howling made her blood run cold. She had been struggling to sleep all night, sick with worry over the werewolf who had brazenly approached her on the porch. Was her uncle safe? The brute must be a Garoul on the lookout for Luc. And *why* hadn't she warned her about the werewolf she had spied that morning? *Because we were too busy rolling over each other naked, that's why.* Emily worried at her forgetfulness and flighty behavior. She had meant to tell Luc about it, to warn her that the Garouls were not far away, but as usual, her intentions had turned to mush the moment Luc got within twenty feet of her.

Alarmed at the howling, she pulled open the blind, certain she would see a huge beast skulking on the lawn, its moonlit shadow stretched hideously across the grass. The howls were so close she was sure it came from her own backyard. It had to be the werewolf from earlier. Luc was too smart to draw attention to herself. Already both wolf and woman were blurring into one amorphous being in Emily's mind. The ebony of Luc's eyes so easily overwritten with that eerie amber glow, the silkiness of her hair hazing into dense black fur, and that silly bent ear that made Emily's heart flip like some dreamy teenager. She was unsure what was happening to her. She felt overheated, overexcited, and in over her head.

The yard below was empty. Beyond the painted fence, the forest was a tangle of shadows, and if she looked hard enough she could imagine anything out there. With no more howling and nothing to see, she turned away and toyed with the idea of locking the window tight. But it was a stifling night and she preferred it left open just a crack to allow a flow of air into the room.

Emily slid back into bed. There was no hope of sleep tonight. She rolled onto her side and lay looking out at a swollen moon hanging lopsided in the sky. The full moon was days away. What would happen then? Bedlam, she supposed, and wondered if she should try to take Uncle Norm away for a short break, just to be on the safe side. At first, she barely registered the creak of the shingles, but her eyes widened at the glint of claws sliding in under the window frame, wriggling through the small crack she had left open to let the air flow.

Emily leapt from the bed and slammed the window down hard on the intruding claws. An angry bellow had her recoiling backward. With an enormous strength fueled by pain, the window flew up and open with such ferocity the glass shook in its panes. The beast leapt into her room. Emily backpedaled to keep clear of it. It snarled and scoured the room with seething amber eyes, its glance barely grazing her, and when it did, she felt scorched. She noticed the misshapen ear and breathed out her tension. It was Luc, but as she'd never seen her before. This Luc was preoccupied and frightening. She was pacing the room, and brushed roughly past Emily causing her to stumble back onto the bed.

Emily lay still and watched as Luc investigated her closet, and the door to her bathroom and tiny shower room beyond. She was looking for something, someone.

"Luc," she said with soft uncertainty. Perhaps it was unwise to draw Luc's attention to her. "What's wrong? What are you looking for?"

Luc turned to her, crossing the floor between them in one stride. She towered over Emily, then leaned in so she was pressed flat to the mattress. She did not react to Emily's words; rather she began an intensive investigation of Emily's prone body, carefully sniffing at her hair and ears and neck. She growled, and it rumbled deep in her chest, her eyes constantly flickering to the left and right as if wary of some danger surrounding them. It made Emily nervous. What was going on?

"Luc," she said again, quietly. "What's wrong? Is it the other werewolf?"

Luc snapped her head away from Emily's throat and held her gaze, her eyes narrowing to glittering slits. Her lips drew back into an evil grimace baring her savage fangs. Emily swallowed. Had she made a mistake in referring to the other Were? Luc returned her attention to smelling Emily again. For some reason, this was of paramount importance to her. Her long claws plucked at Emily's tank top, an old favorite she slept in. She worked a small hole in the fabric, inserted her fore claw and tugged hard. The material ripped as if a sharp blade had run through it. Emily gasped as it fell away from her body leaving her bare-chested.

A wet snout snuffled at the valley between her breasts, burrowing deep into her armpit and eventually pushing in under the breast itself to breathe in the sweat line. Emily gasped as the coolness of Luc's damp muzzle and the coarse scratch of her fur pressed against her flesh. Her navel was sniffed next and a huge wet tongue dipped into it making her leap with surprise and ticklishness. Her underwear was no defense against the curved claws, and soon, her panties lay in shreds on the floor beside her top. Emily froze as Luc buried her face into her crotch and breathed deeply. She explored the crease where thigh met groin.

The folds of Emily's sex were roughly burrowed into as if some prize lay buried beneath. An unexpected flash of arousal ran through her, and she felt dampness between her legs. Her cheeks flamed at

Luc's proximity to this disgraceful, telltale. The large furred head paused for a moment, hovering over this new moisture, the ears flicked, a sign Emily knew to indicate deep thought, and then Luc's nose buried deeper and took a heavy inhalation and then withdrew.

Nothing sexual had happened, yet Emily felt as turned on as she had in the RV when they had slithered over each other's nakedness. She was erotically charged at Luc's proximity to those most intimate parts of her body. Need flooded her, along with a healthy respect for the sharp teeth and claws so casually grazing her body.

As if to underscore the fragility of her human shape, she was flipped over onto her belly. Hot breath burned across her buttocks as Luc resumed her intimate olfactory study. What the hell was she looking for? Emily's thoughts crumbled, and she squeaked with embarrassment as her cheeks were roughly separated and a wet snout examined her butt crease. She squirmed and tried to wriggle away, crawling a few inches up the bed before she was dragged back down and held firmly in place as every inch of her was appraised. She held her breath, uncertain how this would work out, trying to ascertain how much danger she was actually in. And then the huff and puff of inhalation stopped and a rough tongue rudely pressed against the most intimate part of her and licked all the way from her anus, up along her spine to her neck. There the huge jaws clamped around her nape and shook her.

It was a firm shake, letting her know who was the boss, strong enough to make her go limp with an inborn terror, but not hard enough to hurt. She understood this was deliberate. She had no idea why Luc was doing this. And then, without warning, a huge clawed hand came down and slapped her across her buttocks. She yelped, and there was another slap of calloused, leathery skin against the softness of her bottom.

Luc shook her by the neck again, and she whimpered. She had to, out of stunned shock and also because it was the right thing to do. She was slapped across the bottom again, for a third time and more forcefully. Her buttocks stung, and hot saliva ran down her neck from the huge maw holding her nape. She whimpered and was again lightly shaken. Then Luc dropped her and rose to her full height panting and pleased.

From outside, a wolf howled. A real wolf. Emily knew the difference now. It was a lesson easily learned. Luc lumbered over to the window and breathed in the sweet night air in great lungfuls, then she slipped through the window and was gone without a backward glance. *How come she thumps around my bedroom like an elephant then moves like silk once she's outdoors?* The random thought slid into Emily's mind as she began to gather herself.

She staggered to her feet and made her way to the bathroom. She ran the shower and in the long mirror twisted to examine her back. It was sticky and shone with Luc's spittle, and her buttocks were bright red from her spanking. She pulled her hair up and tried to see the back of her neck. She felt more than saw the lumpy rows of raised teeth marks. She couldn't understand what Luc's intentions were but knew she had been branded in some way. If she had intended to hurt Emily, then the slightest bit of pressure would have snapped her neck like the stem of a wine glass. No, this had been about marking and domination. Emily knew there was no going back from this. She had started something she'd be lucky she could finish.

CHAPTER TWENTY-FIVE

W e've come to return these," Marie said.
Jolie slid the brown paper package onto the countertop and had to avert her eyes in case she gave Norman Johnston the good glaring he deserved. Her ears had been battered all night with Hope's scolding about the state of her little dog, and she held him solely responsible. The package contained the newly laundered shirt and the overalls she had worn and also the T-shirt she'd dressed Mouse in, along with the dreadful tartan dog ensemble. She had taken particular pleasure in tying it up with the tightest double knot she could manage. Let his gnarled old fingers deal with that.

"What is it?" he asked suspiciously. He had just opened his shop for the afternoon and they had caught him by surprise. His shifty confusion and discomfort made him even more unapproachable.

"The dog jacket and a few other things," Marie said. "Thanks for looking after the dog, Mr. Johnston. We thought he was gone for good." There was genuine sincerity in her voice.

"S'okay, I suppose." Norm took a grudging step toward courtesy. "You can keep Wilbur's stuff," he added. "It's too small for my new dog, anyway."

Marie's and Jolie's eyebrows rose and they swapped glances. *Wilbur?* But at least the old coot was showing some manners, the first time in years. There came the clip of claws and a rustle from somewhere behind him and he stepped aside to reveal a large Rottweiler-pit bull cross.

"This is Delilah," he said proudly. "We got her from the pound this morning. She's my new guard dog." He shot Jolie a hard look and she glowered right back. "She was to be euthanized," he said with disapproval.

Marie held out her hand. "Delilah. What a beautiful name and what a beautiful dog."

Jolie considered the big, lumpish brute. It looked like a dumped armchair. No one would want to get on the wrong side of it, that's for sure. All in all, a good match for its owner, she decided.

Delilah's docked tail began to wriggle as she sniffed at Marie's proffered hand as if they were old acquaintances. Norman watched it all with uncertainty, then cleared his throat.

"How is Wilbur?" he asked. It seemed that if his guard dog okayed a visitor then who was he to question it. Already, Jolie could see who was the boss of his house.

"Wilbur's fine. He was well looked after," Marie answered, and Norm's withered cheeks gathered color. "Is your niece here?" Marie asked.

A few minutes at the library had revealed all the local gossip. Norman Johnston had a niece visiting, and that just had to be Luc's love interest.

"Emily?" Norm's eyes narrowed.

Marie nodded. "I'd like to have a word."

"What about?" Norm was right back to his usual cranky self. "Is it because of Wilbur?"

"No, not that at all," Marie said.

"Because she couldn't leave him there. She had to take him. He'd a gotten eaten otherwise," he continued, ignoring Marie's assurances. "Is it because she hunts? Is that it? Because she don't go near your place. No one does. Your place is bad news—"

"What's up, Uncle Norm?" With uncanny timing, a woman appeared from the connecting doorway to Norm's house. Delilah nudged her hand for a petting.

"These here folks are from Little Dip," he said. His voice had become querulous again and Jolie braced herself for more ugliness. The redheaded woman was tall and angular. She had a shrewd stare and a confident poise and had obviously been listening in on the conversation from the other side of the door.

"Nice to meet you, Emily." Marie held out her hand. "I'm Marie Garoul." Emily took it, not quite meeting Marie's eyes.

This was interesting, Jolie thought. It was as if the woman knew Marie was an Alpha. As planned, Jolie gathered several items from the surrounding shelves and brought them over to the counter. Norman Johnston, riveted as he was to the conversation, could not pass up the chance of a sale that marked up more than a week's worth of business for his tiny store. He shuffled over to Jolie and the till, well out of earshot of the women.

"I wondered if maybe we could go somewhere to talk?" With her keen hearing, Jolie could hear Marie's persuasive tone. Emily nodded. They walked through the aisles to the exit.

"Do you want to take Delilah with you?" Norm called after Emily, as if the dog offered some form of protection, but she didn't hear him and the shop door tinkled shut behind her.

Jolie dumped a handful of books on the counter. That caught his attention.

"I'll take these, too," she said. They were children's classics— *Anne of Green Gables*, *Robinson Crusoe*, *White Fang*—all dusty as if they'd sat on the shelf for years. It was time Mouse progressed from comic books.

❖

"I think you know my niece, Lucienne Garoul," Marie said, as soon as they were settled on the bench seat under the library oak.

Lucienne? "Luc?" Emily said. "Yes, I do." There was little point in pretense, and anyway, she wanted to find out what this stately woman wanted from her. She was taller than Emily, maybe in her late forties or early fifties, but it was hard to tell as strength and vibrancy zinged off her. She was as dark as any of the Garouls, with silver-streaked hair pulled back neatly at her nape. She had broad shoulders and intelligent black eyes that Emily swore could see straight through her. Something was tugging at the back of Emily's mind. The woman's svelte stature, her muscular grace, the silver laced through her hair. And then it clicked. This was the werewolf that had faced down Luc at the logging camp. This was the Alpha.

"She escaped you, didn't she? And now you think I know where she is. Well, I don't," she said, belligerence began to enter her voice, but she tamped it down. She did not need to goad this woman. Lost Creek may be on its last legs, but there were still enough people around to prevent Marie Garoul from mutating into a monster. That did not mean Emily could push her luck, either.

"Oh, I know where she is," Marie said. "She's hot on your heels."

Emily flushed a little. "I'll be going home to Chicago soon." As if that changed the playing field.

"That won't keep you safe. She'll follow you there and probably flounder." Marie had this habit of holding her gaze when she spoke. "Can you imagine Luc in a massive city like Chicago? I'm surprised she was able to make her way around these streets without causing a commotion."

Emily found herself unable to look anywhere but at Marie when she spoke to her. She saw every word reflected in those pitch-black eyes and knew it was true. Luc would be hopelessly lost in a city. It would be a disaster, and it would be all her fault. Emily's breath hitched and an old familiar clawing returned to her chest. She wanted her pills.

"I don't mean to be intrusive, but has Luc…marked you in any way?" Marie asked. "A scratch, a bruise? Maybe even a…bite?"

Emily's chest tightened even more. "That's none of your business," she snapped, and knew she had given the game away. She was furious with herself. Anger dammed up her throat, closing it over, choking her with unsaid words.

"Are you all right, Emily?" Marie's voice sounded tinny to her ears. "You look very pale."

"I'm fine." Emily rose to leave, then had to sit right back down again. Her world was disorienting and airless.

Marie placed an arm around her shoulders. "Cover your nose and mouth with your hands and breathe with me." She counted as she breathed slow and steady alongside Emily's ragged gasping. After a few minutes, Emily found it was easy to keep pace and her lungs relaxed, allowing her breathing to flow naturally. Sweat slicked her spine, and despite the warmth of the day, she shivered. Marie's hand was warm and reassuring on her shoulder. She watched Emily carefully.

"I'm okay now," Emily snapped. And as an afterthought, added, "Thank you." There was no need to be rude. The woman was only trying to help her.

"Emily, has something happened to make you this tense?" Marie asked with concern.

Had something happened? Werewolves had killed her father. They were everywhere in town and only Emily knew it. And one in particular was stalking her and licking her and stealing all her underwear.

"No." Emily staggered to her feet and drew herself up straight. "I don't want to talk to you, Marie Garoul. I know you from before. I've seen you before."

"Oh?" Marie took up her challenge, no doubt thinking of the logging camp incident where Luc had tried to save her. But that was not Emily's first memory of this enigmatic woman. She had an earlier encounter than that. One when she was nine years old.

"You were at my father's funeral," she said, her voice hard. Here was her chance to finally say it aloud *and* to the person she held responsible. "You were there to make sure they buried him before anyone asked any more questions about you and your family. But I know what you are. I've always known." Emily threw down her trump card, her ace, her threat. It was the only play she had left. "The Garouls are werewolves. And now I have evidence, living proof, and if I have to lure her to Chicago, I damned well will."

Chapter Twenty-six

M arie's gaze flickered for an instant, and that was the only outward sign that she remembered, and was reassessing Emily and her threats.

"I came here to capture a werewolf," Emily said, drawing her strength from the dregs of bitterness that lay curdled in the pit of her stomach. "If you want her back, you better tell me what happened to my father. What *really* happened to him and why you killed him."

"Roy Johnston came onto our land and tried to murder a member of my family. He shot my cousin, twice." Now Marie was standing and she towered over Emily. "And don't tell me he thought he was hunting bear. He damned well knew what he was doing. He'd been creeping around Little Dip for years."

"He knew something was going on in Little Dip."

"He knew something was going on in Little Dip he could exploit!" Marie thrust her face close and lowered her voice. "Your father wanted to cash in on my family. He shot at us, barely missing a cub. That cub was your lover, the one you don't seem to give much of a damn about. Her uncle took the bullet meant for her, and your father kept shooting to finish him off. Luc went for him and he had a heart attack. He keeled over like a felled tree, just as the coroner reported."

Emily was furious. She didn't want to hear this, but she could remember her father's profile as he sighted up his next kill. The steely determination that came over him, his refusal to miss, to come away empty-handed. He hated to lose. He was the winner.

"You bribed the coroner, and the police. Everyone knows that," she said, her anger bleeding into every word. How dare this woman shake her to the core? "My father's body wasn't even in Little Dip when they found him. He was eight miles downstream."

"We gave your father's body to the Silverthread. He should never have been on our land. The coroner confirmed he had died of cardiac arrest before he hit the water. Why would the police even care? It was the truth. Why should there be any bribery? That's the sort of poisonous nonsense your uncle has been filling you with all your life," Marie said. "I mean *witches*, for God's sake. At least your father guessed at the right monster."

Emily turned to go, but Marie grabbed her arm. Her grip was strong and not to be dismissed.

"You've got a werewolf after you, Emily," she said. Her voice was cold. "And you have gone out of your way to create this situation. I know why you've done it. Out of some misguided revenge, I suppose. I'm not sure *how* you've done it, though I'm sure it took more than a piddle in the woods to make Luc forget about her own safety and follow you around like a mooning puppy. She's enthralled, and she's ill. She has a virus and I need to get the cure to her. And now she has this new sickness that you've somehow pressed upon her."

Emily stood stock-still. She did not like hearing this. It rang a little too true. Marie released her.

"If you care for her then why is she running from you?" Emily counter accused. "She's trying to get to Canada. Why was she sent away?"

Marie fixed her with a stare that turned her inside out and examined all the contents. Emily felt her knees weakening. She could barely cope with this conversation.

"She told you that?" Marie asked.

"She told me she was sent away when she was young."

"She was the same age you were at your father's funeral. Luc was not responsible for your father's death. She didn't touch him. My mother was Alpha then. She did not want the possibility of Luc being questioned. She wanted her out of the way. She sent the entire family north and they never came back."

"She's back here now."

"Because she's ill. Because this will always be her natal den." Marie stepped closer. She was intimidating in all her glowering glory, and Emily fought hard not to backpedal away from her. "Maybe she's come home to die?" Marie said, then laughed softly at Emily's stricken face. "Seems you're not as unaffected as you act. Are you sure she didn't bite you, just a bit?"

Emily felt her face blaze but was smart enough to keep her mouth shut. Marie moved away. She looked bored now.

"Go home, Emily," she said. "Luc will keep right on calling, and when you finally come to your senses and realize the danger you're in…" She shrugged. "Well, you know where to find me." She went to walk away, then hesitated. "Oh, and please talk to your uncle. Ask *him* what really happened to your father. Your dad was a smart man. He figured out what we were, the same as you. But his intentions were bad and a lot of people suffered. My question is, what are your intentions, Emily?"

❖

Emily returned to the shop to find her uncle whistling cheerfully and stacking shelves. Delilah lay slumped by the counter blocking an entire aisle. She still felt shaky after her encounter, but the familiar confines of the shop soon relaxed her.

"Where are the regulars?" she asked, noting the empty stools.

"Pension day. They all go to the steak house on pension day."

"You sure Delilah's not putting them off?" she asked, stepping over the dog who had positioned herself perfectly for any possible tidbits.

"Well." Norm paused to suck his teeth. "Pat Crone came in earlier and looked a little nervous."

Emily hauled Delilah to her feet and pushed the lazy animal toward the connecting door. "I think she needs to stay outside on a fine day like this. Honestly, Uncle Norm, you can't have dogs lying all over the shop. Not with food."

"Here, take this through, will ya?" He shoved an opened package at her, all crumpled brown paper and string.

"What is it?"

"Them Garouls returned some stuff. See? Told you she was wearing my pants." He pointed at the contents. "Told you they were thieves. Always take what they want, them Garouls."

"At least she washed and ironed them," Emily pointed out.

"Yeah, they did that, all right," he conceded, and she could see he found the whole episode confusing. Thieves weren't supposed to return stolen items freshly laundered.

"How much did they spend?" she asked.

"Almost two weeks' takings." His eyes gleamed with satisfaction, and maybe a little relief. "They used to spend like that before—" He shut up and began fiddling with the cans on the nearest shelf.

"Before Dad?" she finished for him. The slump of his shoulders spoke for him. There'd been better days here, before the hate had filled all the empty corners of his life. There was an awkward silence. Emily did not want to launch into this particular conversation just yet. She didn't want to take Marie Garoul's advice and talk to Norm about her father even though she knew she should. Pride was rampant in her. She adjusted her grip on the parcel and noticed the tartan.

"Hey. Wilbur's stuff," Emily said, delighted. "Where's the collar gone?" she asked, frowning at this particular discovery.

"Told 'em to keep it. They didn't want the coat though, just the collar."

"You gave them back the collar?" Emily sighed.

"Is there a problem, Em?" Norm asked. "Did I do wrong? What did that Garoul woman want with you, anyway?" She could see the anxiety in his eyes. She set aside her pride. Maybe it was time for them to talk. She didn't want him to worry anymore.

"You did fine." Emily brushed her hand over the back of his. "I'll come back and we'll have some coffee and I'll tell you all about Marie Garoul."

She carted the parcel back to the kitchen nudging Delilah along every inch of the way with her shins. In the end, the dog refused to go outside, so Emily let her sleep on Wilbur's old blanket instead. Once the dog was settled, she went back to the shop. Butterflies swam in her stomach in anticipation of the conversation they were about to have.

"Tell me about Dad," she said as soon as she settled on the stool opposite him. Mugs of coffee steamed on the counter between them, and he was slicing up some pie to share.

"Roy?" he asked. "Roy was great. Great hunter. Clever fella. Cleverer than me," he began his usual spiel, the legends of her childhood. Inventing a brave, wonderful pa for a lonely little girl. "*He* was a school teacher, and look where I ended up. You definitely got his brains, Em."

"He wasn't clever enough to keep away from that valley," she said softly.

He sliced the pie slower and slower until, eventually, he set the knife down on the countertop. Norm sighed.

"I know, sweetheart. I told him a million times, just like I tell you. Stay away. Nothing good ever came out of Little Dip. The place is cursed—"

"In what way exactly?" she pressed. She didn't want the old nonsense about witches now. She needed to understand what he knew. His washed out eyes met hers. Without his glasses, she could see the milky aura around his pale blue irises and the jaundiced color of his eye white. His skin was dry and patchy, and rashed where he shaved badly. His hands were liver spotted, and on wet days, they trembled. He was too old to be running this shop. He should have retired years ago. He should be down at the steak house with his buddies drinking beer and yammering. She didn't want to hurt him, but this phantasm of her father's death had lain between them for too long now. She didn't want that to be the glue that bound them.

"For all his brains, Roy could be damned stubborn." Norm let go. "He had some wild ideas about yetis and all sorts of monsters, and he would talk about putting them in cages or killing and stuffing them and displaying them all over the place. We'd be millionaires, he'd say."

"What did you think?" she asked.

"I think what I always thought, let sleeping dogs lie. Nothing ever came to Lost Creek and hurt me and mine, and in turn, I don't go hunting where I'm not wanted. I let Mother Nature keep the score and set the balance." He didn't say werewolf and she didn't push it. He had enough monsters to work with.

"Did Dad have a weak heart?" She had her father's motive. She needed one more thing.

"All the Johnston men do. We could go in a snap." Norm clicked his fingers, perversely proud of his boast. It sounded familiar to Emily. She had heard him say it before when she was little when the idea of losing him scared her half to death. She remembered being frightened of snapping her fingers in case he would suddenly disappear. The unexpected memory filled her with tears.

"You all right, Em?" He stared at the moisture in her eyes.

"You're my pa, Norm. You always have been, and I love you very much."

He looked stunned. His jaw dropped and his tired old eyes found a sudden rush of moisture of their own. He coughed, sniffed, coughed again.

"Did she say things to hurt you?" he asked, almost fearfully.

"Marie Garoul? No." Emily shook her head. He had just corroborated Marie Garoul's story. "She only said things that helped."

❖

It took some coaxing, but Emily managed to lure Delilah outside with Wilbur's old dog treats. She could see the writing on the wall with Uncle Norm and his new pet. He would spoil the dog rotten, and it would just get fatter and fatter. She was determined to get Delilah into the habit of expecting at least one short walk a day. The exercise would do Norm good, too.

She let the dog waddle out of the yard and into the woods beyond, realizing they were following the path Emily had taken with Wilbur. It would be a short walk then. Wilbur could hardly be called a walking machine either, but he had his stubby legs as an excuse. Delilah was plain lazy.

Emily mused over the day's exposés. She was an intelligent woman, and the separate stories she had received on her father's fate felt more like a balm on an old, tired bruise than the acidic sting of an unwanted truth. She had seen him hunt. Hadn't he taught her all he knew? And he'd been ruthless and efficient. She could imagine him doing the things Marie Garoul accused him of. Hadn't she come close to the same barbarity herself? A chip off the old block. Her old man would have been proud of her with her traps and drugs and surgical tools. Marie Garoul had looked her in the eye and told her a hard story, but she had her uncle to turn to for corroborating the truth of it. He had not failed her.

Before Roy Johnston's death, relationships between Little Dip and Lost Creek had been cordial enough to benefit the town. The Garouls were a well-heeled, but very private family, and her father had been fascinated with them, to the point of obsession. He began to spy on them and stalk them in their own valley despite the cautions of his brother. When Roy's body was found in the Silverthread, Norman Johnston called foul play and soured the relationship between the town and Little Dip forever. The Garouls funded the local library and that was all. Their other charitable concerns were focused elsewhere.

Emily considered Marie's other news that Luc was mesmerized with her. *Enthralled* was the word she'd used. Emily was less sure of this. Luc had behaved bizarrely last night. Emily's body was still bruised; the nape of her neck bore a parade of blood red blotches. Marie had somehow sensed their intimacy, and she had indicated Emily might not be safe.

Up ahead, Delilah growled. Her growling increased in rapidity and volume until she was in a full-on barking frenzy. Emily hurried to see what had stressed the dog. She did not know Delilah that well and hoped she could calm her.

At first, she could see nothing.

"What is it, Delilah?" She glanced around. Delilah fell back into uneasy growling. Still, Emily couldn't see what had alarmed the dog. Then the trees caught her eye. The poor disfigured trees. Their trunks were pulled to pieces with huge chunks torn from the living wood. Score marks so deep and livid they wept sap.

"Shush," she whispered to the dog. Delilah stopped growling and moved close to her, pressing hard against her leg. The animal was spooked. The place was horrid. Emily had no other words for it. Her head began to pound and she clung on to the nearest tree for support. For several moments, she had to stand in that hell and count her breaths until she was in control again.

Then it dawned on her that this was the spot where she herself had behaved strangely, rubbing against trees and...Her face burned. She had scented this place, too, and intimately. Once again, she turned in a slow full circle drinking in the malice, the brutality. In her mind, on some deep, subconscious, almost primeval level, she knew this to be the work of Luc. It slotted into perfect place beside her bestial behavior last night. This was what they were doing to each other, the collar and the key. Emily had devised a trap for both of them.

The breeze turned chill and clouds crowded the sky. The shadows around her lengthened and the forest grew darker, sullen, and unnaturally quiet. Shaken, Emily turned back the way she had come. She felt utterly lost. She had dabbled in something she had no hope of understanding. Pride and anger had led her here, to a place where all her old truths were spinning away from her, and new terrors replaced them.

"Come on, girl," she encouraged Delilah to follow her home. Marie Garoul was right. She was out of her depth. Luc was feral and savage and capable of any cruelty Emily could imagine. She had to stop this now before she placed herself and Uncle Norm in any more danger. She had to go to Little Dip.

CHAPTER TWENTY-SEVEN

"L uc found my tracks around Emily's pee," Ren said.

They were walking back along the old logging road away from Lost Creek and toward Little Dip. It was a beautiful day. A day when the sky fell open, flat as a big blue blanket and the sun shone down unhindered by a single cloud. Not even a bird cast a shadow. They were all rustling furtively in the underbrush or busy building nests. Spring had arrived, and every animal was either courting or homemaking. Jolie felt the urge, too, and couldn't wait to get home to Hope. Mouse had moved back in with Ren so they had the cabin all to themselves, and Jolie planned to raise the roof a little tonight.

"She didn't like it," Ren added. "She pulled the trees to bits." She had been out scouting again, while Jolie and Marie visited the general store and found Emily.

Jolie snorted. Luc was caught up in the same springtime extravaganza as the birdies whether she liked it or not.

"I still can't figure out how Emily managed it," Marie said. "There's no pattern to this that I can see. Luc is acting so unpredictably that I'm worried for Emily and her uncle. I want patrols around Lost Creek tonight. We need to make ourselves visible to Luc, and maybe keep her at bay."

"What!" Jolie was aghast. Her plans did not include hanging out around the general store trying to keep Luc away from her girlfriend's liquid calling cards.

The splutter and burp of an engine that had seen better days came rumbling up behind. All three turned and watched a battered bright orange RV rumble around the bend and make a steady course toward them. It drew up alongside Marie, and Emily Johnston stuck her head out the window.

"Can I give you a lift home?" she said.

"Only if you stay for dinner." Marie smiled in greeting.

"I think I would like that," Emily said, and waited while they all piled into the small RV.

The sun slipped below the rim of the valley as the afternoon shadows dissolved into dusk. Emily leaned her forehead against the windowpane wishing she were outside on the porch, watching moths patter against the lanterns and catching the early evening breeze. Instead, she was suffocating in Marie Garoul's cabin. She could see the woman reflected in the glass, sitting behind her watching Emily right back.

The claustrophobic squeeze on her lungs tightened. The cool glass against her forehead brought no relief from the headache slowly developing. How had her life become so insane, so ridiculous, for her to end up here of all places? What journey had she taken, corners had she turned, for this valley to represent shelter? She had lost all control, the one thing that mattered most to her. Without control, she would spin away into oblivion.

"We'll eat in about ten minutes." Connie Fortune came through from the kitchen wiping her hands on a dishtowel. Emily turned from the window and strove for normality. She smiled at Connie.

"Thank you," she said. "It was kind of you to invite me to dinner."

"Nonsense. I'm glad to finally meet you," Connie said. "Though I'm afraid with this one, it'll be more work than pleasure." She poked at Marie's shoulder.

"Can you remember the year of the almanac?" Marie asked, proving her partner's point. She was watchful, as if aware of the struggle Emily was going through.

"Eighteen eighty-two."

"That's an old one. I'll be back in a moment." Marie left the room.

"She keeps a copy of every Garoul almanac ever published," Connie explained. "I'm surprised you found one outside of the family. They rarely leave the clan, and if one does turn up in the sale catalogues, it's usually snapped up by a family member."

"This one was far from collectable. All the botanical plates had been ripped out," Emily said. "It looked like a tattered old recipe book."

"Ah." Connie nodded. Marie came back into the room holding a pristine version of Emily's battered book.

"Is this it?" She opened the covers, which squeaked of tight, clean leather and under use. A glimpse of the cover plate drew Emily forward like the moths around the porch lanterns.

"It's beautiful," she breathed, reaching out to touch the rich colors of the belladonna that adorned the first plate.

"What was the name of the recipe?" Marie asked.

Emily tore her stare away from the pages. "Silver collar," she said.

Marie hesitated then laughed. "Of course. Luc was wearing one. I've never seen one before. It's an ancient thing. I thought she'd stolen some jewelry."

"She's capable of it. I can see her in diamond earrings if the notion took her." Connie also smiled, and Emily could feel the sincerity of their concern for Luc. "Let's eat now. We'll start our research later."

"Tell me how the hell you got that thing on her?" Marie led Emily to the table. "We found your traps but nothing to do with silver."

"Drugs," Emily said. "She's a sucker for a ham sandwich."

Over dinner, she told them of the traps and the mudslide. She didn't reveal that they had saved each other's lives, or tell about the night spent in the RV nest. On some things, she didn't want to be judged, on others, like the torn up trees behind her house, she needed advice. Throughout the meal, she had a feeling she was not fooling Marie and Connie at all. The true depth of her experience with Luc did not seem a mystery to them, and even though Emily had no name for it as yet, she suspected her hosts did.

Now Marie Garoul's silvered hair hung over the open pages of the almanac. She read intently, sitting slightly offside so Connie could read over her shoulder. Emily fiddled with her coffee cup and stared surreptitiously at Connie. She knew her, well, knew of her. Had even seen her shopping a few times in Lost Creek, or visiting the library there. This was the famed Connie Fortune, the reclusive wildlife artist whose work adorned gallery walls, and glossy magazine covers, and about a million billion T-shirts. It was obvious she and Marie were more than work partners. The air around them hummed with an energy that made the tiny hairs on Emily's arm stand at attention.

So this was what being in a relationship with a werewolf looked like. Basically, like any other healthy relationship Emily had known. The normality of their home, of sharing a meal with them, watching them try to help her…Emily had not expected this. Luc's family was not what she expected at all.

The yellowed vellum crackled, and Marie sighed. Emily was disconcerted by the weightiness of it. She caught Marie sharing a conspiratorial glance with Connie.

"What? What is it?" Emily asked. She wanted them to know she had caught the look and nothing was to be kept from her. She squared her shoulders and raised her chin, prepared for either a lecture or an argument. Instead, she received a sympathetic look and her bluster faltered. She had a feeling she was not going to like their news.

"This spell." Marie's long finger tapped the opened page. "Silver Collar. This is definitely the one you used?"

"Spell?" Emily said. "That's an alchemic formula. Okay, so there are elements of medicinal herb lore in it, but they're mostly allegorical."

Connie gave a grin that lit up her whole face. "Well, you're not wrong," she said, "but that's only the surface value. There's a whole strata of subtext here. As with most things Garoul, you never get what you think you will. Unfortunately, these guys have hidden depths." She squeezed Marie's shoulder.

"What subtext?" Emily asked. This was not making sense. She knew what she had read, and it was alchemy. The text was alchemical in its entirety. She was not mistaken in that.

"This is not an alchemic silver bullet," Marie said. "It's a coded text for something else entirely." She tapped the text. "Emily, this is a love spell."

It came upon her in waves of slow motion. Emily felt her jaw slacken, her eyes widen. Her arms hung uselessly at her sides. She knew she looked like an idiot. Sweat began to bead on her scalp. She was slipping, losing control, and nothing could stop the wild tilting.

"It is not," was all she could manage to say.

Connie gave an ungodly snort of laughter, and Marie tried to suppress a smile under a very convincing frown.

"I'm afraid it is," she said. "You've cast a love spell on Luc. She's bound to you whether she likes it or not. Whether *you* like it or not—"

"I d-don't like it. I don't like it at all!" Emily could hear the scratchy panic in her voice as her chest closed over, trapping the last of her words. With a shaking hand, she grappled at her pocket for the Lexotanil. Connie watched with growing concern.

"Are you okay, Emily?"

But Emily was beyond speech, beyond stammering. She was on automatic now; she had to pop her pill. Had to. Her hands were shaking. The foil wrapper was fidgety and awkward in her slick, sweaty fingers. She just needed a pill. One goddamn pill! How hard was it to pop one fucking—

"Here." The coolness of Connie's fingers brushed against her own and the packet was gently pried from her hands. A pill was dispensed into Connie's palm.

"How many do you need?" she asked.

Emily grabbed at the pill and gulped it down dry, shaking her head at the offer of another. One should do.

"Drink this." Marie appeared at her side with a glass of water. She took the foil from Connie, and with a cursory glance at the wrapper, pushed it back in Emily's pocket. "Come and sit down."

Emily was guided to a soft, squishy couch that all but swallowed her when she sat on it. Connie fell in beside her, and Marie took a nearby armchair.

"How long have you had the panic attacks?" Connie asked.

Cooling sweat glazed Emily's skin and she shivered. She shook her head, not prepared to answer.

"It's not as bad as it u-used to be," was all she said. "And I felt this one building on me all day. Once I'm on a roll, it's easy to tip over. And believe me, I've been on a r-roll for days."

"I'm sure our news didn't help," Connie said. "So you have a history with this?"

"S-since my dad died," Emily said. "I also stammer if I'm stressed. I'm low on the PDSS scale." She used to be a lot higher, but she didn't want to share that.

"Panic disorder severity scale." Marie brooded over the words. Her mind seemed to be elsewhere. "And you use Lexotanil." It was a statement not a question.

Emily nodded but turned her attention back to Connie. Already, she felt calmer, and she'd rather not talk about her health. There were far more urgent problems to discuss.

"I did *not* cast a love spell on Luc. I d-don't believe in that mumbo jumbo anyway. I made a replica of an artifact from that goddamned book—"

"A silver collar that enthralls the beast you place it on," Marie said. "*And* you dedicated it to Luna, our moon goddess."

"I did not."

"Yes, you did, whether you know it or not," Marie said, straight to the point. "Luna is the soul of a Were being. She is the power that draws out our secret nature, our true selves. And every time Luc mutates into her Were being, you become irresistible." She sat back in her chair and stared at Emily with a mixture of admiration and censure. "That is *not* how the recipe is supposed to be used."

"How is it supposed to be used?" Emily was angry at her own misunderstanding. Her queasiness was subsiding, and if she could concentrate on this argument, the residual symptoms of her attack would recede still further. Her stammer had already slipped away unseen.

"It's an ancient recipe. Out of use for well over a century. Where the hell did you find that almanac?" Marie asked.

"A dealer tipped me off. Lucky for me, it was a quiet day at the auction, and I was able to get it for an affordable price. And you're telling me it's some sort of grimoire?"

"It's not a grimoire. The Garoul almanacs accumulate knowledge over generations, and we send a coded copy out each year to respective family members. It's our clan lore book, if you like. It changes each year. Some content is more relevant to the way we live while other stuff falls out of fashion and is omitted. Like silver collars."

"What is a silver collar supposed to do then?" Emily asked.

"You were right in guessing it's a containment spell. But it's medicinal. It's for a loved one to manage a werewolf in pain. If it's in enough agony, a wolven is a crazed thing. Imagine a silver collar as a sort of analgesic. It enthralls the beast within."

"So tell me how to stop this obsession thing. What do I have to do to get Luc off my scent?" Emily was growing impatient. She had to resolve this and soon.

"Take the collar off," Connie said. "And good luck with that, by the way."

"Can't you help me?" Even as she asked, Emily knew the answer.

"I'm afraid there is little we can do. You put it on, and you have to take it off."

"There's a key. It's part of the spell. But I'd have to get close enough." Emily was worried about this. Luc wasn't that approachable these days.

"Is there a ritual for using the key and opening the collar?" Marie asked. "There's usually a reversal procedure with old stuff like this."

Emily looked at her blankly. Her ratty old almanac seemed like a joke now compared to the pristine article on the table before them. So many pages were missing she had no idea if there was a special ritual for using the key. She hadn't seen anything written about it. She felt ill again.

"Remember. We know very little about this, and you can't break a spell and not pay a penalty. Luna only knows the price you may have to pay for breaking this one." Connie's voice was soft, making her warning all the more dire.

"Then how the hell am I supposed to get the collar off?"

Marie tapped the almanac. "Research," she said. "Research and bait."

"Bait?" echoed Emily.

"Yes," Marie told her. "Bait. And that would be you."

Chapter Twenty-eight

L uc was furious.

There were Garouls everywhere, guarding Emily's den, barring her from it. Not that she would go within a hundred yards of the place now that they were there stinking it up.

Adding to her foul mood, Emily's RV had gone. Emily had driven off and Luc had missed seeing her go. Was anyone with her? Had she packed up and gone for good? This made Luc panicky. And to top it all, there was a new dog at the house. A big, mean bitch of a thing that had a slight cystitis infection, judging by her urine, which probably made her even meaner.

Luc didn't know whether to roar her throat raw in discontent or huff silently up a tree. She decided on the latter where she could keep an eye on the house and on the motley wolven patrolling it. The stupidity of the Garouls amazed her. They didn't look up even once. For them, the whole world was at ground level with the rustle of animals, and the smell of plants, and the pattern of paw tracks. That was only fifty percent of *her* kingdom. *She* was as mighty as a gorilla, as agile as a chimp! How she wished she could throw branches at their stupid heads and wake them up.

She scratched her neck. The collar was getting itchy. Time for it to come off. She was cured now. The magic in the collar had taken away the virus; she was sure of it. Now she would take Emily into the woods and show her the tree nest, and bite her. Emily was strong and clever; she would not succumb to the virus. Luc's ears flattened. At least she hoped not. But the time had come. Emily was the one for her. Luc had to turn her, to make her a full-blooded wolven mate, and then they would head for the border and home to Lonesome Lake.

❖

"Can I see inside your RV?"

Emily hadn't seen the little girl approach. She looked up from her seat on the porch and smiled. "Sure," she said. "It's not locked."

She was surprised to see a child here. She had that definite Garoul look, all dark hair, sallow skin, and wild, black eyes. Their Nez Perce heritage ran close to the skin.

Then again, the Garoul compound was nothing like what she had expected. A small vacation village would be the best description. There was a central meeting and eating area around a massive fire pit and barbeque, big enough to hold a heifer. And each cabin seemed to be well equipped for family living, some more permanent than others. Emily could see where some family groups, Marie and Connie for instance, lived here full-time while others came and went. Where children fit in, Emily was unsure. Did they attend Covington schools or were they home taught? She wasn't sure how werewolf families operated over the minutiae of everyday living, but now that she thought of it, she was sure she had seen some of these men and women at the Covington Mall shopping for food and shoes and household products like everyone else.

The child ran over to the RV and Emily followed.

"The side door slides open," she called.

"Cool." The kid's nose was already pressed against the glass looking inside. Emily's heart lurched at a memory of a very muddy Luc doing exactly the same thing. The kid even managed to leave grubby hand marks on the door as she slid it open with all the excitement of entering a secret cavern. Emily smiled.

"If you check out that drawer to your right, you might find a bar of chocolate," she said. The chocolate was found and devoured in two bites and the wrapper dropped anywhere handy. Emily frowned as she picked up the litter and placed it in the trash. She was having full-on déjà vu, and it involved Luc and her nasty habits.

"This is great. Do you sleep in it? Where's the bed? Hey, look, it's the tiniest bathroom in the world. Is that the stove? What do you eat?" The kid's chatter was incessant and soon had Emily grinning.

"What's your name?" she asked.

"Mouse," the girl said. "What's yours?"

"I'm Emily. I'm visiting Marie and Connie."

Mouse continued to poke in drawers and cupboards.

"Luc was here, wasn't she? I can smell her." Her words were so matter-of-fact Emily was stunned into wordlessness. The smile dropped from her face. Of course, the child was a werewolf. Why should Emily assume they were all somehow initiated and not born into lycanthropy?

"Um. Yes, Luc was here for a while," she said faintly, aware the child expected an answer. Mouse was sniffing at the bench seat now, actually sniffing it.

"She marked this," she said with authority. "She says this is her RV, too." Mouse seemed happy with this.

"You know Luc?" Emily asked, and her chest tightened despite the Lexotanil. She could see what was coming and it felt like a slow-motion car crash.

"Luc's my mom," Mouse said proudly.

I knew that. I really did. They're so alike.

"Here comes Taddy." Mouse had moved on to another topic, unaware of the bomb she had just dropped.

Emily turned to see a small dog bustling across the compound to greet her.

"Wilbur!" she cried, and scratched his head in welcome while his tail wagged itself ragged.

"Wilbur?" Mouse asked.

"He looks like a dog I once knew," Emily said keeping her explanation simple. "You called him…what? Taddy? Is he your dog?"

"Taddy is short for Tadpole. He's Hope's dog. Come see Hope. She's cool." And Mouse was running away assuming Emily would follow. Tadpole went after her without a backward glance. Emily threw a quick look over her shoulder at Marie's cabin. She had stepped out for a breath of fresh air while her hosts pored through the almanac. She supposed five more minutes in this fascinating place would do no harm and fell in behind the dog.

Hope was the most welcoming person Emily could ever imagine. She was sunny and happy and had Emily drinking a glass of homemade lemonade minutes after saying hello. Hope's cabin was small and cramped, but she soon explained it was a makeshift home until she and her partner, Jolie, finished building their own place down by the river.

"Does Mouse live with you?" Emily asked, unsure of the family setup.

"She lives with Ren. She stays with us sometimes if need be." Hope shooed Mouse and Tadpole out of her kitchen with treats of their own to be taken in the other room. Emily noted she and Hope were now alone and braced herself for a serious conversation.

"You know Luc?" Hope asked outright.

Emily nodded but said nothing.

"Everyone's talking about this collar you put on her." Hope fixed her with a steady, no-nonsense gaze. "By everyone, I mean the whole Garoul clan on two continents." She smiled. "Werewolves are awful gossips."

Emily relaxed at the small joke. Hope seemed genuine. "Are you a werewolf?" she asked. She had to know.

Hope shook her head. "Not all mates choose to be."

"Choose to be?"

"Yes. Once you marry into the Garoul family, there is always the option to become wolven, but only if you want to."

Emily was amazed at this news. Here was a mixture of wolven and human, all living in the same community, and no one was savaged or eaten? Hope laughed at her expression.

"I felt exactly the same way when I found out about Jolie. But you're different," she said.

"How am I different?"

"That's what all the gossip is about. You didn't wait for your Garoul to choose you; you chose Luc with your silver collar. It's all very romantic and thrilling. Werewolves love a good romance. Not exactly the passive type, are you?"

"Oh, it's not like that," Emily hurried to explain. "The rumor mill's got it wrong. I wanted to snare a werewolf. I can't deny it. I found an old almanac and thought I understood a way to trap one, but Marie has just pointed out to me I got it slightly back to front."

Hope frowned. "You were hunting werewolves? Are you mad?"

"I guess I had something to prove." Emily felt no need to mention her father. That was water that would run under the bridge for many miles before she could bring herself to examine it again. And she knew she would, but not now. Today, she had another Garoul mess to untangle. "Marie is going to help me unlock the collar and release Luc."

"Is that because you want Luc to be free, or because you want to be free of her?" Hope made busy pouring more lemonade in an attempt to hide her expression. Emily knew her answer was important. She liked this woman, and in different circumstances, she'd have hoped they could be friends. She had a more intelligent and mature attitude to the Garouls than anything Emily had come across in an entire lifetime of studying them.

"If," she began, then sipped from her glass as her mouth went dry. "If Luc is happier, then it's worth it. I don't know her any other way than in the collar. To me, she's a complex, totally stressed out entity. She's also funny, and in a strange way has some charming quirks. I guess I'll miss her. Miss the connection with her, I mean."

"The connection?"

"I think the collar works both ways. There's the collar wearer and there's the key holder. I can't say I've been unaffected by the experience." Misery crowded in on her. The adventure was ending. She was glad the danger would be over, but sensed she was losing a lot more.

Hope reached for her hand. "Silver clouds things, Emily," she said. "If it's smooth like a bowl, it never reflects true, but if it's sharp, it can cut to the heart of the matter. The Garouls believe it draws out the soul. Perhaps once that collar is off little will have really changed?"

"I'm not so sure about that. It's been a day for hard truths." She glanced toward the living room where Mouse and Tadpole were watching cartoon DVDs. Luc had a daughter, a history, a past that included other lovers. She thought of Marie's revelations about her father, and her new honesty with Uncle Norm. The day had been full of lessons. The Universe had roared its lessons at her today. "Once that collar comes off, everything will change."

CHAPTER TWENTY-NINE

"Do we need to go over this again?" Emily shuddered at the whine in her voice, but she was exhausted. Marie was relentless in gathering her details.

"Yes. Nothing can be overlooked. The slightest thing could be a clue as to how we go forward." Marie was stern.

Emily was back at Marie and Connie's cabin. Other family members whom Marie had specifically invited had joined them. She was planning her own trap for Luc and had assembled those Garouls best suited for the task. Emily was pleased to see Hope was there, along with her broody partner, Jolie. They sat together almost leaning in on each other. Emily was very aware of the physical closeness all the couples displayed. They were very sensitive to each other's presence.

Emily sat opposite Ren, Luc's twin, and couldn't resist casting surreptitious glances in her direction. It was spooky to see a broader, fitter, heavier example of essentially the same person, and it reminded her again how sick and undernourished Luc really was.

"When I first put the collar on her, she was a werewolf, and out for the count," she repeated her opening line for the second time.

"Because of the ketamine?" Ren said.

"Yes. I now realize she succumbed to it because she was so ill," Emily continued. "And when she turned to human form, she was even sicker."

"And you think it looked like an influenza?" Ren was pressing her for answers as she had been all evening. Emily knew she was a vet. Luc had told her that, so she was not surprised that Ren was more interested in hearing about her sister's health. "Do you think the silver may have helped her recover?" Ren continued with her questions.

"I do," Emily said. "It sure as hell didn't freeze her into Were form. She seemed able to change at will, and I hadn't expected that."

"You wanted her to stay in wolfskin," Marie said. It was not a question.

Emily nodded. "Yes. I wanted to take tissue samples from her for nucleotide research. But she never held still long enough." She was still a little embarrassed by this confession even though the shock it had engendered had long past. When she had first admitted wanting one of their kin for a lab rat, the Garouls had been understandably perturbed. Connie and Hope had been dismayed, though she suspected more at the lack of romance than the research element. The scientists in the room, Ren and Marie, had been intrigued, and she knew they would have questions for her later. While Jolie had whispered a little too loudly in Hope's ear, "What's a nucleotide?"

But Emily was being honest here, even if she said things that upset her hosts. The deal was she would give them the truth, warts and all, and they would help her undo the silver collar. She was pleased to see that whatever their differences, the Garouls would not abandon a pack member. Luc would be safe with them.

"I've been checking over older almanacs," Marie said. "Going further back than Emily's edition, and the collar charm was used for another contagion before the turn of the last century. I'll need blood samples from Luc, of course, but I feel confident that this is not the first time this virus, or something like it, had done the rounds."

"You think the collar is a cure?" Hope asked.

"More like a medical instrument. I won't know until I see what Emily has constructed, and she'll have to show me how she charmed it." Marie turned to Emily. "I'll need your copy of the almanac to compare to mine."

Emily knew this request would come sooner or later. "You'll get that as soon as the collar is off Luc."

"You're bargaining with us?" Jolie sounded shocked.

"You bet I am," Emily said coolly. "I'm handing over a lifetime's work, all my research notes and my almanac, and in return you assure the safety of my uncle and get Luc off the streets. I think you're doing okay."

"You're giving up a lot to keep your family safe," Hope said. Her eyes met Emily's and they held warmth and knowing. "Family is the most important thing. We understand that here."

"I think we need to break for coffee." Connie stood and moved to the kitchen. Emily was glad to stand and stretch. She had called her uncle and told him she was with friends and would be back late, and was content to know that Marie had Lost Creek under wolven patrol to deter Luc and her house calls.

"Have you seen changes in Luc's behavior over the past few days?" Ren came over and handed her a coffee cup, but instead of moving away, she stood with her. "I'm asking because I know there have been changes in yours." Her dark eyes shone kindly on Emily's fervid blushing. She'd been honest about her irrepressible need to mark the woods behind her house. She'd even admitted to placing her mouth around Luc's throat, much to the Garouls' interest. But she would not, could not, reveal the details of Luc's last visit. Some things were only for herself and Luc to know.

Hope drifted over and joined them. "They're courting, Ren. Remember your own blundering attempts," she joked. Now Ren's cheeks colored and she managed to twitch her lips in a half smile. Ren was so serious and reserved, totally different from her exuberant, larger-than-life sister.

"You have a partner?" Emily asked her.

"Isabelle." And the light in Ren's eyes deepened. "She's in Bella Coola at the moment. My pack is up there. We've been hit hard with this virus, and she's organizing bringing them back here."

"Luc was always going on about Canada. She wanted me to drive her there."

Ren laughed. "Luc, in a car! She can't sit still for a minute. You'd have been demented."

It struck Emily as odd that the joke wasn't about a werewolf in the car but rather Luc and her obsessive behavior. Her family knew the quirkiness of her, the good and the bad, the things Emily, in her own way, was beginning to see, too.

Marie called for Ren, and Hope and Emily stayed where they were, comfortable in their corner.

"How do you feel about the way you've been behaving recently, Emily?" Hope asked the million-dollar question. "It's strange, isn't it?"

Emily was going to deny it. Instead, she said, "Yes. It is strange. Strange and confusing, and I'm not sure what will happen next. Once Luc and I are free from each other, I'll have to walk away. I don't think it will be easy."

Marie called them all back to the table.

"It's never easy," Hope said as they moved away. "Werewolves act on instinct. They have knee-jerk reactions. There is no such thing as emotional finesse. I don't think it will be easy for you to walk away either, but for a different set of reasons. After all, you've crossed a line, Emily. Broken the taboo. You're loving the monster. But what will you do if it loves you back?"

Luc watched the patrol. They were young and inexperienced, slinking about under the careful eye of Claude. He was a wily whiskered old thing, and Luc wouldn't dare an attempt on Emily's house with him there. Besides, the RV had not reappeared and Luc was beginning to get testy. First, Emily disappears, then a new guard dog arrives, and now the whole town was thick with Garouls. She knew Marie was behind it, and she had a damned good idea why. Marie had just upped the stakes. She had lured Emily away to Little Dip.

Luc was frustrated. What could she do? It was much too dangerous for her to go anywhere near the home valley. She retired to her nest to think. Lying on her pallet of twigs and leaves, she gazed up at the starlit sky. Usually, it would thrill her on a clear cloudless night like tonight, but now even that annoyed her. The lack of clouds, the cheerful brilliance of the stars, would supply no cover, and her stupid collar would shine like a beacon.

And then the full moon crested over the distant mountain rim, hovering over her world of forest and sky, round and wild and totally fantastic. It was a sign! Luna smiled on her, and in an instant, Luc knew what to do. Her mind was spinning with the simplicity of it. She would go to Little Dip. She would sneak and slither and use all her wonderful skills and steal back Emily. It would be easy. The Garouls thought she was skulking around Lost Creek, hence the patrols. She would let them think that. Let them look for her in all the wrong places while she stole back her mate from under their stupid snouts.

CHAPTER THIRTY

Luna hung low, hugging the mountaintops, urging her on. Luc thundered through the forest, bowling toward Little Dip, gleeful in the knowledge that the Garouls were all over at Lost Creek guarding Norman Johnston's grumpy old ass.

She swung past Big Jack, the boundary tree, and skipped over the roadside ditches onto the lower slopes, all the while moving down into the heart of the valley. She was a blur, she was lightning, she was…lost. Luc stopped under a basswood for a breather and to take her bearings. The compound was about a mile ahead of her; the Silverthread rumbled to her right. Should she cross it and loop around behind? Now that she was in the depths of the forest, Luc was calmer and was thinking straight. She suspected when the full moon hit her collar, she went a bit moon happy. Best to watch out for that. She needed a proper plan now that she was in the heart of enemy territory.

The moon winked at her through the boughs of the basswood. Luc leapt to her feet. Planning be damned! She was a creature of the night, a creature of instinct. She was wild; she was nature at its rawest and at its finest! And she was off like a crazed hare, zigging and zagging through the trees at full speed, the powerful muscles of her thighs pumping, the night air running silky fingers through her fur. Hooting at owls, snapping at night moths, and howling with wonder at the glorious full moon.

❖

A sharp rap at the cabin door quieted conversation. Marie opened the door and stepped outside. Emily could hear the mutter of voices and then Marie reappeared.

"She's on her way," she addressed the room. "Claude's sent word that Luc has left Lost Creek and is coming in along the Big Jack trail. He's following her with the others and will try to hem her in."

"Luc's coming here?" Emily was on her feet.

"It's part of the trap," Marie assured her. "There's no way Luc could sit back knowing you were in Little Dip. She had to follow you here."

"I didn't expect it to be happening so soon." Emily was troubled. Now that the trap was in motion, she felt nervous and out of her depth.

"Nor did we, but I think Luc's calling the shots with this one," Connie said. Around her, the Garouls were beginning to move as if they all knew what they were doing and where they were going.

"What about me?" Emily asked. "What can I do?"

"You need a Garoul with you at all times," Marie said. "We'll drive your RV out to the clearing by the creek. The RV is full of your scent. It will be like a red rag to Luc. We'll be watching and ready to move in as soon as she appears."

"And we need the key." Ren put out her hand. Emily looked at her.

"I don't have the key," she said.

"What?" Marie was stunned.

"I know where it is," Emily hastened to reassure her. "I couldn't keep it on me in case Luc found it. I couldn't even keep it in the house, as she was pulling everything apart and snooping everywhere. So I attached it to Tadpole's collar."

"Tadpole has the key?" Hope sounded incredulous.

"He gets his big snout in everywhere," Jolie muttered.

"It was the best hiding place I could think of," Emily defended herself. "I didn't know he was your dog or that he would run off to Little Dip. As far as I was concerned, my uncle had as good as adopted him."

"Where is the dog?" Marie asked.

"I'll go get him." Hope moved to the door. "It's on his collar? I noticed that and thought it was an ornament. I took the bell off but left the key on. Lucky, eh?" She turned to Emily. "Why didn't you grab it earlier when you were at my place?"

"Because I hadn't had this conversation with your Alpha yet," Emily said. "And he was glued to Mouse in the other room." It was true. To her, the key was another bargaining tool. She had to be careful when she disclosed its whereabouts, and Luc's premature arrival had not given her time to retrieve it.

"Get the key and meet us at the creek," Marie ordered Hope out, then turned to the rest of them. "Claude and his pack will cut off Luc on the north side. If we park the RV by the creek, the Silverthread will act as a natural barrier to the southeast. I've put some Weres on the other bank in case Luc tries to cross the river. We'll ambush her as soon as she approaches the RV. She won't be able to resist it, especially as Emily will be there, too."

"Where will I be?" Ren asked.

"And me?" Jolie pushed to the fore.

"Jolie, you stay with Emily," Marie said. "Ren and Connie are with me. I don't want your scent in the mix, Ren. Luc will be leery enough at scenting Jolie. If she smells you, she'll be sure it's a trap."

"She'll recognize my scent from the nest," Jolie said. "I touched her stuff, remember?"

"I know. And now you're with Emily. She'll see you as a love rival and be livid. Hopefully, too livid to pay attention to anything else going on around her," Marie said. "Now out, everybody. Out and change."

The compound was deserted, but the energy in the air around it was electric. Even the trees seemed to crackle. The valley bowl echoed with rambunctious howling, and the Garouls stood for a second, heads cocked, listening to the reverberations.

"Sounds like she's on the north side." Ren sounded anxious; her worry for her sister was palpable.

"Having a party," Connie added.

"That's good. That's where we want her. Gives us time to get in place," Marie said, and then began to casually pull off her clothes and drop them on the porch table.

Emily stood on the porch step surrounded by a mass of writhing flesh and fur. Before her amazed eyes, her companions disrobed and fell to the floor, bones grinding, skin stretching to near tearing point, and muscles and sinew twisting into heinous and unnatural shapes. They rose to their full majesty, four huge werewolves with gleaming coats and snapping jaws and eyes of bright amber. She could not take her eyes off Connie. She knew this woman was not born a Garoul but had come into the clan as a chosen mate. Once, she had been fully human; now, she was wolven. Emily would never have detected this abnormality in Connie, and had she not seen her transform with her own eyes, would not have believed it.

They seemed to converse in their own way and soon split up. Jolie, now a big ebony beast, strode over to the RV and waited for Emily to join her. Rather than get in with her, Jolie was content to run before the weak headlights of the old RV and guide Emily down a rickety old track that led to a bend in the river. Here the Silverthread had been channeled, and a sliver of it poured into a man-made waterhole used for swimming and sport. *This must be the creek they talked about.* Emily swung her RV into a tight turn and cut the engine. *Here is where it happens.*

Jolie stood beside the small RV dwarfing it. Unsure what to do next, Emily slid open the side door and perched on the step.

"Guess we wait for the others, huh?" she said.

Jolie raised her muzzle to the trees beyond and Emily took that to mean everyone was in place already.

Emily was nervous now. The night had become cooler and what had once been a clear sky was scudded with rain clouds. She pulled the sleeves of her top down over her cold hands and wrapped her arms around her stomach. She was chilly, but shivered more from emotional discomfort than the temperature drop. The wind had begun to whip up. The treetops shook and shimmied and filled the night with ghostly whispers, breathing words of malice into Emily's tortured thoughts. *Traitor. Father. Lover. Gone.*

Emily hoped she was doing the right thing by Luc, but there were few other options left, and she trusted the Garouls. It had been a hard and speedy lesson, but there was solidity to them. They were rooted in a code of honor, a way of being that though it was ancient, still strived for harmony and balance with everything around them. Whereas Luc sparked like a firework fuse, she carried that same essence but in an unruly, unschooled way. She was a keen predator with a cold, cunning mind, but she was more wolf than woman. Emily had to agree with Marie. Luc was out of balance.

The distant howling had faded away some time ago, leaving only the whistle of the rising wind and the murmur of the nighttime forest. Minutes dragged by, feeling like hours. Emily's nerves tightened, and beside her, she could feel Jolie, coiled like a spring, cast anxious glances into the shadows.

Someone was coming! Even Emily could make out the shift of movement along the edge of the track. Jolie did not seem worried so Emily assumed it was one of the hunt party. Sure enough, Hope stepped into the clearing. She had Tadpole's collar in her hand.

"Sorry I'm late," she whispered. "I can't run in the dark. I couldn't get the damned thing off, so I brought the entire collar." She handed it over to Emily then rubbed Jolie on her muzzle. "I better get on back to Marie. Good luck, and don't worry. It will all be fine. You're doing the right thing." She gave Emily a quick hug.

"Thank you," Emily whispered back, needing the reassurance.

Hope headed back to the tree line and was soon swallowed up in the shadows. The waiting game began again. Emily gripped the dog collar, twisting it around in her hands. Barely five minutes had passed when there came a woman's scream.

It was Hope!

A stone flew through the air and smashed the RV's windshield. And then all hell broke out. Emily ducked the flying glass and leapt to her feet. Jolie bounded off into the woods in the direction of Hope's scream, roaring in anger and panic. Emily waited a second before chasing after her, thinking it wiser to stay as close to Jolie as possible.

"It was Luc! She jumped out at me." They found Hope several yards into the thicket. Jolie gathered her into her arms, sniffing her tenderly to make sure she was unhurt. "She came up on my blindside. I didn't see her until the last minute and then she just vanished." Hope was part apologizing and part fighting back tears.

Around them, the forest seethed as the Garouls on this side of the riverbank moved in on the fracas.

"I'm all right," Hope reassured them. She grasped Emily's hand. "Look at you. You're as white as a sheet."

"We thought you'd been hurt—" Emily's sentence was never finished. From the boughs above, Luc reached down yanking her off her feet and up into the tree in a split second. Emily screamed in fright. She was tossed over Luc's wide shoulder and the world spun crazily. Branches, leaves, sky, and then the ground below whirled around her. She saw the shocked gaze of Hope looking up at her; she heard Jolie bellowing, and the distant howls of the other Garouls. Luc had her in the trees, and everyone else was all over the place on the ground, running toward screams, running toward broken RV windows, running in circles. Luc had won. Luc had stolen her, and Emily knew she was lost.

❖

Jolie couldn't believe it. One moment, Emily had been standing right in front of her, the next, she took off skyward like a rocket.

"Go get her." Hope was poking her in the back, herding her toward the tree. Jolie bellowed with anger and annoyance. She hated trees! Now she had to climb another freakin' one because Luc Garoul would not play fair. Jolie was outraged. Nevertheless, she succumbed to Hope's prodding and began to lurch up the tree trunk, grabbing for handholds and praying the damned tree could take her weight. Luc may be part ape, but she was also a lighter build than Jolie, and when Jolie got her claws on her, there'd be a whole lot less.

Through the branches she could see Emily fighting. Luc had her over her shoulder and that was a mistake. It left Emily's hands and arms free, and she was making good use of them by clinging on to everything within reach and slowing Luc down. Unless Luc wanted to hurt her, there was no way she was going anywhere fast. Luc would learn soon enough that human mates were the most frustrating, obstinate creatures on the planet. They never made things easy.

Jolie's ears twitched as she judged her advantage. If she could just make up these last few yards, she'd be on top of Luc before she knew it. Hopefully, Emily would see her coming and manage not to get in the way.

She was close enough to see Luc snarl in frustration and give Emily a nip on the buttock to still her. *Big mistake there, buster.* Emily yelled in outrage and flew into an even greater fury. She began to pull on Luc's ears, twisting them viciously. Luc howled in protest and almost let Emily go. Emily slipped off Luc's shoulder to the side and tried to lever herself further away using all her body weight. Luc paused to push her back into position, so distracted with her squirming captive she did not see Jolie leap.

Luc took the full force square on her back. The thump knocked the air out of her and Emily jarred free. Jolie grabbed her by the arm and shoved her toward the lower branches and safety as she and Luc began to kick out at each other. Luc roared at the loss of her mate and swung a vicious roundhouse at Jolie that caught her on the left temple. Her vision blurred in that eye and Luc delivered another series of blows to her blindside, sensing the weakness.

Luc was smaller, but she was fast. Jolie lashed out with her left claw. She was hanging on to the tree like grim death with her right. Several swipes missed Luc completely, and Jolie was becoming desperate Luc would slip away from her. Below, she could hear Marie and Ren arriving and hoped they could get up here quick. She was unsure how long she could stand and swap blows. Luc was merciless on attacking her left side and her kidney was already hurting.

To handicap her more, she was wobbling all over the place, her head swimming from the blow and from an all-invasive rush of vertigo she could not ignore. If Luc decided to turn tail and run,

Jolie knew she couldn't go after her. She gave up on punching back and let loose with a swift kick to Luc's knee. It was a good strategy; it took the leg out from under Luc. She lost her footing and fell face-first onto the bough she was perched on. Jolie heard the crack of her face hitting the wood and without hesitation stomped hard on Luc's shoulder, rolling her out of the tree.

❖

The pain shooting through Luc's face was all-encompassing. Time became disjointed and she wondered if she'd passed out for a second. And then another vicious kick had her crashing through the tree boughs to the ground below. Everything was cedar scented. She had splintered half the tree to pieces in her fall and the sharp scent exploded into the night air. Several Garouls surrounded her and moved as if to help. She struggled to her feet, roaring, slashing wildly at the air, spittle foaming on her muzzle. They pulled back and gave her room to vent.

Behind them, she saw Marie watching her with calm, calculating eyes, beside her stood Emily, and Luc faltered. Her gaze flickered from one to the other. She had lost Emily. What would Marie do next, have her killed? Surely she would not kill Emily for knowing their secret?

"Luc, nobody wants to hurt you." Emily took a hesitant step forward. Luc snorted. It wasn't Emily's snout that had just been stomped on, or Emily's ears that had been practically ripped off her head.

"Sweetheart," Emily continued to entreaty, and Luc's sore ears twitched at the unaccustomed endearment. Luc heard her heart thump. Her muscles ached so much they felt as if they were sliding off her bones. Her hearing was fuzzy, her sight blurred. She was exhausted. The madness of the past few hours had spun out. Her moon goddess had abandoned her under a dark and cloud filled sky without even a star to guide her. Luc's ear's drooped. She had lost her mate. Life could not get any worse.

"Mom!" Mouse appeared at the edge of the crowd, pushing her way through, the stupid dog at her feet. Luc whined in despair.

"Taddy wanted to see why Aunt Hope wanted his collar," Mouse explained her misdemeanor to anyone who would listen. She looked at Luc with such pride and delight that Luc was certain she heard her own heart break. It cracked like an egg. A huge splintering sound…followed by a bellow? Luc looked up in time to see Jolie Garoul fall on her.

And then there was nothing but Emily, her sweet, warm scent suffusing everything. Her cool hands soothing her. It had to be a dream. But it wasn't, and then her muscles began to cramp and reshape, and her skin bubbled and boiled over her useless, broken, human bones.

Luc could hear Marie talking, though the pain in her head made her sound tinny and toy-like. "…too weak to stay in wolven form. Turning back to human is her body's way of conserving energy." And her fur retreated, leaving her naked and shivering with cold and prickled by the forest floor.

"But she'll be okay?" Emily asked. Luc's eyes opened on hearing her voice. She was crouching next to her, gazing at her anxiously, stroking her bruised and swollen hand.

"Look, she's conscious already," Marie said. "Werewolves are strong, Emily."

"Luc?" Emily leaned in close to her. "Luc, there's something I have to do. Stay still a moment, sweetheart, please?" She picked up a dog collar and Luc stiffened.

"I'm NOT wearing that."

Emily tsked. "It's the key for the collar, idiot. Keep still."

But Marie stilled her hand. "There's not as much urgency now," she said. "Why don't we get your almanac and see what it says about using the key?"

Emily nodded. "Ren?" she called, and Luc's sister came into the periphery of her blurred vision. She peered down at Luc, as if she wanted to peel everybody away and examine her for herself. *Damn vet.* Luc would never forgive her for siding with the Garouls, two-faced, underhanded, smart-assed…twin.

"…you'll see the stash in a net hanging from the cottonwood. The almanac is in an oilskin wrapper," Emily was giving Ren directions to collect the stupid book that started all this mess in the first place. Luc was becoming crankier by the minute. Why couldn't they all fuck off and leave her alone?

"Hey, Ren," she called after her sister. Ren came back at once, her face full of concern. "If you find a ham sandwich, eat it."

"This is all nonsense," Emily said. "If I put the collar on you, I can take it off." With a twist of the key, the collar split open and slid from Luc's neck.

"That thing weighs a ton," she groused and laid her head on the ground, exhausted. She sniffed. She sniffed again. And then she coughed, a big, wet, guttural hacking cough that made her shoulders heave.

"Looks like the virus is still present," Marie said. "Interesting that the collar suppressed it. Now we'll have samples for the lab."

"So glad to help," Luc growled. She grappled weakly at the collar lying at her side. "Put it on," she said between coughs. Emily removed it from her hands.

"No. Marie has medicines." She brushed the hair back from Luc's damp brow. "You're home now, and you're safe. And I think it's time you allowed your pack to look after you."

CHAPTER THIRTY-ONE

Luc was sitting up in bed, her leg cast resting on a pillow. Mouse played with a jigsaw on the floor, hammering pieces that could not possibly fit into place with her fist.

Emily frowned at Mouse's banging, her concern deepening when she saw the tiredness in Luc's eyes.

"Here," she said, "I thought you'd prefer this to more grapes." She handed over the paper bag she was carrying.

"I ate the fruit you brought yesterday, didn't I?" Luc pulled out the dead mouse by its tail. "Gee, thanks."

"I'm getting criticism from a woman who leaves dead squirrels in my bed?" Emily laughed.

"Cool." Mouse stopped banging and came over to look. "Did you kill it?" she asked.

"No." Emily shook her head. "I found it out front, stone-cold dead. Why don't you go see if you can catch some live ones?" Mouse took the dead rodent with eager fingers and ran for the door.

"Catch an army of them," Luc shouted after her. "And make sure you take them to your Aunt Marie's cabin and set 'em all loose."

"Is Marie still torturing you?" Emily settled on the side of the bed and brushed the dark strands of hair away from Luc's face. Her eyes were still puffy and discolored, and her nose was swollen under its bandage.

"That woman has filled every orifice with any old muck she can lay her hands on. And then she gives me injections to make even more holes."

"You're such a wonderful patient. I bet she loves working with you." Emily couldn't keep the smile from her face.

"I'm a lab rat. I bet if you left that critter you found on this pillow instead of me she would barely notice."

"Except it was a dormouse and they're quiet, timid creatures." Emily's fingers had now begun a light massage of Luc's tense neck and shoulders. "But you're feeling better?"

"Oh yeah. I'm healing so fast this cast can come off by Friday. Jolie has to wait another week to get hers off." This seemed to cheer Luc up. "And the gloop in my lungs is nearly gone. Marie thinks the silver did its job."

"It did," Emily said. "Your relapse was slight. Most likely the shock to your system when the collar came away." She was currently assisting Marie. It was impressive to see the working lab Marie kept in the valley. She had not neglected her studies when she became Alpha. If anything, it gave her more resources to pour into her research. She knew Marie enjoyed her company in the lab. They had many overlapping areas of interest.

"You smell different," Luc announced. "Sweeter."

"I'm not taking the Lexotanil anymore. Marie gave me an herbal remedy for when I feel an attack coming on. But I haven't really needed it these past few days." Which surprised her. This week had been fraught with worry over Luc's health, and massive upheaval in her own life, a perfect time for a panic attack.

"Oh?" Luc said. "What hole does she shove it in?" Underneath the general grumpiness, she sounded pleased at this news.

"You are so bitter," Emily said. "I never noticed before as you were so busy being insane. She gave me a tea. *I* have the luxury of drinking my medicine along with a nice cookie. No injections for me."

Luc's head nodded sleepily. "And you're massaging me," she said.

"So? I like massaging you."

"What's up? People are only nice when they want something," Luc said.

"People are nice when other people deserve it."

"Do you have another injection hidden down there?" Luc indicated Emily's pockets.

"No, silly. But let's talk." Emily pushed further onto the bed until they sat hip to hip. "Marie has asked if I can stick around awhile and help her out with this research. It doesn't stop because you have no more gloop to give. Ren's pack is arriving from Singing Valley soon and some of them are in a bad way."

"What's that got to do with me?" Luc asked a little sulkily, and began plucking at her bedclothes.

"You know Ren's pack." Emily saw she'd have to spell this out. "You taught them how to hunt and to survive?"

No answer.

Emily pushed on. "Ren says you turned most of them yourself. They were runaway kids and you thought you could give them a new start?" Emily wasn't so sure about the ethics of this, and Ren assured her that she and Luc had many fur-flying arguments over it. But she was not here to drag up old fights. She was trying to forge a new way forward for the two of them.

"It's not called Lonesome Lake for nothing," Luc grudgingly answered. "Those kids were destitute when I found them."

But Emily did not need Luc to qualify what she had done.

"Those same kids trust you and they'll need your help settling in here," she said.

"They'll have Ren and Isabelle." Emily could sense Luc grubbing around in her head, putting up imaginary barriers.

"Ren is busy in the lab. And Isabelle is new to this, too." Emily was losing patience. "Will you do it?" she said. "Stay here?"

No answer.

"With me?" Emily asked.

"With you?" Luc looked at her; her bruised, blackened eyes were guarded.

"I'm trying to be nice here," Emily said, "but now you've gone and made me pull rank. I claimed you, Luc Garoul. Everyone knows it. I claimed you first so I'm the boss."

"What!" Luc all but squawked.

"You can't deny it. I made the collar; I made the first claim in the RV. I've been talking to Ren about it, and I have it on the utmost authority that I'm the boss of you."

"What does that big blowhard know about anything? If Isabelle hadn't come along, she'd never have found her love teeth. She's clueless!"

"She's been very kind and helpful to me. She knows a lot about everything," Emily said.

Luc snorted at this.

"It's all in the almanacs," Emily continued. "But there probably weren't enough pictures for you to bother reading about it."

Luc blinked at her, for once keeping quiet at the appropriate moment.

"Luc, will you help those kids?" Emily asked again, the answer was important to her.

"Course I will. Someone has to warn them about Marie and her orifice fixation."

Emily suspected she was being played with, so she moved straight to the heart of her argument.

"Luc, I'm moving back to Lost Creek to help Uncle Norm with the shop. He needs me around. This visit showed me that. He's been an anchor to me all my life and now it's my turn to look after him. And on my days off, I'll be helping Marie in the lab. It's a done deal," Emily said. "I just need to know where you'll be."

"I'll be in the county jail doing time for sororicide. How dare she say you made the first claim?" Luc found her voice. Her cranky one. "You didn't even know what you were doing. It was just a lucky chomp."

"Luc. I want to be with you, but I need to be here. Will you help me out? Will you stay here with me?" Emily asked.

"I'm going nowhere without you. But you're not the boss. It was just a lucky chomp," Luc said. "Now rub lower, more to the right."

"You were going to stay all along, weren't you?" The truth dawned on Emily. Luc's sly smile corroborated it. "When did you decide that? When were you going to tell me?" Emily demanded. "I've been working up to this all week."

"I was talking to Marie. We do speak when she's digging holes in me with a needle. She wants me to be with Mouse. Seems Mouse wants that, too." She smiled shyly, looking very pleased, as if this was something she had never expected for herself. Emily squeezed her hand, delighted for her.

"But..." Luc's voice trailed off and she shot Emily a sideways glance. "But we agreed that Mouse needs a proper family den. When I left her with Ren, her pack was a lot older than Mouse. It was more of a community than a real family. Ren did her best, but Mouse missed out on a lot of things."

"I think it's wonderful news," Emily said.

"Wonderful enough to want to be part of it?"

"It's more than I'd hoped for." Her lips grazed the bruises along Luc's jawline. "Seems Marie has set us both up."

Luc turned her head and captured Emily's lips. "We never kiss enough," she murmured.

"Then we'll start to," Emily whispered. "We've got to start all over again, this time with no silver coming between us." She broke the kiss. "Luc? Tell me about Mouse's father?" She held Luc's dark gaze trying to surmise if she had crossed a line. Luc stiffened then relaxed against her, and Emily realized they were sitting in that close way she had noticed all the other Garoul couples doing and she had secretly been envious of.

"His name was Miller, and he was a big gray rogue who had a roaming range from B.C. to Alaska. I was young and out of control when we hooked up. I had no sense and soon fell pregnant. I was pleased enough though. It was all part of the adventure for me. He wasn't. He attacked me when I was near my time. Some feral males do that. They smell a change. The cubs came too early as a result. Ren helped, and because of her, Mouse made it, but her twin didn't."

Emily cradled her close. The story was a simple one.

"I got depressed afterward, and as soon as Mouse was weaned, I left her with Ren. I was always more wolven than woman, and I knew that Ren, with her job and the farm, and all her stability would be the better parent." Luc had gone back to plucking the bedclothes. "Ren didn't argue. She didn't want Mouse raised feral. You can't bring a cub back from that. And Ren was the one who tried to keep to the Garoul ways more than I'd ever done." She looked over at Emily for judgment. "I was always around though. I made sure I was there for her as best I could."

Emily had no judgment to make. These were wolven ways, and the Garouls had a culture and society too complex for her to, as yet, fully understand. Ren, Luc, and Mouse had worked it out for themselves. They were still close, and none of them seemed damaged, except perhaps for the woman in her arms.

"Mouse will always have a home with us," she said. "She'll just love her uncle Norman, once he gets used to having witches in the family." These last words were muttered.

"So this is it," Luc said. "This is what I came all the way down from Canada for. I wanted something, but I never knew what I was chasing."

"Ren says you wanted to get Mouse to Little Dip."

"The virus was scaring me. Ren was baffled. She had no idea how to deal with it. Little Dip was the only place I could think of. But, as usual, it all went wrong."

"That's another story for another day. I think you need to sleep now." Emily heaped the bedclothes around them into a little nest and slid down beside Luc so they lay cradling each other face-to-face. "This is how we sleep. Already, we have a tradition."

"We're building our own lore." Luc smiled back. "And our own den. I want it to be in a tree."

"Bit by bit, we'll build our life and our home together. And I don't care if it's in a tree, a cabin, or a hole in the ground, as long as its foundations will always be here in Little Dip." Emily kissed her Were on her human snout and watched over her as she fell asleep in her arms.

The End.

About the Author

Gill McKnight is Irish and moves between Ireland, England, and Greece in a non-stop circuit of work, rest, and play. She loves messing about in boats and has secret fantasies about lavender farming.

With a BA in art and design and a Master's in art history, it says much about her artistic skill that she now works in IT.

Books Available from Bold Strokes Books

Crossroads by Radclyffe. Dr. Hollis Monroe specializes in short-term relationships but when she meets pregnant mother-to-be Annie Colfax, fate brings them together at a crossroads that will change their lives forever. (978-1-60282-756-1)

Beyond Innocence by Carsen Taite. When a life is on the line, love has to wait. Doesn't it? (978-1-60282-757-8)

Heart Block by Melissa Brayden. Socialite Emory Owen and struggling single mom Sarah Matamoros are perfectly suited for each other but face a difficult time when trying to merge their contrasting worlds and the people in them. If love truly exists, can it find a way? (978-1-60282-758-5)

Pride and Joy by M.L. Rice. Perfect Bryce Montgomery is her parents' pride and joy, but when they discover that their daughter is a lesbian, her world changes forever. (978-1-60282-759-2)

Timothy by Greg Herren. Timothy is a romantic suspense thriller from award-winning mystery writer Greg Herren set in the fabulous Hamptons. (978-1-60282-760-8)

In Stone: A Grotesque Faerie Tale by Jeremy Jordan King. A young New Yorker is rescued from a hate crime by a mysterious someone who turns out to be more of a *something*. (978-1-60282-761-5)

The Jesus Injection by Eric Andrews-Katz. Murderous statues, demented drag queens, political bombings, ex-gay ministries, espionage, and romance are all in a day's work for a top-secret agent. But the gloves are off when Agent Buck 98 comes up against The Jesus Injection. (978-1-60282-762-2)

Combustion by Daniel W. Kelly. Bearish detective Deck Waxer comes to the city of Kremfort Cove to investigate why the hottest men in town are bursting into flames in broad daylight. (978-1-60282-763-9)

Silver Collar by Gill McKnight. Werewolf Luc Garoul is outlawed and out of control, but can her family track her down before a sinister predator gets there first? Fourth in the Garoul series. (978-1-60282-764-6)

The Dragon Tree Legacy by Ali Vali. For Aubrey Tarver time hasn't dulled the pain of losing her first love Wiley Gremillion, but she has to set that aside when her choices put her life and her family's lives in real danger. (978-1-60282-765-3)

The Midnight Room by Ronnie Black. After a chance encounter with the mysterious and brooding Lillian Gray in the "midnight room" of The Griffin, a local lesbian bar, confident and gorgeous Audrey McCarthy learns that her bad girl behavior isn't bulletproof. (978-1-60282-766-0)

Dirty Sex by Ashley Bartlett. Vivian Cooper and twins Reese and Ryan DiGiovanni stole a lot of money and the guy they took it from wants it back. Like now. (978-1-60282-767-7)

Raising Hell: Demonic Gay Erotica edited by Todd Gregory. *Raising Hell*: hot stories of gay erotica featuring demons. (978-1-60282-768-4)

Pursued by Joel Gomez-Dossi. Openly gay college student Jamie Bradford becomes romantically involved with two men at the same time, and his hell begins when one of his boyfriends becomes intent on killing him. (978-1-60282-769-1)

Young Bucks: Novellas of Twenty-Something Lust & Love edited by Richard Labonte. Four writers still in their twenties—or with their twenties a nearby memory—write about what it's like to be young, on the prowl for sex, or looking to fall in love. (978-1-60282-770-7)

The Storm by Shelley Thrasher. Rural East Texas. 1918. War-weary Jaq Bergeron and marriage-scarred musician Molly Russell try to salvage love from the devastation of the war abroad and natural disasters at home. (978-1-60282-780-6)

Ladyfish by Andrea Bramhall. Finn's escape to the Florida Keys leads her straight into the arms of scuba diving instructor Oz as she fights for her freedom, their blossoming love...and her life! (978-1-60282-747-9)

Spanish Heart by Rachel Spangler. While on a mission to find herself in Spain, Ren Molson runs the risk of losing her heart to her tour guide, Lina Montero. (978-1-60282-748-6)

Love Match by Ali Vali. When Parker "Kong" King, the number one tennis player in the world, meets commercial pilot Captain Sydney Parish, sparks fly—but not from attraction. They have the summer to see if they have a love match. (978-1-60282-749-3)

One Touch by L.T. Marie. A romance writer and a travel agent come together at their high school reunion, only to find out that the memory of that one touch never fades. (978-1-60282-750-9)

Night Shadows: Queer Horror edited by Greg Herren and J.M. Redmann. *Night Shadows* features delightfully wicked stories by some of the biggest names in queer publishing. (978-1-60282-751-6)

Secret Societies by William Holden. An outcast hustler, his unlikely "mother," his faithless lovers, and his religious persecutors—all in 1726. (978-1-60282-752-3)

The Raid by Lee Lynch. Before Stonewall, having a drink with friends or your girl could mean jail. Would these women and men still have family, a job, a place to live after...The Raid? (978-1-60282-753-0)

The You Know Who Girls: Freshman Year by Annameekee Hesik. As they begin freshman year, Abbey Brooks and her best friend, Kate, pinkie swear they'll keep away from the lesbians in Gila High, but Abbey already suspects she's one of those you-know-who girls herself and slowly learns who her true friends really are. (978-1-60282-754-7)

Wyatt: Doc Holliday's Account of an Intimate Friendship by Dale Chase. Erotica writer Dale Chase takes the remarkable friendship between Wyatt Earp, upright lawman, and Doc Holliday, Southern gentlemen turned gambler and killer, to an entirely new level: hot! (978-1-60282-755-4)

Month of Sundays by Yolanda Wallace. Love doesn't always happen overnight; sometimes it takes a month of Sundays. (978-1-60282-739-4)

Jacob's War by C.P. Rowlands. ATF Special Agent Allison Jacob's task force is in the middle of an all-out war, from the streets to the boardrooms of America. Small business owner Katie Blackburn is the latest victim who accidentally breaks it wide open, but she may break AJ's heart at the same time. (978-1-60282-740-0)

The Pyramid Waltz by Barbara Ann Wright. Princess Katya Nar Umbriel wants a perfect romance, but her Fiendish nature and duties to the crown mean she can never tell the truth—until she meets Starbride, a woman who gets to the heart of every secret, even if it will be the death of her. (978-1-60282-741-7)

The Secret of Othello by Sam Cameron. Florida teen detectives Steven and Denny risk their lives to search for a sunken NASA satellite—but under the waves, no one can hear you scream… (978-1-60282-742-4)

Finding Bluefield by Elan Barnehama. Set in the backdrop of Virginia and New York and spanning the years 1960–1982, *Finding Bluefield* chronicles the lives of Nicky Stewart, Barbara Philips, and their son, Paul, as they struggle to define themselves as a family. (978-1-60282-744-8)

The Jetsetters by David-Matthew Barnes. As rock band the Jetsetters skyrockets from obscurity to superstardom, Justin Holt, a lonely barista, and Diego Delgado, the band's guitarist, fight with everything they have to stay together, despite the chaos and fame. (978-1-60282-745-5)

Strange Bedfellows by Rob Byrnes. Partners in life and crime, Grant Lambert and Chase LaMarca are hired to make a politician's compromising photo disappear, but what should be an easy job quickly spins out of control. (978-1-60282-746-2)

Dreaming of Her by Maggie Morton. Isa has begun to dream of the most amazing woman—a woman named Lilith with a gorgeous face, an amazing body, and the ability to turn Isa on like no other. But Lilith is just a dream…isn't she? (978-1-60282-847-6)

Summoning Shadows: A Rosso Lussuria Vampire Novel by Winter Pennington. The Rosso Lussuria vampires face enemies both old and new, and to prevail they must call on even more strange alliances, unite as a clan, and draw on every weapon within their reach—but with a clan of vampires, that's easier said than done. (978-1-60282-679-3)

Sometime Yesterday by Yvonne Heidt. When Natalie Chambers learns her Victorian house is haunted by a pair of lovers and a Dark Man, can she and her lover Van Easton solve the mystery that will set the ghosts free and banish the evil presence in the house? Or will they have to run to survive as well? (978-1-60282-680-9)

http://www.boldstrokesbooks.com
Bold Strokes
BOOKS
victory
EDITIONS
Drama
LIBERTY
EDITION
AEROS
e
e-Books
Mystery
C
CRIME
Sci-fi
SF
SPEC FIC
HE
erotica
Erotica
BSB
SOLILOQUY
Young
Adult
MATINEE BOOKS
Romance
BOLD
STROKES
BOOKS
WEBSTORE
PRINT AND EBOOKS